CAROLINA CRIMES

D1158935

TRIANGLE SISTERS IN CRIME
PRESENTS

CAROLINA CRIMES

*21 Tales of Need,
Greed and Dirty Deeds*

EDITED BY
Nora Gaskin Esthimer

Introduction by Jeffery Deaver

Down & Out Books
3959 Van Dyke Rd, Ste. 265
Lutz, FL 33558
www.DownAndOutBooks.com

Cover design by Liam Sweeny

ISBN: 1-943402-95-7
ISBN-13: 978-1-943402-95-3

CONTENTS

CONTENTS

Dedicated to Karen Pullen, with gratitude from her Sisters in Crime, the Triangle Chapter.

Introduction
Jeffery Deaver

Although I live in North Carolina, I suppose I'm not as Tar Heel as some. I think back to what I heard a native, somebody who *was* born and bred in the state, say once: "Just 'cause your kittens curl up in the laundry basket doesn't mean they're socks." I love too the winking observation about a town not far from me, Cary, NC. The saw goes that the name stands for "Containment Area for Relocated Yankees."

But that doesn't stop me from loving the state and the Triangle area—Raleigh, Durham, Chapel Hill and environs—in which I live. It's got everything: an eclectic blend of North and South, Silicon Valley and tobacco farming, the world's only decent barbecue recipe—it involves vinegar and brown sugar and NO tomato sauce—and sports to die for, including the best basketball team in the ACC—no, make that the country (I'll keep my opinion on that otherwise to myself, except to point out I live in Chapel Hill, so enough said).

The area also boasts some of the finest crime writers ever to set ink to paper and pixels to disk, as this Sisters in Crime anthology attests.

1

I was particularly delighted when J.D. Allen asked me to pen an introduction—not only because I knew of the quality of the writers involved, but because I have always felt that SinC is one of the preeminent writers' organizations in the nation. I've been involved with various chapters since the beginning, and I know the group has not only been a true champion of, obviously, women authors, who've been historically underrepresented in the world of crime fiction, but of improving the art of writing in general. Through its advocacy and through hosting programs on tradecraft, community literacy, marketing, publicity, the changing and often inscrutable nature of the publishing business, and many other topics, SinC has made untold contributions to our profession.

I can't think of a better collection of stories to illustrate the diverse voices of SinC writers. Just like a Carolina Sunday supper, these stories dish up a variety of styles, tones and tastes, from procedurals to cozies to dark psychological thrillers.

We start with a fitting tale: Sarah R. Shaber has created a formidable protagonist, who patiently does her job in the face of attitudes like: "A woman policeman. It ain't natural."

If I may belabor the dining metaphor, Jennifer Riley treats us to a dinner table story that starts homey and ends, well, a bit differently than we might be suspecting, while the more dangerous side of dessert is addressed, deliciously, by Bonnie Korta. One of my favorite books, Julie Child's *Mastering the Art of French Cooking,* makes an appearance in Ruth Moose's twisty offering.

Fashion, in various forms, is the motif in several of the stories: Courtney Carter uses perfume to delightfully ominous advantage, while Jamie Catcher does the same with footwear. Britni Patterson takes us to a cosmetics convention—who would have thought what shenanigans might go on there?—and Sharon Bader takes on both fashion and siblings in her story.

Sisterly rivalry is also a centerpiece of Caroline Taylor's tale here, and I think we can all relate to the revealed twist at the end.

Classic psychological suspense radiates from several of the stories: Su Kopil's, for instance, which is chillingly reminiscent of *The Twilight Zone*. Linda Johnson gives us a new look at bullying—and nails life in the office cold—while Don Marple writes about a sentimental trip back home that takes a decidedly troubling turn. The world's oldest profession is a theme of Robin Whitten's story, a classic noir.

In this day and age, technology often appears in crime fiction. A research lab is the scene of some troubling happenings in Bonnie Olsen's tale. And you'll never look at alternative energy the same after you read Gina Lea's. A simple computer game leads to some disquieting consequences in Judith Stanton's.

Another type of gaming is the theme of Karen McCullough's story—think twice before going to a casino again!

Media are such a part of our world now, too, that we might expect an anthology to contain at least one offering on the subject, and Liz McGuffey steps onto our stage with winning results.

The line between cozy and thriller can be a fine one, and there are elements of both in Antoinette Brown's story, which is, forgive me, a truly "crafty" one.

All crime anthologies *must* have a P.I. tale, and J.D. Allen has given us an evocative and compelling one; you'll love her gumshoe.

And if any of you are writers and have ever been troubled by writer's block, well, there's a suggestion or two for you in Toni Goodyear's tale.

As a suspense writer, I believe my job is to tease, not tell, so I've left these snippets a bit vague. I hope I've succeeding in whetting your appetite for the brilliant offerings contained in this volume. So, in keeping with my admittedly overused Tar Heel supper metaphor, I encourage you to do what I did: pour yourself a tall sweet tea or a couple of fingers of bourbon, sit back and dig in.

— Jeffery Deaver

ALL THAT GLITTERS
Sarah R. Shaber

I left my truck lights on, trained on the shack. The place was as desolate as ever. A shack cobbled together from logs and ragged boards, a rusty pick-up parked out front, the yawning mouth of a worthless mine a few yards away. And Dusty. Years ago, the old mule had passed away. The animal was too big to bury, so Zeke had piled rocks, dust and sand on his corpse. All that was left of him was skeleton with a few bones poking out of his makeshift grave.

"Hello the camp," I called out. There was no answer.

I pulled my gun from its holster. I hated to. Zeke was an old, sick man, but the folks in town had said he was drunk and brandishing his shotgun, shouting about killing the imaginary outlaws he insisted were trying to steal his silver mine. As if anyone with any sense would want that barren hole in the ground. Just about as long as I could remember Zeke had insisted a bonanza of a silver strike was just days away and he'd die a rich man. There was sure no sign of it yet and he didn't have many years left.

"Zeke," I called out. "It's Chief Jensen. Come on out. You know you got to."

The shack door opened a few inches. "I'm nekkid," Zeke answered. "Just give me a minute to put my trousers on."

I holstered my gun and climbed out of the truck. He met me at the door to his shack carrying an old lantern and tucking a greasy shirt into a threadbare pair of trousers with his free hand. His bare feet were dirty and what grey hair he had stuck out around his ears.

"What do you want?" he asked.

"I got to arrest you," I said.

"Oh, hell. No you don't."

"Zeke, you threatened to shoot up the mercantile. And you were drunk. You scared the cashier nearly to death."

"If the store had had them little Baby Ruths I like I wouldn't have lost my temper. Come on, Mariah, you don't need to take me in. You know I wouldn't shoot nobody."

"Go put your boots on. And don't call me Mariah when I'm in uniform. It's Chief Jensen."

Grumbling, Zeke set down the lantern and went over to an unmade cot heaped with an old Indian blanket and a pillow that had never been washed. I could hear him mutter as he groped under the bed for his boots. "A woman policeman," he said. "It ain't natural. It just ain't." He found his weathered and cracked boots and struggled to pull them over his bare feet.

While I waited, I looked around his shack. How could

someone live like this, I wondered. The dirt floor had been swept recently, but that was the extent of Zeke's housekeeping. A pot-bellied stove that must have dated from the time of the Comstock stood in a corner. A cast-iron pot caked with cooked-on food rested on its single burner, while a crate of supplies sat on the floor nearby. An almost empty bottle of Four Roses whiskey rested on a three-legged table propped up on a stump.

Zeke'd lived like this as long as I could remember, bringing slivers of silver scraped out of his old mine into town to buy his simple needs. It was a common belief that Zeke had been driven plain crazy years ago, obsessed by silver fever. No one dared to approach his property without hollering first because the old man was sure claim jumpers were after his mine and he intended to shoot first and ask questions later. He needed a bath, a decent hot meal, clean clothes and a serious talking to. Which is why I'd driven all the way out here to arrest him.

Zeke jammed his battered felt derby on his head and followed me out to the truck. I wished I'd remembered to bring a blanket for him to sit on. His trousers were black with the charcoal he used to smelt his ore.

We followed the track from Zeke's claim a couple of miles to where it met with the state road, guided by a line of rocks painted white picked out by my headlights. Once we got into town, I pulled up in front of the police station, a small white-washed stucco building with bars over all its windows and *Police* painted in black letters over the door.

"Where is everybody?" Zeke asked. "The whole damn town looks deserted. There ain't no lights any-where."

"It's the blackout, Zeke. Don't you remember?"

"Remember what?"

"The Japanese bombed Pearl Harbor. We're at war now."

I helped the old man down out of the truck. His arm felt like a stick of dry kindling.

"You're ribbing me," he said. "When did this hap-pen? Where's Pearl Harbor?"

"About three months ago. Pearl Harbor is a port in Hawaii."

"No joke."

I wished it was a joke.

Vernal, the only other police officer in our tiny town, was waiting for us. Well, I had sworn in Coral, the girl I'd hired to take my place as secretary and dispatcher, but she wasn't in uniform. I'd been able to hire Vernal because a childhood bout with polio left him with a bad arm so he couldn't enlist or go work in the bauxite mines. He was just a kid but he had a lot of promise as a peace officer. Lord knows he was eager enough.

"Hey, Zeke," Vernal said.

"Hey, boy."

Vernal took Zeke's arm to lead him to the bathroom. "Come on now, I turned on the boiler so the water's nice and hot," he said to Zeke.

"Don't forget the carbolic soap and scrub brush," I said.

"You two is a barrel of laughs," Zeke said.

While Vernal supervised Zeke's shower I sorted through the piles of old clothing in our storage room. We'd collected it for years for the hobos and drifters who used to come through town on their way to Reno looking for work or a soup kitchen. Since the war started we hadn't needed used clothing like we used to. It seemed like every man and a lot of women in the country had enlisted or found a job. Which is how I got to be Chief of Police and Vernal got to be a police officer in spite of a crippled left arm.

I handed a pile of clean clothes through the bathroom door to Vernal. Zeke was singing "The Last Round-Up" in a thin squeaky voice while he soaped himself up.

"I'll call the café to bring something over for Zeke to eat," I said.

"Don't forget he ain't got but five teeth."

So I ordered up green pork chili with fry bread and coffee for Zeke's dinner. Tomorrow morning, when I released him, he'd be clean, dressed in fresh clothes and have a full belly. Which was all I could think of to do for that loco old man.

I groped my way across the desert along a dirt road, again guided by a long row of white-painted rocks, to my family's ranch house. It was just me living there now. I hadn't been born to be a rancher. I didn't inherit my father's fondness for stepping in cow pies, harvesting hay in the blistering heat and stringing barbed wire. Neither did my brother, who got a job in a bank in Sacramento as soon as the economy perked up. Since I was the daughter of the family I stayed home to take care of our parents. Once my folks were gone I enrolled in secretarial school and then got hired by the police department. I leased out our grazing land to a neighbor and accepted a butchered steer for my freezer as part of the payment. My brother complained, but I told him if he wanted to come back and chase cattle around the desert all day he was welcome to it. He didn't.

I loved living alone under the tall desert sky. Unnatural for a young woman, I'd been told, but I didn't care a whit what people thought of me. Never had. Which came in handy when I got appointed police chief of Desperation, Nevada.

I stopped by the stable with an apple for a chat with Dickie, my dapple-grey cow pony. Then I opened the ranch house door and groped around in the dark for the light switch. I flicked it on and checked to make sure that my blackout curtains were drawn. I hated them for blocking out my view of the desert sky at night, clear and high and blinking with thousands of stars. So stupid, really; if the government thought that the Japs could bomb Nevada, they wouldn't have built so many airfields and training camps out here. But maintaining a blackout was good for morale, they said, and as police chief of my little town I had to enforce the law. Which meant I had to obey it too. I might as well get used to it.

I had a feeling that before this war was over, the government would think of a lot more rules and regulations.

It wasn't against the law to sit out on my own front porch yet, so after I put on my pajamas, made a leftover steak sandwich and poured a tumbler of scotch, I went out there and rocked a while. After I finished my sandwich I poured myself another scotch and rocked some more, thinking about Zeke.

Should I confiscate his shotgun? I hated to do that. On the one hand the old-timer was unpredictable when he was drunk, but on the other a man, and a woman for that matter, needed a gun out here. To kill rattlesnakes if nothing else. And Zeke did own a silver mine. A poor one, but still some wannabe outlaw might take it into his mind to try to steal what little silver the man had. If he couldn't defend himself Zeke could get hurt and no one would know for days. If he would just quit going on a bender when he came into town for supplies it sure would be a help to me.

As it turned out I didn't have to worry about disarming Zeke. When I walked into the office the next morning Vernal met me at my desk. He touched his hat to me, like always.

"Good morning, ma'am," he said.

"And good morning to you. How's our prisoner?"

"Not too good. He's dead."

Vernal opened the cell door. Zeke's body lay face up

on his cot with one hand dangling out from under the blanket that covered him.

"I found him when I brought him a cup of coffee this morning," Vernal said. "Lying there just like that. I reckon he died in his sleep."

I pulled back the blanket from Zeke's face. He looked real peaceful. I covered his face again and turned to Vernal.

"Have you called the doc?"

"Yeah. He said he'd come when he could. Should I notify the undertaker?"

I shook my head. "Not until Doc sees him. He's got to sign the death certificate saying it was a natural death before we can move the body."

Vernal looked disconcerted. "He's just going to lie there? For how long? I mean he must have died in his sleep. He was locked up in a cell."

"It's procedure, and procedure exists for a reason."

We closed and locked the cell door behind us before going back into the front office we shared with Coral. She'd just gotten into work, her tiny frame lost behind her desk. Some folks thought I shouldn't have hired her since she had a Japanese grandparent, but I didn't have any time for that mess.

"Coral," I said, "would you call the mayor's office and leave a message with his secretary for him to call me?" Mayor Jonah Moss was a cattle broker and would be at the stockyards outside of town at this hour. "Tell her that we had a prisoner die in his sleep in one of our jail cells overnight and I need to talk to him."

Coral, her black hair swinging just below her ears and her glasses resting on the tip of her nose, picked up the telephone receiver. She didn't seem surprised or upset to learn there was a dead man in the jail. Her composure was one reason I hired her.

"Who died?" she asked.

"Zeke Smith," I answered.

"That crazy old prospector?"

"That's the one."

I liked to patrol the streets of Desperation first thing in the cool of the morning, when people were out and about going to work and running errands. Sheriff Porter, my predecessor who'd hired me six years ago, impressed on me the need for the law to be visible to the public. "Let the citizens know you're working," he said. "Keep your eyes open and ask questions." I was visible, all right. I was the only woman police officer anyone in town had ever seen. Hell, I was the only woman police officer I had ever seen.

The townspeople muttered behind my back plenty when I was appointed Chief of Police. But they knew the town was short of manpower and expected I'd be temporary until a man could be found for the job. They didn't know I had no intention of giving it up. I liked the job and the salary that came with it.

I saw the doc across the street and flagged him down.

"You look at Zeke yet?" I asked.

"I'm on my way there now," Doc said, mopping his

neck and bald head with a bandanna. "But I can tell you right now he died of old age and alcoholism. His liver must be rock-hard. Once I look him over I'll tell Vernal that he can call the undertaker."

When I got back to the office I found Coral sorting through a pile of wanted posters that had come in the mail. Most of them went into the circular file. She'd learned quickly that I didn't give a damn about some bored teenager who took a joyride in a borrowed Jeep. He was his ma and pa's problem, not mine.

"Vernal's out at the high school," she said.

Another thing Sheriff Porter taught me. "Let the kids at the high school see you every week. Boys that age, and sometimes girls, need to remember that a lot of the stuff they'd like to do is illegal."

"And the mayor returned your call. He said he'd meet you at Martha's for lunch."

I scooted into Jonah's booth at Martha's café. He stood up until I was seated and then sat back down, tucking his napkin into his neck. "Good morning, Chief. What's this about a man dying at the jail?"

Jonah Moss ran a cattle-buying business that employed a dozen men even during the Depression. He'd been mayor of the town for twenty years. He still dressed like a working cowboy in denim trousers and checkered shirts and fastened his belt with a silver buckle he'd won at some rodeo when he was a kid.

"Zeke Smith," I said.

"That addled prospector that's been around since the Flood?"

"That's the one. I'd locked him up for a night to get him clean and fed after he waved a shotgun around the mercantile yesterday. When Vernal brought him a cup of coffee this morning he'd died in his sleep."

Jonah gulped from his mug of black java. "We should all be so lucky," he said.

"So what do I do now?" I asked. "I mean after the doc looks at him and we call the undertaker. I reckon his funeral will be on the town."

"We'll plant him in the pauper's section. For sure he ain't got no money."

The waitress appeared and I ordered a tuna fish sandwich and Jonah asked for a bacon sandwich with French fries. The waitress topped off our coffee before she left.

"I guess all that's left for you to do is notify the next of kin."

That took me by surprise. I hadn't even thought that the old man might have relatives. Where would I start to look for them?

"You don't think he left a will, do you?" I asked.

Jonah laughed. "One with the name of his closest relative and a current address?"

"Yeah, that one."

"I had Lucille and her ma check the town files before I came over here," Jonah said. Lucille was Jonah's secretary and her ma was Mrs. Orelia Neeley, although the

Mrs. was honorary. She never was actually married to Mr. Neeley. There were no preachers and no law back when they set up housekeeping.

Orelia arrived in town decades ago to work as a saloon girl. She was one of those elderly people whom you expect will live forever. Though her mind was clouding up, her memory of the old days in Nevada was legendary. When she got bored with porch-rocking and biscuit-eating she'd go over to Jonah's office and help Lucille out.

"Did Lucille and her ma find anything?"

"Nothing at all, not one word on paper, but Orelia remembered when Zeke first came to town and staked his claim. She says he didn't have any family."

The waitress poured us fresh cups of coffee and carried off our plates. Jonah lit a Camel, inhaling it deeply and exhaling circles of smoke that floated up to the tin ceiling.

"I reckon the state gets Zeke's land then?" I said.

"Not right yet. We need to search Zeke's property for any sign of family, letters, a will, legal papers, whatever."

"Okay."

"Oh, and Zeke had a partner, Orelia says. She doesn't recollect his name. Had quite a horse, she said, a black gelding named King he decked out in a Mexican bridle. Anyway, Orelia said the two of them argued just a few months after they set up their claim and Zeke bought the partner out. Remembers the guy riding out of town on that horse. When you're at the shack see what you can find out about him."

I never knew which was worse, driving out in the desert with the truck windows rolled down so sand and dust blew all over me, or closing the windows and getting baked alive. For this trip, I chose dust. I tuned to the local radio station and turned the volume up loud to listen to country music. Once I was most of the way to Zeke's place I heard the chirrup which meant that Coral was interrupting the commercial frequency. "Chief Jensen, call in when you can," she said, and then the music resumed. She'd said "when you can," which meant it wasn't important enough to interrupt what I was doing. After I was done at Zeke's I'd go over to my own place to clean up and use the telephone.

When I got to Zeke's I walked down to the crick that ambled by the mine and practically took a bath. I filled my hat with water and doused my head, then sponged the worst of the sand and dust off my face and neck with my bandanna. Then I drained my canteen and refilled it.

I passed by Dusty's resting place on the way to the shack. Poor old guy, I thought, he must have had a hard life even for a mule.

Once inside the shack I had to wait a few minutes for my eyes to adjust to the dimness of the single room. I pulled on work gloves. If I were Zeke's papers, I thought, where would I be? In an empty cigar box or coffee can, probably.

I started at Zeke's sleeping area, lifting the blanket and pillow off the dirty mattress. I got down on my hands and knees and checked under the bed where Zeke's boots had been. Lifting the lid on an old carpetbag I found some dingy underwear, holey socks, a couple of towels wrapped around a bar of soap and a rusty razor. An extra pair of pants, two shirts and a nightshirt hung on pegs in the wall. Circling back toward the door I found a slicker and a flannel jacket on two more pegs. I went through every pocket, turning up a pocketknife with a broken blade and a bandanna. In the kitchen corner, I sorted through Zeke's box of supplies. It contained three cans of beans, two of peaches, coffee, sugar and white bread. That left a shelf of dishes, mugs and old coffee cans over the stove. One of the cans held forks, knives and spoons, another a few packages of Hostess CupCakes and then I hit pay dirt. A third and final can hid a thin sheaf of papers. I squatted on the floor and leafed through them. No will, no letter, nothing, except a signed and notarized deed to Zeke's mine in the name of Zeke Smith and William Pardee. Pardee must have been Zeke's partner, the man Orelia remembered. I fanned through the papers again. I didn't see a new deed, the one Zeke should have gotten after he bought out Pardee. Maybe he didn't bother. I checked the date on the original claim—1907. Which meant Zeke had been living out here with just a mule for company for more than thirty years, and the mule had been dead part of the time. No wonder he was loony.

I guess the town would need to check state records in

Carson City to see if the mine was still deeded to both Zeke and Pardee. If it was, we might have to search for Pardee or his relatives. I was sure they would be thrilled to know that they'd inherited a patch of desert in Nevada. Zeke probably owed taxes on it, too.

I tucked the deed into my shirt pocket and went outside. I had to answer a call of nature, so I went behind Zeke's old truck, which was ridiculous since there was no one within miles. On the way to my vehicle I passed Dusty again and couldn't help stopping to look at the sorry thing. I saw a pathetic hoof poking out from the sand and paused, surprised. Dropping to my knees, I picked up the hoof and held it in my hands. Still attached to a sturdy leg bone, the hoof was large and real wide, bigger than any mule hoof I'd seen before. I carefully laid it back down in the sand, jumped to my feet and went back to the shack where I collected a ragged broom. Back outside I began to brush sand and dirt away from the creature's skull and backbone. Once they were revealed I stared at them. The skull was small, the jawbone narrow, and the backbone wasn't straight. The vertebrae near the shoulder were jammed together, forming the rise of the withers of a horse. A horse, not a mule. A horse. This wasn't Dusty.

Why was there a horse skeleton outside Zeke's mine? Why had he told everyone it was Dusty's? What happened to Dusty if he didn't die here?

The sky rotated above me and dark spots crowded my vision. The heat, I thought. I needed to get out of it to think. I went to sit in my truck, but it was too hot.

Taking up my canteen I drank half the water in it. I still felt dizzy, but I couldn't bear the thought of going back into Zeke's filthy shack.

I glanced over at the mine opening and hesitated. I hated tight spaces, but the shaft looked dark and cool. It was the only shade around. I slung my canteen over my shoulder and headed for the mine. I'd rest for a few minutes and then head home to call the office.

Once out of the sun my vision cleared and I began to feel human. I knew I was dehydrated, so I drank the rest of the water in my canteen. Sweat dried on my body while I wondered about Zeke and his damned mule.

As my eyes adjusted to the interior of the dark mine I noticed something white gleaming further back in the shaft. Curious, I stood up and went to see what it was. When I saw the heap of animal bones I had to lean up against the wall and catch my breath. It had been a mule once, no question. This was Dusty. And lying in a heap nearby was a mound of decaying horse tack that had once been quality. The bridle had silver medallions, black with tarnish, mounted on it. I wondered what the hell had gone on out here.

I found a lantern filled with lamp oil at the mouth of the mine. I lit the wick and turned the flame up as far as I could. I headed further into the mine. I proceeded slowly around a corner into the pitch-black tunnel keeping my eyes on the ground so I didn't trip over something. When I stopped and looked up again, the biggest damn vein of silver ore I'd ever seen stared me right in the face. Buried in a wide blue-green swath of copper-oxide, the silver showed dark and sooty. And floating in the vein were specks of gold.

Zeke and Pardee had been rich men. But the old skinflint couldn't spend the money. For years he lived on beans and white bread in a filthy shack in the desert rather than let anyone know he'd struck it rich.

Holding the lantern up, I went further into the mine, and just a few feet along the shaft I found one of those depressions in the dirt that I'd read about in the FBI manual I'd found in my desk after I became chief of police. A rectangular depression in the dirt caused by burying a body. Decomposition releases gases that cause a human body to shrink, and the dirt piled on top of it is never as dense as the original soil.

I had a shovel in my truck, but not a probe. I could dig the body up myself, but I wanted help and a witness.

Back at my house I showered off the dust, sand and dirt from my body and changed into a fresh uniform in less than fifteen minutes. The revulsion I felt after my discoveries at Zeke's claim would take longer to dissipate.

I called the office. Coral answered. "Is Vernal around?" I asked.

"Yeah, he's right here."

"Tell him to meet me at Zeke's place as soon as he can," I said. "And make sure he brings a shovel. Did you have something you needed to tell me?"

"The Mayor called. Orelia had a lot of free time this

afternoon so she went through all the town files again. She found a couple of letters from William Pardee's niece in 1909 and again in 1911, asking if anyone had seen or heard from him. Appears he'd disappeared and they were trying to find him."

I didn't say anything more to her. I needed to collect my thoughts before I told the world the unlikely tale of Zeke Smith, miser, who had killed his partner, a horse and his own mule rather than share untold wealth with another man.

I wondered if Pardee's niece was still alive, or if she'd had children. If so they were about to become very rich.

WRITER'S BLOCK
Toni Goodyear

Once upon a time on a dark and stormy night I dreamt I went to Manderley again where someone called me Ishmael and all the knights in the kingdom were...what?

Sitting on the crapper?

Murdering children?

Out raping damsels in distress?

I have no goddamn idea. All I know is here I am again, slogging through the daily torture session, fingers whacking away at the laptop keyboard like some desperate form of masturbation. Hollow words, meaningless crap. My novel still stuck like a dragonfly in mud.

Never mind. Keep going. Don't analyze, just write.

Stream of consciousness: Shit, shit, shit.

Shit on a shingle...what was that, anyway? Oh yeah, that's what servicemen in World War II called chipped beef—the hind end of a cow probably—in ugly gray cream sauce served on stale toast. Thirty years later my father was still steamed about it. Once, when they tried to serve it to me in the school cafeteria, I threw up and they had to call my mother to take me home. At least that part was cool.

Maybe fuck is a word that can save me—an entire page of the f-word like a new-world "shazam!," magically pulling something from nothing, like a rabbit from a hat. Thinking about magic reminds me of my long-dead childhood friend Arnold who grew up to be a Vegas magician and who one day actually disappeared in his twirling cabinet and was never heard from again. That is until his body turned up in a desert canyon with a sign that read *Deadbeat Douchebag* chained around his neck. But thinking about Arnold doesn't get me very far with this shitshitshit constipated, deadbeat, no magic, no movement, no hope, no wisdom, no craft, fuckfuckfuck of a novel.

I raise my fingers from the laptop keys and stare out the French doors of my study. So much for stream of consciousness. If I took my paper rantings to a hypnotist would there be a breakthrough? Would some deeply twisted thing slip through the cracks in my writer's block and straight into my bored mistress of a novel, *she who lies there* waiting for me to excite and arouse, make her shudder with pleasure?

Yeah, yeah, yeah.

My publishers, who keep mumbling about breach of contract if I don't deliver them Bestseller Number Twelve by next Friday—yes, it's four months late already—might find it at least mildly amusing that I'm stuck on page six-six-six of this rambling crud-dump of a book, this demon with whom I need to make a new pact. "I'd sell my soul to finish this novel!" I would cry, and in a puff of smoke and he/she/it would be there at my side, whipping a business card out of the air, and *voilá*, the right words would pour into the keyboard from my curved fingers like they were copper faucets on newly plumbed lines run from endless underground springs, pumps, pumping, pumped.

I need torrents of words. I write spy thrillers that need to be fat enough to sell for eighteen bucks in my paperback-first, signature trade format. And there are other criteria. Things must explode, crash, speed. The violence-drenched plotline must twist and turn like the old Coney Island Cyclone—insatiable suck holes of action are required. Action is college for the kids and filters for that friggin' swimming pool pump out back, so I must write, write, write. If my old pal Arnold could have pulled money out of hats instead of rabbits he'd still be happily screwing hatcheck girls today.

But it's not just about money. I'm known, celebrated, somebody. Writing is identity, and my writing is as dead as Arnold. No words, no me. Just terror—and blame. On least on that score I have no confusion; I know exactly who's to blame. I look past the French doors, past what my wife calls our butterfly garden with its pebbled pathways, cool modern fountains, and riotously colored plants, to the treed fence line that separates my property from my neighbor's. The sight of his house through the greenery sends a cold shaft of anger up my spine.

Oh, yes. I know damn well who's to blame.

I hear a click as the door of my study opens. I can tell without looking that my wife, Ellie, has opened it just enough to peer in, checking to see if The Genius can be disturbed. I wave her in without taking my eyes off the yard. A patch of columbine has self-seeded by the base of one of the fountains. Pink bells, willowy.

Ellie comes around behind me and lays her hands on my shoulders. "Having a better day, hon?"

Her voice is quiet, meant to calm.

"The best," I snap, and she begins to knead. Her touch, loving and gentle, quickly breaks me. I lean my head back against her. "I can't take this much longer, Ellie. I've got to do something about him."

Instantly, I realize my mistake. I'd meant to say "I've got to do something about *this*," not "I've got to do something about *him*." I hold my breath and wait.

Her fingers stop moving. I feel her body stiffen, like it's pushing back against an ill wind that has suddenly sprung up from a fault line that runs under our house.

"You promised you would never talk about him again. I can't bear it anymore, Porter. I won't have it in our lives."

I swivel my chair around to face her. Her normally rosy cheeks have gone pale and tight in what I call the "the bastard fade," said bastard being me of course.

She is not finished. "Ted Breen has done nothing to you. This obsession of yours is insane, it has to stop. Our next-door neighbor is *not* the reason you can't write."

I know better than to argue. Especially since she's right. After weeks of ranting, I had promised not to say another word about the cocksucker next door—ah, a good "c" word.

But that's all she's right about. Ted Breen is a demon.

I stand and take her into my arms. Her head drops to my shoulder and I feel the warm, sweet breath of her. A woman worth fighting for.

"I'm sorry, Ellie. I misspoke. I'm so damn frustrated. I'm not crazy and I'm not obsessed with Ted Breen. I'm just a little worried, that's all."

"You're not going to do anything, are you?"

"Of course not. Just venting."

After a long moment, she raises her head to look at me. She wants so much to believe me. "I'll make us a couple of brandy alexanders?"

I wipe her tears, manage a smile. "Alexanders would be great. Just another half hour's work, then I'll come."

She nods, but I see the shades of dread in her eyes, the muted terror that her normally rational husband has gone 'round the bend.

"I love you," she says hopefully.

When Ellie's gone, I lock the study door and pull my new binoculars from my desk drawer. They're real beauties from the Bird Store, blue-black 76Z Winstock Premiers with Delimore lenses and 11x70 magnification. (This is the kind of detail you care about when you write spy novels for a living.) With these babies, I can see a blue jay take a dump on a mailman's head halfway down the street. I fiddle with the focus and stare at the house next door.

Our gated subdivision is typical upscale suburbia.

Houses are set on five-acre lots with most of the land to the rear, three-quarters of an acre between Him and Me on my eastern side. Mine is a corner lot. Only one side is exposed to neighbors. We keep a manicured front lawn and enough of a landscaped backyard to hold a slate terrace, pool, and outdoor kitchen and seating area, in addition to the butterfly garden outside my study. The rest of the property we leave natural woodland. A row of newly planted cedars on my land will someday deliver full privacy between Him and Me. For now, we can still see one another through the still smallish trees and a decorative fence of wrought iron and brass.

He often keeps his motorized blinds raised, drapes open. With my binoculars, I can see him moving around inside his house. I can also see into his garage. A row of windows at the top of the garage wall that faces the patio at the rear of the house—what the subdivision marketing material calls "the new, natural-light ap-proach" to garage facilities—lets me monitor movements there as well, lights on and off, car in and out. I can also watch him swimming in his pool, cooking on his grill—the man never stops—filling his garbage cans, raking his leaves. Sometimes I can see the naked women who occa-sionally share his bed but I'm not interested in watching them. Only Him. I can confirm that at such times he appears totally normal: no tail, no cloven hooves, no raw squirrels for dinner. But we all know how that works. Humans are easy to fool.

He'd certainly fooled me when he first showed up on my doorstep four months ago.

"Hi, my name is Ted Breen," he'd boomed with a wide, toothy smile, thrusting his hand toward me like it was something he'd learned in "How to Be a Great Guy" class. "I'm the new neighbor moving in next door. I thought I'd start right off annoying you by coming over to borrow something."

He threw his head back and laughed as if he'd just landed a joke that would've made Groucho cream.

Okay, larger than life and not too bright, but probably harmless, I thought dimly. Six-footish, maybe in his fifties, solid, no flab, dusty brown hair, clean cut, square jaw. What Ellie would call "handsome enough not to shoot."

I smiled and shook his hand. "Nice to meet you, Ted. Name's Porter. Welcome to the neighborhood. That's a nice-looking house you've got there. I've always liked it."

"Got it for a great price. Will Barker and I went to school together." The Barkers were the previous owners. Nice guy, a CPA, with a sweet wife and three kids. "Hope you'll come 'round when I'm settled. Have a beer, cook some steaks, maybe solve all the problems of the world." His grin was infectious.

"Sounds like an idea," I said.

"I was thrilled when the lady down the block told me my new neighbor is Porter Kitredge, the guy who writes those spy novels. I read your books all the time. They're great."

Did I cringe? I don't know. "Thanks. It's good to know people enjoy them."

He continued to grin at me.

I hastened to change the subject. "And what do you do, Ted?"

"Oh, nothing as exciting as you. I'm sort of a cleanup man. I bury bodies."

This took a beat or two to process—I am, after all, a writer of thrillers. He saw the look on my face and barked another laugh. "I sell coffins for the funeral trade. Housing for dead people. If you want to wipe your hand on your trousers now, go ahead, I won't be offended. Happens all the time."

He was right on the money. I *did* want to wipe my hand. I smiled and shook my head. "Sorry. That seems to be some kind of reflex. Let me lend you something to make up for it."

"Thought you'd never ask. Just so happens I'm in need of a long-handled tree saw. I want to trim a few branches off that big elm up front and my saw didn't survive the move."

"Done," I said, and stuck my hand out again. This was my redemption move. Show him I'm over it. Unafraid. "Just happen to have one."

"Done." He gripped my palm enthusiastically, holding it for a second—or was it two?—longer than he needed to.

It took me three weeks of not writing to realize that was the moment he'd zapped me.

I don't believe in demons, actually. I don't believe in spooks. I don't believe in little green men or great hairy ones for that matter, or that cloned aliens are lunching on lizards in Area 51. I'm a sane, thoughtful, average sort of guy who doesn't write horror stories or sci-fi and isn't afraid of the dark. But I know this too: On the physical plane of life there can emerge slits in the fabric of reality, chasms in everyday bedrock, hairline fractures that spread like plague, spider web mazes of compromise. Ellie would say I'm obsessed with identifying the faults at the heart of things. Maybe all writers are.

Ted Breen is one such fault, a fissure I can't explain— a Jonah, a jinx, a Something Coughed Up from a probabilistic universe of synergies and anti-synergies. From the day we shook hands, my words have been fated to fail like so many idiot sperm heading up a wrong channel after what should have been a pro-creative lay.

And other things have happened, though Ellie would call me mad to say so. Like Breen never failing to dash out of his house with his big Mr. Friendly waves the moment I step into the yard, those giant grins flashing like warning lights. There are repeated invitations to cook-outs, steaks and beer, hot dogs and football, all politely declined, so sorry, too busy working. When I try to water my backyard, he sprints to a break in the tree line at the fence and shouts out to stop and chat. Sometimes I can wave him off but sometimes I can't—he's quite insis-tent—and he always tries to put his hand on my arm or shoulder like we're comrades-in-arms battling the dread-ed rye weed, but I stay out of reach. I am not fooled.

I've modified my routines. I work in the yard only when his car is gone, retrieve my newspaper only when

I'm certain he's not about. I put my garbage cans out a day early to avoid chance meetings at the curb, and I've hung shades on the French doors in my study and all windows facing east. Two months ago, I rented a post office box at the local packaging store to avoid accidenttal meetings at the mailbox. This worried Ellie a lot, but I told her it was because I want a locked box for general security reasons. It broke my heart to watch her struggling to buy that.

A month ago, she caught me spying. Breen had arrived home at dusk accompanied by two long-legged model-types, one blonde, one brunette, both stunners. He'd let his hair grow long, had it tied back in a kind of pony tail, a baseball cap on his head. I'd doused the lights and pulled the shades in my study, leaving just enough of a peephole for the binoculars to do their work. My heart pounded like a Sousa march; visions of the *Witches of Eastwick* flooded my mind. Weird book, but a threat that was more believable than most, the simple Power-of-Three focused on One like a needle piercing a voodoo doll.

"What in God's name are you doing?" Ellie had cried, hitting the lights.

I dropped the shade and the binoculars. She scooped up the latter and stood there with rage and panic distorting her face like in a Dali painting. She had endured my endless ravings but this was something else entirely. I rushed to reassure her. Yes, sweetheart, yes, I would stop this crazy behavior immediately. I would quit obsessing about the neighbor. I would never spy on him again—

you keep the spyglasses, hon—nor even mention his name. And yes, yes, certainly, I'd be glad to see a shrink.

That was a month ago. A few days later, driving back from pretending to attend a therapy session, I bought my new Winstock binoculars. They're a thousand times better than the old ones.

So here I sit again, filling my journal. "Today is the 113th day of NO WRITING, six days to MS DEADLINE, no way found out of the maze." These benchmarks are noted in caps in the spirit of historical eras, a dying message left behind by an ice-bound explorer on Everest, the final squeaking cry of human courage. *To whomever finds this...*

I close my laptop. The time has come.

Today is Saturday, and I can tell by the closed-blind stillness of the place that Breen isn't home. Winds calm, nothing stirring. At three in the afternoon, I watch the mailman wrestle two big manila envelopes into Breen's mailbox and conclude the oversized box is crammed with mail from the day before. In fact, I hadn't seen evidence of life since Thursday night after supper, when Breen had dragged his recycling to the curb.

At five, the purple-haired teenager who lives one street over shows up with earbuds in his ears and a cord running down to a shirt pocket. He bobbles his head to what looks like a hard rock beat as he moves Breen's recycling bin to the back of the house, then rolls out a hose and waters shrubs. Gone for a long weekend? I can't be sure, but it's a damn good bet, and I've got to take the chance.

I'll make my move at twilight. Astronomical twilight, that is. Sunset—civil twilight—comes at seven thirty, too risky for my purposes. Nautical twilight, the time of night one gets a star to steer by, isn't terribly useful for navigating subdivisions. It's astronomical twilight that brings the darkness that reveals all the heavenly bodies see-able on a given night in a cloudless sky. In our neck of the burbs, this is around ten p.m. Ellie will be out for girls' night until well after midnight. And what I have to do won't take long.

I eat a sandwich for dinner, drink a glass of wine, return a phone call to a distant cousin. At ten, I head to my garage, to my small toolbox. I cram a tiny Maglite, a flathead screwdriver, and a small wrench into my pockets.

The route to next door is short and familiar. I have no trouble picking my way to Breen's property under cover of night, no tell-tale light necessary.

An advantage of McMansion developments from a skullduggery point of view is that while each house has a distinctive look, the infrastructures are identical. I know exactly where to go. On the far side of the rear patio, tucked into the ell formed by the garage wall, is what our subdivision developers call the "Yardman's Shed," an attached storage unit just like the one I've got at my house. Eleven feet long, nine feet deep, climate controlled, with a sliding door—tight seal, good protection against critters and moisture—that lets lawnmowers, gas grills, and other yard beasts roll easily in and out. Tucked into one corner of the shed is the home's gas-fired water heater, good to have outside the house in case of leaks.

Most of us in this gated community never bother to lock our sheds. For one thing, there's no crime here—it's against HOA rules. And if some disgruntled landscaper did boost a mower or grill, who in this moneyed enclave would need to care?

As expected, Breen's shed door is unlocked. I enter quietly, slide the door closed behind me, and pull out my little high-intensity Maglite with its tightly focused beam.

Breen's sleek, stainless steel gas grill—the kind that makes lesser men coo with envy—is already primed with a twenty-pound canister of propane. I see a spare tank inside the cabinet at the bottom of the grill. On the workbench nearby are two more backups. I'm not surprised; I know firsthand that the man makes a vocation of grilling.

What most people don't know about propane is that it's heavier than air. If there's a leak, either from an improperly closed tank valve or a grill knob not fully in the "Off" position, the gas falls to earth and gathers in a deadly cloud at one's feet. In an enclosed space, the pressure builds and builds. Any electrical event can cause the cloud to spontaneously ignite, with spectacular results. People have had their faces blown off by opening the grill top and hitting the electronic ignition to get started on their Fourth of July hamburgers. On a

Philadelphia street, a food truck blew into a thousand pieces, scatter-bombing the neighborhood with hot debris. Twelve people injured, two critically. Cars driving nearby burst into flame from the intensity of the heat. In California, a pickup exploded when the tank in its bed overheated in the sun. A buildup of pressure caused the valve to leak. When the driver tried to tighten it with a wrench, the spark from metal on metal ignited the gas.

These are not freak accidents; about six hundred a year are reported. And when propane blows there's nothing polite about it. It erupts into a mushroom cloud of flame, at its center a sinister acetylene torch blasting for the sky.

I turn the knob on Breen's grill ever so slightly toward the open position. That takes care of the tank connected to the grill. I squat to the cabinet below and remove the small wrench from my pocket. I know from my own grill—it's the suburban-dude's obligatory apparatus, after all—that a slight twitch of the wrist on a propane tank valve can begin the slow release of gas. For good measure, I twitch the valve on the two reserve canisters on the workbench. We all get our propane tanks from Connors Hardware down the road. Surely, if there was one bad tank valve, there could've been more, a kind of a bad-batch phenomenon. Though I expect there will be little left in the way of definitive evidence to worry about. A propane explosion in this shed would soon be joined by the natural gas lines that feed the appliances in our upscale houses.

All I need now is an igniter. I turn my attention next to the water heater. Just above the catch basin at the foot of the heater is the drain valve. I use the screwdriver on the screw in the center of the valve and loosen until I'm rewarded by a steady drip.

I stand up and stretch my back. Cold water will be drawn into the tank as the water level falls. When the water temperature descends far enough, the water heater's ignition will spark to light the element and make more hot water.

And blow the Writing-Wrecker's lair to smithereens.

I make my way back across the yard and return my tools to my toolbox. I turn my television to a late-night movie, *Home from the Hill*—great old flick—and stretch out on the sofa. A part of me wants to be asleep, mostly to avoid Ellie when she comes home. The rest of me wants to stay alert, listening and waiting. Eventually, the adrenalin crash wins. I drift off thinking that Robert Mitchum was our true American male hero, a guy who made John Wayne look like a sissy.

I bolt awake to an infomercial on how to flatten your tummy. Ellie's purse is on the coffee table. She didn't wake me, didn't shut off the TV because she knew the sudden silence would wake me up.

The mantel clock says four-thirty a.m. A little more than two hours until dawn.

I hurry to my study and peer around the shade. Breen's muted yellow porch light is on.

In my groggy state, I struggle to register this. A porch light? On?

Just outside its glow I see the outline of a car in his driveway.

A car. Holy shit.

Details emerge as my eyes adjust. Breen's big-ass Hummer.

Oh God. Breen. What's the bastard doing home?

I dive for my binoculars and wriggle farther under the shade. I see ambient light, dim, in his second-floor bedroom. Either a small lamp—or spillage from the master bathroom?

The master bathroom. Hot showers.

Oh crap.

I get only this far. A rear section of his house, where the garage meets the kitchen, erupts like the launch exhaust of a Saturn V rocket. Flames soar upward and outward, giant storm clouds bursting into the night sky, roaring pillars of fire. Seconds later there's another explosion, then a third, and half of the house—including Breen's bedroom—explodes into flame.

Chunks of siding and brick, joists and furniture careen through the night like meteors from hell, flaming debris slamming into my house, crashing onto my roof. The glass doors of the study shatter as the twisted remains of a refrigerator door punch through the wall to the left of me. I cover my head with my arms and run screaming for Ellie.

We spill into our front yard, clinging and sputtering. Neighbors scurry around with flashlights and sirens shatter the night. Soon, fierce halogen lights split the darkness and firemen drag Ellie and me farther away from our house, wrap us in blankets, and deposit us across the street on the front steps of our grandmotherly neighbor, Mrs. Jameson. We submit without protest, staring numbly at the nightmare around us. Smoke and madness blur time and space.

Eventually, someone says they've cut off the gas lines, that there's nothing to do now but wait for the fires to burn out. Breen's house is still aflame. Ours has been mostly quenched, the damaged third of it red-smoldering, including my study and the guest bedroom suite closest to Breen. The remainder looks oddly unscathed, like a computer graphic not yet finished.

Ellie and I sit silently, covered in soot, patches of hair charred from burning debris. As dawn begins feebly to break through the fog of grey smoke, I can tell there will be very little left of Breen's house. Very little left, I'm sure, of Breen.

I'd never meant to kill. I'd only meant to drive him away. His existence next door had reduced my writing life to ash, as I've now reduced his.

My wife turns her face toward me with the dazed slow-motion of shock. Beyond the unfocused incomprehension that accompanies all tragedy I see something else—a pure, fearful certainty that we both understand must never, ever be named.

"I had nothing to do with this, Ellie," I say, my tone quiet, even. "You simply must believe that."

The glazed look retreats further into itself. Slowly—ever so slowly—she dips her head. Once. Yes, it says.

That's exactly what I must do—for as long as I possibly can.

Mrs. Jameson appears with mugs of coffee. She asks again if we want to come inside, use her bathroom, lie on her beds. I again say no, but Ellis accepts. She stands and turns to follow our benefactress.

"Mrs. Jameson," I say. "Do you have a pad and pen?"

Her surprise at the request quickly segues to an understanding nod. She takes Ellie into the house and returns a moment later with a spiral notebook and a pen. She hands them over wordlessly, then backs away, like an acolyte making an offering to a distant god.

I remove my blanket and take in the destruction around me. I can barely fathom the devastation I've wrought. Breen. Two houses. Ellie. Me. Our marriage doomed, our privileged enclave in tatters. And yet...

I take a sip of Mrs. Jameson's bracing coffee and set the coffee mug down beside me.

As the strengthening rays of morning sun cut their first tentative path through the murk, I open the notebook and begin anew.

LOU'S DINER
Su Kopil

From her station behind the counter at Lou's Diner, Betty taps the end of an unfiltered cigarette and listens to the young couple in the corner booth.

"What I said back there. I didn't mean it," the man says.

"I know," the woman answers.

It's half past midnight. The only other customer is a man with a cane, shuffling toward the register. Betty places her unlit cigarette back in the pack and drops it into her apron pocket. She rings up the man's coffee and hands him his change.

He nods, glances at the young couple, and limps out into the night. His exit brings a draft of cool air. It weaves past the empty tables and chairs until it finds the corner booth.

Betty watches the woman pull her thin jacket tighter.

"What I said, it just came out. You know it didn't mean anything." The man tosses aside a half empty sugar packet. "It just came out."

"I know," she says.

He stirs his coffee, and watches the woman, but she's

not looking at him. Her finger pushes the few granules of sugar that spilled.

She starts to speak and Betty has to strain to hear. "Do you always take what you need and abandon the rest?"

He swipes the bits of sugar onto the floor. Betty frowns. She's the one who'll have to clean up his mess.

"Forget about the sugar." He begins again, "Look, I don't know why I said it."

"We don't need to talk about it," the woman says.

He turns away from her and stares out the window.

Her gaze follows his.

From her vantage point, Betty can see the man with the cane leaning against the lamppost, haloed by the circle of light. He's facing the diner, his hat brim shadowing his eyes. Is he waiting for someone? Or is he watching the couple through the window? She wonders if he saw the evening news—the announcement of another murder not far from here.

Her gaze returns to the couple, their attention back on each other.

"I like you, Mary. I do." The man is speaking again. "But love…"

Betty catches Mary's eye. Can't he see the woman's mortified? *Shut up*, Betty wants to yell. Instead, she brings out the pack of cigarettes, her hands unsteady as she shakes one out, smells it. Lou won't let her smoke up front. She's not even supposed to have them with her. Teases the customers, he says. Well, if no one likes the rule, why enforce it, she counters. It's the law, he says.

Betty didn't have to like the law, but she needs the job, so she compromises. She keeps her cigarettes close, but doesn't light up while on the floor. She looks out the window again. The halo of light is empty.

"I shouldn't have said it." The man's voice is pitched higher now.

"Richard, please." Mary's hand hovers in the space between them.

He stares at her across his half empty cup. "I don't love you."

Scream, cry, beat him, Betty wills the woman across the diner.

"I know." Mary's shoulders slump.

Betty puts the cigarette away, slips the pack back in her apron, and grabs the coffee pot. What is it about the Richards of the world that attract women? She's known her share of Richards. They're as addictive as tobacco— taking you higher one minute, killing you the next.

"More coffee?"

Richard's cup rattles.

Mary's knees hit the table.

Betty smiles, neither of them heard her approach.

Richard recovers first, points to his cup, and pulls a pack of smokes from his jacket. "May I?"

Betty points to the *No Smoking* sign on the back wall. The one Lou insisted on hanging.

Richard peers around the empty diner before producing a smile meant to charm. "Who's to tell?"

"Me," Betty answers.

Richard slaps the pack on the table making Mary jump.

"Tempers aren't worth the time you put into them." Betty refills Mary's cup, eyeing the abused pack.

"Let's get out of here, Mary."

Mary's face is pale, pinched. She wavers, then suddenly stands. "I need the restroom."

Betty points to the far corner.

Mary nods and scurries past.

Richard scowls as Betty tops up his coffee, swipes a rag across the table, and returns the pot to its station. When he pulls out his cellphone and makes a point of ignoring her, she follows Mary into the bathroom.

The door on the second stall is shut. She can see Mary's shoes—brown, flat-heeled, serviceable—shoes for a woman who expects nothing from life, who takes what she's given.

Betty taps out a cigarette and places it between her lips. The lighter was her grandmother's, an old Zippo that flips open and snaps shut to extinguish the flame.

The first draw is heady and sweet—a coming home, a sense of peace. She holds the smoke as long as she can, unwilling to let it go, until finally she's forced to breathe. She opens her eyes, unaware that she closed them, and stares at the stall door.

"I had a Richard once, promised me the moon and back, promised to love me forever, until he promised himself right down the aisle to another woman. When I told him I was pregnant, he denied it was his." She picks a piece of tobacco off her tongue. "Not that it mattered.

I lost the baby, my daughter. Doc blamed the cigarettes. Men stick together. Remember that. You're not pregnant, are you?"

The stall door swings open. Mary steps out, clutching her bag, and shakes her head.

"Good." Betty inhales a lungful of smoke, anticipates the shiver of pleasure.

"Why did he say he loves me, if he didn't mean it?" Mary stares at her serviceable shoes.

"Honey, we're just dolls to them. In their minds, we're plastic, without a lick of feelings."

"May I have one of those?" Mary gestures to the cigarette.

Betty shrinks back against the sink, cradling the half-empty pack against her chest, her eyes narrowed from the smoke. "It's a bad habit," she says. "Don't give him the satisfaction of starting because of heartbreak." She studies Mary through the smoke. "If I could quit I would have, long ago. It gets under your skin, in your blood, same as guys like your Richard." She gestures toward the front of the diner where they'd left Richard waiting. "Quit while you still can. I would give my own daughter the same advice, if I could. You can go out the back way, wait in the alley for a cab. Lou's in the kitchen but he won't mind. We're about ready to close up anyway."

"I thought this was a twenty-four-hour diner." Mary relaxes her grip on her bag, holding it with one hand at her side.

"Not since the murders. We stay open until the movie theater lets out the last show. We get a few couples, like yourselves, but most hurry on home."

"I can't just walk out on Richard."

"Honey, men like him need to be taught a lesson." Betty snuffs the end of her cigarette against the sink, then slips the stub back into the pack.

"Mary," Richard yells. "You fall in? Let's go."

Mary pales. "I don't know. I don't know what to do."

Betty puts a hand on the girl's arm. "Head high, Mary. He can wait on you until the cows come home. Not that he would. And that's no mark against you. It's just what he is. Women deserve better. You scoot out the back. I'll handle Richard."

Mary hesitates, then leans into Betty and gives her a shy hug.

"Lou might look like a bear," Betty whispers, "but he's not one of them. Tell him I said you want a cab." She opens the restroom door and gently pushes Mary to the left, toward the kitchen, while she turns right, into the dining room.

Richard is standing near the corner booth searching the area.

A thrill of pleasure moves up Betty's spine. "Lost something?" she asks.

He spins around, relaxes. "My smokes. Where's Mary? Did she take them to mess with me?"

"Maybe you kicked them under the next booth."

He grumbles but squats down to look.

"Shall I ring up your bill?"

"Where's Mary?" His voice floats up from beneath the table.

She ignores the question, rips their check off her pad, and takes it to the register. She scribbles his name on top of the check, sticks it in her apron next to her cigarettes, and rings up the two coffees.

"Find them?" she asks when he approaches the counter.

He shakes his head and looks toward the restroom. "She crying in there?"

"Who, Mary? No, she left. Went out the back."

"She what?" His brows lift then drop back into a scowl. "Just assumed I'd pay her way, did she? Well, good riddance." He taps his jacket pockets searching for his smokes.

"Here." Betty reaches under the counter and carefully pulls out a cigarette from the second pack she keeps in her bag—her own special blend, shared with a select few.

"Thanks." He takes matches from his pocket.

Betty holds up her hand, points to the sign. "Not in here."

He snorts. "Right." He tucks the matches away and tosses her a five-dollar bill. He waits for his change.

She drops two quarters into his outstretched hand.

He gives them a little flip then shoves them into his jeans pocket. With a last scowl toward the restroom, he walks out of Lou's Diner. He pauses under the halo of light, a match flares, and he moves on.

* * *

The next morning, Betty wakes before the sun. She rolls over, feels for her cigarettes and lighter on the nightstand, and brings them into bed with her. The flame from the lighter momentarily brightens the small bedroom. The tip of her cigarette glows a warm red. She inhales, smiles contentedly, and tosses the empty pack onto the floor.

She feels along the bed, finds the remote and turns on the television, switching to the local news. "A body was found late last night on Baker Street. Although it's still too early to know for sure, police believe this to be yet another victim of the killer, dubbed 'The Exterminator' by police." An image of Richard fills the screen.

Betty swings her feet over the side of the bed, turns on the lamp. She retrieves a thumbtack from the nightstand drawer, finds the slip of paper she left on top, and stands to tack it to the wall above her bed. Richard's name stares back at her from the diner check, along with the names of three other men scrawled across their own checks.

That thrill of pleasure moves along her spine. She takes the cigarette from her mouth. It's getting so she can't tell what she craves more. She looks at the empty pack on the floor and makes a mental shopping list: cigarettes and cyanide.

ROLLA
Jennifer Riley

Dinnertime.

With his sweetheart Viola and courtin' on his mind, Rolla White studied his face in the clouded mirror. He was a decorated war hero, 22nd Infantry, but would that help when he went to courtin'?

He scraped his hair over his forehead. He surveyed the result, didn't like it, made a scalpel of the comb, dragged it over his scalp, attempted a side part just so. He stepped back, looked again. "Tck." Began again.

He tried one final time. At last. He nodded into the mirror, certain the 22nd Infantry would approve. He went to the kitchen in time to see his mother pull a pan of cornbread out of the stove and smile at him. He nodded to his father, brother, baby sister, and grand-mother as he wrestled his chair back.

"Dinnertime, Rolla," Mother said. "Gotta eat before you walk to Viola Symmington's. I won't have you eatin' there." The cast iron pan clattered on the table.

"Hoo, he and Viola will warm it up," James said from his place across from Rolla's seat at the oak table.

"James, leave your brother alone," Mother said.

"Help yourself to the ham, James, then pass it to Grandma. More pork chops? More sliced tomatoes? Collards, take some and pass them. Grandma, pass Rolla the butter and, Rolla, pass the butter around the table. Everbody's drinkin' buttermilk tonight."

"James and I churned this morning," said Grandma White.

Father nodded, "Good. James is becoming a man. Takin' Rolla's place soon." He piled a small heap of collard greens. "Passa cider vinegar, please."

Through the open back door, Rolla heard frogs cranking into their own full-throated courting, seeking partners. Courtship drifted from the backyard through the screen door and into the kitchen, where Rolla's family gathered to sit for dinner.

He pulled back his chair and sat at a forty-five-degree angle, poised to bolt through the front door as soon as the meal was over. As he stroked butter onto his first piece of cornbread, in his imagination he saw the slab of oak he'd make into his own table, his and Viola's. He caught Grandma looking at him. Grandma White nodded at him and said to his siblings, "James and Susanna White, mind your manners."

"Passa cornbread again," Rolla said and added, "please. Butter. Thank you. Cornbread, best in the county." Rolla lathered another piece of cornbread with butter churned today. Underneath the table, his toes in polished shoes tapped up and down but he kept his feet still, didn't fidget, as he tried to improve his manners. He was no longer a 22nd Infantry demolition soldier, and needed to up his manners to go courtin'. James pushed him the fried pork chop platter. Rolla tucked his dinner napkin into his collar. He caught his dad looking at him and wondered if his dad would understand improving table manners during courtship. Rolla thought again of the 22nd Infantry. Should be good enough for Viola's father to approve me courting Viola. Sure it would be. And that wasn't all. He had that oak slab picked out, planed, polished, and ready to be his table, his and Viola's. He cleared his throat. "Thanks for fixin' a good dinner, Ma." He lifted his glass and drank buttermilk.

"Like?" James said. "You mean 'love.'" James warbled in delight while hiding his laugh behind his napkin. "Love," he said again in a trill of half-step notes. To distract James, Grandma pointed to his napkin then made a downward motion James dared not ignore.

"Buttermilk," said his mother, "fresh this morning. Drink up."

"You need buttermilk before courtin'," James said, and smooched the air, smoothing his napkin across his lap.

"Hush," said Rolla.

"Hush," said Grandma and Mother.

"Take your time, Rolla," Father said. "Too early in the evening to go courtin' anyway." He glanced at James and Rolla in one stroke. Rolla knew his brother wouldn't dare snigger or smile when their father spoke. Grandma nodded and patted Rolla's hand.

Rolla split a second piece of cornbread. Buttered it. "It's good, Ma," he said again. He saw her look at his father and he wondered, how had courtship been for them.

"Eat more than just cornbread, Rolla. It's a walk to Chestnut Street." Ma passed him collard greens. Rolla heaped collard greens over his plate and reached for the cider vinegar. He caught his mother's eye.

"'Scuse me, didn't mean to reach." He thought, Can't be nervous already, 22nd Infantry. Grandma smiled. Mother nodded once. Father didn't look up. James puffed out his chest trying too hard not to giggle. The baby sister lowered her head and made smacking noises. Out the backdoor, frogs continued chirping, seeking courtship.

After three more bites, Rolla pushed back the chair and stood up. "Thanks, be going now." He thought he sounded like a nervous man in his own house; stop it. He nodded to the rest of his family and silently blessed them. James looked ready to burst with a hiccup and cough to hide the giggles.

Courtship. The awkward moment in every man's life. Had 22nd Infantry been this scary? Maybe. Rolla thought briefly about his mother and father's courtin' time. Then he grabbed his cap and stopped one more time in the doorway to look at his family, all sitting at the table.

Father kept his head lowered to feed scraps to the hound. Grandma fed the baby from her plate. James pulled a face. Ma got up and followed Rolla to the front door.

"You look nice, Rolla." She smoothed down the collar of his best shirt. "Aunt Mina's has already put in a good word for you with the Symmingtons."

"Tck, I wish women folk would mind their business," Rolla mock-wailed, as he kissed his mother's cheek. "'Bye, Ma." Secretly he was grateful. He tipped his cap to her.

"Rolla, tell the Symmingtons we'll see them in church this Sunday. Courtship isn't the end of the world," Ma said.

Rolla nodded. "I'll tell them you said hello. If they need help plowing their next field, they can let me know."

Rolla knew the way to the Symmingtons' house. Just last fall, he'd helped clear stumps and rocks from a new field Mr. Symmington wanted cleared, and Rolla hadn't taken any pay for it either. That and his time in the 22nd, they ought to make him good enough for any man's daughter.

The walk offered him a few more minutes to practice his speech, almost like a prayer now. Pray every day. He walked past the churchyard. Under his breath, "Mr. Symmington, could I pay court and come to see your daughter? Ask her out of an evening? I'm asking for your permission, sir." Rolla had designed the words and the expression on his face. What he'd do with his hands. He was confident of his statement, as confident as three years of high school, the 22nd Infantry, Demolition Division, his handiwork skills, and working season after season on various farms could make him. His family was upstanding citizens, finest people in the town. Preacher Bob told them so every Sunday as they exited the church.

Rolla took one last secret feel of his cap, his shirt collar, his shirt front, best he could manage, and headed toward the Symmington house on the next street. He saw success blooming around him in the evening air. With her father's permission, Rolla could court sixteen-year-old Miss Viola Symmington.

Shank of the Evening, Reckonings

"One more time, don't come near my daughter Viola. She's too young for you. I appreciate the 22nd Infantry, but you're a man of the world," said the father, edging even closer to Rolla and whipping his finger in Rolla's face. "Plus, our family is of the merchant class. What's your family, son?"

Symmington and Rolla had excused themselves from the front parlor to the railroad tracks that ran across Center Street, out of the hearing range of everyone else. Man-to-man conversations took place at the railroad tracks. Iron will and iron horses. Power, iron rails, spikes and steam.

"My family are farmers and proud of it, sir." Rolla looked Old Man Symmington right in both eyes. In his past, Rolla had pinned his knife through eyes meaner than those. "I'd take care of Viola, sir. Treat her with respect." Rolla's chin almost touched Old Man Symmington's chin in a lover's nudge. They could have rolled a cigarette between their chins and noses.

"Don't come near Viola. Don't ask me again." Old Man Symmington spat and turned his back on Rolla.

Rolla stood up two inches taller and started calculating firepower.

Almost Midnight

Boom. The dynamite Rolla White used forced apart wooden planks, iron nails and propelled them skyward. Small flames babbled like tongues and grew. Smoke roiled skyward. The Symmington General Store shelves blew up, blasted their treasures with them. Cans of Clabber Girl baking powder, pepper, salt, cloves, cinnamon, crocks of pickles, the cracker barrel, the bag and string holder, the counter, the Indian cigar statue, chewing tobacco, bolts of fabric, planking, OXO soup, George Mugridge & Sons Biscuits, J.G. Ivers & Son Steam Bakery, fishing tackle, coffee pots, the cash register, the telegraph key, all blasted outward and upward. Debris whirled skyward, telescoped outward to blacken the evening.

Rolla enjoyed the sight for a few seconds. He thought the 22nd Infantry might not approve, but his heart was black and broken. Then he sensed townspeople waking up coming outside to look, starting toward the scene, scattering in first waves of panic but then summoning the volunteer fire department.

I served in the 22nd Infantry, he thought, but I'm not good enough to court Viola Symmington. I'm not good enough for her father, on this late Day of Our Lord, June 17, 1867. He had never thought he'd be denied the pleasure of courting Viola Symmington. His heart was broken into more dirty pieces than the explosion he created.

All the contents of the Symmington General Store, all blown to smithereens in a skyward blast of anger, youth, and denial. Rolla turned his back. Who would he tell first? Words failed him again as people pushed past him to see the commotion. He kept walking, oblivious to spraying as the boom settled itself back into a harrumph over the astonished town as he walked away.

I had an itch to hitch, Rolla thought, still walking toward Preacher Bob's house. No more. He opened the churchyard gate and then closed it. Then he thought of what had been his last act as a free man in his parents' house: pushing open the screen door and saying good-bye to his mother.

The fire bell was clanging now. Men were stumbling over each other, vying to be first to put out the fire, yelling, turning, twisting, a human flame struggling for direction, panic before purpose in the only general store in the county.

"Nothing to put out," Rolla said, squared his shoulders and marched up the stone path. Ma had said they'd see who on Sunday? Oh, yeah, by Sunday he'd be dead or in jail.

A CALCEOLOGIST
HAS A BAD DAY
Jamie Catcher

"Faerie Culpepper. The woman of the shoes, they call you."

The detective introduced himself as Detective De-ranged-kangaroo, or something like that. I was too distracted by his shoes and their gleam to pay attention. I will think of him as Detective Shiny Shoe.

"I didn't do it."

A red shoe sits in a clear plastic evidence bag on the table in front of me, and I inch forward in the desire to save it. This all began with a missing shoe and now here I am—defending my life—with a found shoe in an interrogation room that smells of lemon floor cleaner and faint cigar smoke.

Or did you do it for the *heel* of it? That's what he'll say next. I imagine the words forming from his pillowy lips, the fleshy pink pinched with a nice Cupid's bow, but he purses his lips together instead, and only nods. They are prize lips; I noticed them immediately when he came to arrest me. I appreciated the tiny touch of beauty in the ugly moment of being surrounded by cops and handcuffed while sitting at my kitchen table, having coffee with the vice president of the Junior Ladies Bonne Society Club. We'd been planning a charity shoe auction and I'll never, ever, forget the look on her face.

He sits across the table from me and says nothing, his face stony as he grinds his teeth back and forth, then sucks his bottom lip in. I wonder if he notices me staring at his lips. Maybe that's why he continues such grand lip activity.

I also wonder what he thought of my shoe collection.

My beautiful, beautiful shoes. Did he walk into my shoe room and look around in awe? Did he touch the white wooden cubbies that lined the wall from floor to ceiling? Maybe he flicked on the lights above the protective glass of the showcase for the Chosen Four. While rows and rows of my shoes are tiny representatives of past times and cultures, those four pairs of shoes meant my future.

Coco Chanel said that with four pairs of shoes, she could travel the world. So, I had four pairs chosen for my trip. There was a pair of tall brown boots for attitude and bad weather, and a pair of burgundy ballet flats for naps on mass transit and good measure. A pair of utilitarian black loafers rounded up the pack—my sightseeing heavyweights—and then there was *the pair* of cherry red stilettos. I daydreamed of wearing *them* on a hot date. All were patiently tanned and hand-sewn, and met my criteria of sturdy yet beautiful.

The detective taps his fingers, and I hear his watch tick as the walls of the interrogation room seem to tighten. My throat is dry and the urge to swallow hits, but I fight it off in front of his stare.

Tick.

When I blink, images blur and turn like the glass in a kaleidoscope. When I saw the left shoe of my red pair was missing, I screamed and I screamed. I clutched my head, the screams spinning around me, mingling with Jack's laughter.

Tick.

"There was an old lady who lived in a shoe," Detective Shiny Shoe says under his breath as he rustles papers and adjusts in his wooden seat.

The sense of humor I hear in his voice wants to spill now, but he's holding it together. I bet he's actually a fun guy, but as if I haven't heard that old shoe line before. I smile and sit up straighter in my posterior-numbing wooden seat to play along with the game.

"Who had so many children, she didn't know what to do," I say. I hope he knows I'm the victim here. He has to see it and let me go home to my shoes so I can finish packing and print the train tickets for Venice to Florence. I paid extra for two nicer seats: one seat for me, and one for the Chosen Four.

He raises his eyebrows at me and I keep talking.

"Women do like their shoes, as do many men. I see you're wearing an Italian-made loafer in a US size 12, but I'm sure it's marked Euro size 46. They appear to be hand-constructed, which is rare these days. Probably in Tuscany. Florence, specifically. Did your wife buy them secondhand? I doubt on your salary you could afford them new. You should be proud to wear an Italian cobbler's work. They're not Salvatore Ferragamos, but they're close."

He glowers during my spiel and then raises his leg to plop his foot on the table. He stares at the shoe, pulls it off, and looks inside. "Well, now. Made in Italy. Size 46. I never noticed. Bravo, Madam Shoe." He puts his shoe back on, lowers his foot to the floor, and looks down at the loafer, perhaps with new appreciation.

As he should. They were a fine pair of shoes, a remnant of the days when shoes were made lovingly by hand over hours and hours in a small room with scattered mounds of leather, wooden shoe forms, and tiny tools.

"I've always wondered if it was true that the cobbler's wife went barefoot, as the old adage goes," he says. He pulls two Chapsticks out of his coat pocket and applies one and then the other liberally to his lips in a very exact process, one that took him some time.

I watch, thinking he seems quite preoccupied by his lip activity in general. "If I married a cobbler, I'd want the pick of the lot." I say, then remember I've sworn off men, even shoemakers.

The air conditioner turns on, mingling the lemon cleaner and cigar smoke with the smell of someone's curry take-out dinner, and the hairs on my arms rise. I feel sick. To calm myself, I imagine the feel of a new Italian shoe on my foot, one with tender leather molded to my foot.

"Your ex," the detective says, "what did he think of

you and your shoes? Living like that in a self-made shrine of shoes? Or did he not care because you supported him, that is, until he met her, and she made more money than you?"

Living like that. Why was I being judged for admiring beauty? For loving the smell of buttery soft leather and a hand-sewn sole with the heel stacked and pressed with exactness? For admiring centuries of artisans and craftsmanship? I want to knock the detective's Chapsticks off the table.

"I don't care if she made more. I do just fine in cybersecurity at the hospital. And I think of my collection as being a shoe museum. I collect many shoes of the past. You can learn a lot about an era and about a person from their shoes. Their income. Their personality. The style of their culture and the technology of the time period. It's called calceology."

"Calceology, hmm." He leans back and crosses his arms. "Our cyber guy has heard of you. Spoke well of you. He says he sees you at conferences."

I fidget. I sit taller, cross my legs, and concentrate. My bladder passed its emergency mark at least an hour ago, and I feared standing up meant a water show. Maybe that was why the floor cleaner reeked so strong in here.

Now he leans toward me. "Have you always tucked shoes into little beds and pulled up the covers on them like they were babies? Did you give them some broth without any bread, whip them all soundly and put them to bed?" he sing-songs, finishing his page in Mother Goose as if he just can't help it.

So now it begins—the questioning of my sanity. I nod. "Yes, I have. And when do I get my shoe back?"

"You mean the murder weapon found at the scene? You don't. It's evidence. Your ex tells us you sleep with shoes in your bed, and I did see shoes there. Did you just scoot them over when he was around, or did they replace him after he left you for her?"

Funny how you can take a moment in time, a bad moment, and wall it away in your brain, this dark little room that your day-to-day thoughts ignore as they waltz on by. And then *boom*. The door bursts open, spilling the dark out into your every thought, and taking over your brain in a rush that leaves you struggling for breath while your brain screams.

I feel the heat flush my cheeks at the memory of seeing two people smile at each other in the park. I had followed him there, suspicious that he would meet someone. I hid in the trees but once I saw them, I had to look straight to her shoes. She wore pleather size sevens from the fall collection at the corner department store. Machine-made. Cemented-together soles. But a fine knock-off of a famous designer who had her shoes handmade by some the world's best shoe artisans. I wanted to hate her for her shoes, but I couldn't. They were actually a good choice for today's assembly line market. So, I hated him instead.

"Witnesses say there was a loud confrontation last night at his apartment. You accused your ex and his lover of stealing a single shoe."

That part *is* true, but did he have to say lover?

"I did go to Jack's, but I left both of them alive," I say. Again I think, I am the victim and I will the detective to see it.

"When I returned home from work yesterday, the left side of Pair One's cubby sat empty. Jack had been over to get his things, and by the lingering smell of perfume in the house, I knew she came with him. They were the only people in my house yesterday." *She* had already admitted she loved my shoe collection months ago. She'd once been my so-called new friend, all chatty and asking a zillion questions, and then Jack walks in, and her eyes pop.

"Of course, I accused them of stealing my shoe. It's completely like Jack to take one shoe just to piss me off."

"It must have been hard. Being replaced by a younger woman."

At least he hadn't said a younger, thinner woman. "Well, if we'd had anything worth anything, he wouldn't have left me for her. Best to know where I stand right now than continue living a life that's a charade."

The detective tilts his head in apparent thought at this, and then rubs the dark stubble flecked with red that lines his jaw. He closes his notebook, and I think, This is it. I'm free to go. I've surprised him with my coolness, my acceptance. I'm not crying and blubbering and raging around slamming my fists to the table like a dumped partner. He knows I'm innocent. *I am the victim.*

"Your fingerprints were all over the murder weapon."

"You mean the shoe. Of course, they were. It's my shoe."

"You suspected Jack and his new girlfriend stole a single shoe to taunt you. A joke sent you into a rage. I think you hid in the bushes and tackled her, then you stabbed her repeatedly with the high heel of the stolen shoe's mate."

Okay, now this guy is just an idiot in nice shoes.

"Its five-inch heel was plunged into her carotid artery, according to the medical examiner."

I look to the table. My poor baby sitting in the evidence bag without air. I hate how it looks now, the heel soaked in her blood, and blood spatters all over the upper.

"After the screaming match over the stolen shoe, the one the neighbors reported, you waited outside in the garden, and when she went for a jog, you took out your revenge, didn't you?"

"Did Jack tell you all this? Are you going to believe everything Jack says? Maybe I didn't care as much about Jack as Jack thinks. And his new girlfriend and I were surprisingly cool around one another. We both like shoes and I know she really liked my collection. I didn't hate her and I didn't kill her."

He leans back, his lips apart, and his eyes squinting.

I cross my arms, wincing as I sink down into my chair, the hard wood slats making my lower back twinge with pain. My thoughts scramble from *I need a lawyer* to *My plans for tomorrow are absolute rubbish now* to *why didn't I buy trip insurance?* I don't know of anyone who would post my bail, so I'll probably be sleeping in jail tonight, and there'll be no one to tuck my shoes in. I picture the tiny white cubicles, unkempt and alone.

I weep.

Detective Shiny Shoe nudges a box of Kleenex at me.

"I understand you have a big trip planned. You understand, if I let you go tonight, you can't take that trip. You have to stay in town."

I blow my nose with more power than I intend, the loud honk much like a horn in the tiny interrogation room. He's really letting me go.

"Yes, I've been planning a trip around the world. I go to Paris tomorrow to search the antique markets for a 1960s' Chanel nude pump with a black toe. It shortens the foot while elongating the leg, you know. And then–"

"And then, you continue your elaborate escape while shoe shopping in Paris."

"No. I was going to say, I'm going to Florence to shop leather. Did you know you can stay in a centuries-old villa overlooking Florence where Dante himself stayed? From the villa, I can walk to the bus stop and go to a variety of artisan shoemakers and then the Duomo. I have it all mapped out. It's my dream come true."

"You're not going on your dream-come-true trip now. Understand?"

"You can check the booking dates. You'll see my plans were made long before last night's events. Why would I risk my trip? Why would I want her blood on my shoe?"

"I did check, which is why I'm not arresting you now.

Lock your doors tonight and call me if anything out of the ordinary happens. And I mean anything." The detective stands, pockets his Chapsticks, and places his card in front of me, suddenly in a rush to leave the tiny room of *eau de lemon cigar curry.*

"I can leave? Just like that?"

"Uh-huh. Like that."

"Free," I say, though I don't know how I'll get home without my car. They carted me up here, wide-eyed and annoyed, all my neighbors peering out their windows

"And Faerie? I don't have a wife. I buy my own shoes, possibly secondhand at times," he says with a slight shrug and a grin before glancing at his loafers.

He taps them once as if beckoning me. I squeeze my legs together and waddle to the bathroom, my heart pounding. I'm free. Free! But what did he mean about locking my door tonight? The detective sounded like he thought I might end up with a stiletto in my carotid, with all his *call me for anything.*

When I step out of the precinct washroom, he waits. He leans against the wall in a black leather jacket. Combined with his growing stubble, it gives him a rugged look that makes me suck in my stomach and swear off Lay's potato chips.

"I'll take you home, Faerie."

I follow on the heels of the Italian loafers.

"It's the house that looks like a giant shoe, right?" he says, giving me a side eye.

"Shut up," I say under my breath, unsure if he heard and unsure if I care.

On the silent drive home, I count fourteen Chapsticks in his car. He parks and I go to open my car door, but he holds up a finger for me to wait.

"I mean it, Faerie. If anyone comes to the door tonight, don't answer it. Call me—immediately—don't even think."

Don't even think. I nod and grimace, choking down a hysteric laugh. I wander into my empty house, the faint smell of bacon lingering in the kitchen. I try to remember something, but the something's out of reach and all I can think of is my shoes. I lock the door behind me and peek out the window to watch the detective walk away.

I go straight to my shoe room and gather my favorite pairs, my arms full. I drop them on the bed as they're sleeping with me tonight for safety. I arrange them on the bed, placing them at careful angles so I can see them all, and try to decide on Pair One's replacement for the trip. So torn between a navy patent with a gold heel and a black studded stiletto, I'm about to choose my Chuck Taylors when out of the corner of my eye, I see that my closet door sits ajar. I rush over and shut it, annoyed by a memory. Then an icy thought crawls up my spine and it's *the* something out of reach: I don't remember cooking bacon this morning.

A blinding light floods my bedroom window, making my heart race. I lunge forward and crawl across my bed to crack open the blinds and peer out. Despite Jack's arguing it was unnecessary, I had installed the brightest motion detecting lights I could find a few years ago. Now, anyone who steps into my backyard after twilight gets a nasty—*click.* A figure stands there.

"It's Detective Bergeroo, Ms. Culpepper. I'm checking out your grounds. Can you turn your lights off?"

So, that's what his name is. "The lights will go out on by themselves in fifteen minutes." I turn back on my pillow, ignoring the bleaching white light, and waiting for his reply to that. *You didn't say please, Detective Bergeroo.*

Something rustles. I sit up. The rustle's followed by a metallic zinging sound. Outside? *No.* Inside. Unless he's capable of teleportation, it can't be the detective, and now my heart thunders in my ears as I squeeze the covers between my fists. A muffled male roar follows the zing. I now realize it comes from a cubicle off its track in the shoe room.

I grab the baseball bat that I've kept by my bed ever since Jack moved out. On tiptoe, I ease toward the shoe room, realizing I hear breathing that's not my own.

Someone's in my house. They left my closet door open and they ate my bacon. I need to get to the door and call Detective Bergeroo-Shiny Shoe. He has to still be nearby, doesn't he? I make it out of the room and down the hall.

Ooomphf. The impact of a hand over my mouth slams my head to the wall. I drop the bat from the force, the aluminum pinging as it rolls away on the wooden floor of the hallway.

"You crazy bitch."

Jack, with bacon breath and the stolen cherry leather stiletto in his hand, is red-faced and fuming. He shakes the shoe heel at me and squeezes me to the wall as I struggle for air.

"We were just playing a joke on you. Why'd you have to kill her? How sick are you? You killed her with a shoe!"

I manage to gather enough of his flesh between my teeth to bite until he releases me, and I then scream for Detective Bergeroo. I try to run, but Jack drags me down and gets on top of me. He presses the shoe heel against my neck. I get hold of his thumb and bite again.

My front door busts open, the wood splintering, and I hear running footsteps coming toward us in the hall. I picture Detective Bergeroo, his service weapon drawn, but all I see is the looming face of mad Jack, howling in pain. The shoe heel and its sharp edges are only inches from my throat. Jack presses it down and I feel it pierce my skin.

"Drop the shoe, Jack." Detective Bergeroo grabs him by the shoulders and twists him off of me. "Faerie, are you all right?"

To my horror, I see Jack raise the shoe over the detective's head and start to swing.

A boom. My ears vibrate in pain, the shock waves pulse through me, and time slows. Jack freezes. He falls on top of me.

Liquid warmth grows between us, and I'm not sure if it's his blood or mine. I try to breathe under Jack's weight and I watch the ceiling morph black around the edges until I hear Detective Bergeroo's voice again, calling me, and then I feel his hands prying Jack's hands from my neck. He shoves Jack's body to the side, the metallic smell of blood rising in the air.

He pulls a handkerchief out of his pocket, and presses it to my throat as I stand up, flinch to get away from the dead body, and swipe up the fallen stiletto along the way. *What a kill shot, Detective Bergeroo.*

"Well, Miss Culpepper. I guess you see now why I let you go tonight. We already had dirt on Jack. Something to do with his girlfriend having another boyfriend, some damning emails, and a rank search engine history."

I let out a low whistle.

"Oh, thank you, Detective Bergeroo," I say. I throw my arms around him, and with shoe dangling in tow, I kiss those hot lips so he can't see my face or read my mind.

It sure didn't take much to get rid of those two.

No one messes with my shoes.

THE UNBEARABLE SWEETNESS OF ICE CREAM
Bonnie Korta

Clare Sanders opened her refrigerator and pulled out a pint of Red Raspberry gelato and another of Dark Chocolate Fudge Brownie. She returned to the rocking chair in front of the window and spooned alternating flavors directly from the cartons into her mouth. She ate and watched and rocked. Snow transformed the cityscape of Richmond with its Confederate statues and converted tobacco warehouses into ghostly shapes. The rocking and the ice cream did its usual trick, and induced Clare into a trance that carried her above the urban condo and the dilemma that plagued her.

As always, the sweet cold made her think of her grandmother. Summers, Mamaw churned ice cream every few days. In winter, when it snowed, she made snow cream with fresh snow, raw eggs, cream, sugar, vanilla. The memory made Clare feel loved.

If it snows all night, Clare thought, I'll make myself a batch, if I can find any snow not speckled black by Richmond pollution.

She hugged herself, happy at the idea. Maybe her

Mamaw witched her with that snow cream. Maybe that was why her freezer was so crowded with Breyer's, Turkey Hill, Häagen-Dazs, and her new fave, Talenti, that she barely had room for a healthy frozen dinner. When Blue Bell was taken off the market due to listeria, Clare had rushed to another county to buy up the last carton of Banana Pudding. She still hoarded it. She mourned the loss of that brand and any retired flavors like a death in her family.

Her ice cream was arranged by flavor, but she shoved the Ben and Jerry's behind the others so she would not have to look at them. They brought back too many memories of Edmund.

Just thinking his name jolted her out of her ice cream-induced trance. She looked at her bookcase and realized she hadn't read a book since she met him, hadn't even wanted to. While he was in her life, for the first time ever, reality was better, more compelling, than fiction. *The Elegance of the Hedgehog*, *All the Light We Do Not See*, and *The Trail of Crumbs* lay on her coffee table, awaiting her attention. She wished she could pick one up and dive in, but it was too soon.

She did not write anymore either, although she still collected journals with beautiful covers. She picked up one from the table beside her chair. Its cover showed a green woman with red hair flying through a swarm of butterflies and feathers. She wanted to be that woman and fly away from this condo. She heard the empty pages call to her: "Write on me, write on me, write on me." But not yet.

When both cartons of gelato were gone, Clare felt the walls of her condo close in. She'd grown up on a four-hundred-acre farm and often felt trapped in the four-hundred-square-foot space with its trendy Shockoe Bottom address and its exorbitant adjustable-rate mortgage.

Even her life felt confining. By day, Clare worked as a kindergarten teacher. She loved children although the likelihood of having her own family at thirty-five seemed dim. She was sick of being an old maid, a spinster, a thirty-something bachelorette who lived alone and was contemplating getting a cat. That's what led her to kismetmatch.com. Kismet Match seemed so much more thorough than other services, considering astrology and food preferences as well as multiple domains of compatibility. She began to spend her evenings on her computer, hoping to make a love match.

She suffered through dozens of awkward first dates. The men who sounded so good on paper, perfect matches for her, were duds, peculiar looking, no gift for gab, no sense of humor. She was beginning to doubt Kismet Match's whole system and question her own self-awareness. Then she had an idea. She created an alter ego, Fleur Doucet Sandoval, poet, trust-fund baby, world traveler, and philanthropist. It worked.

Enter Edmund Carpentier, professor of philosophy and religious history at Randolph College in Lynchburg. They met for coffee in a public place, and found they had everything in common. Just as she'd always dreamed, Edmund wrote poetry for her and did not understand why she could not get hers published. Edward gave her helpful critiques of the poems she pilfered from other poets' collections. They had long conversations about books and ideas and walked hand-in-hand as they toured Poe's house and Patrick Henry's church and picnicked along the James River. He bought her a Queena Stovall print of a baptism in Pedlar River after she told him how she dog-paddled out of that same river after her own baptism. And he shared her love for ice cream.

Even on this night, alone in the condo, after all that had happened, her earlobes tingled with memories of Chunky Monkey and Woodstock Fantasy painting her nipples and Cherry Garcia drizzled over her body. She shivered, remembering how Edmund whispered, "You are so delicious."

Their affair flourished from June until December on Edmund's weekly trips to Richmond, random weeknight evenings, early Saturday mornings, never on a Sunday. Although Edmund had not proposed, Clare was so sure about their future, she wondered if he might surprise her with an engagement ring for Christmas. But no, he was going to make a presentation in Boston, then visit his parents in Maine.

"Take me with you," she pleaded.

"Next year." When he promised her that they would spend New Year's Day together, she swallowed her disappointment and allowed herself to get high on the Rum Raisin ice cream he spooned into her mouth.

However, in a way, Clare felt relieved because it gave

her more time to consider how and when to reveal her true identity to Edmund. A confession was overdue. The longer she waited, the more enmeshed she became in her assumed identity and all the lies she told to build and support it. She wanted to be sure that he was as committed as she was before she showed her hand. Surely, Edmund would see it for what it was—an innocent little charade, the creation of a more interesting existence, just pretend.

She imagined Edmund putting his hand under her chin. "How could you think you were not enough for me? Fleur, Clare, I don't care what you call yourself. It's you I love, you I want."

She imagined the name Fleur braided into their love story over the years, something they could laugh about with grandchildren, something Edmund could incorporate into a toast for their fiftieth wedding anniversary. New Year's Day was the perfect time for new beginnings.

She spent Christmas with her widowed mother on Pedlar Farm, near the farm where Clare had grown up. They reminisced about the past and gossiped about the present, but Clare did not tell her mother about Edmund.

They dressed to go to church on Christmas day and Victoria Sanders told her about the new young minister at the church. "He's way too smart for Pleasant View, but he seems to have a knack for dealing with country people. He's about your age, I think."

"Maybe you should introduce us. Can't you just see

me as a country minister's wife?"

"I do think you would like him, but he's got a darling little wife, pregnant with their first child."

"I'm working on finding someone," Clare said. "Might bring you a big surprise when I come home for Easter."

As they passed a sign in front of the church, Clare noticed the name of the minister, Edward Campbell, had the same initials as her prospective husband.

She and her mother slipped into the back pew. Clare scanned the crowd for familiar faces, waved at her friend Wanda Foster there with her husband and two children. The choir processed down the aisle, followed by the right Reverend Edward Campbell.

Clare stifled a gasp. Edward Campbell and Edmund Carpentier were one and the same. How could she have been so stupid? Professor of philosophy? How could she have been catfished at her game?

A common Southern Baptist minister was all her Edmund—no, this other woman's Edward—was. Clare looked up at the painting of Christ as Good Shepherd that always comforted her. But this time, Jesus looked right through her. Clare felt completely alone in a crowd of people she'd known all her life. She wondered if Edmund used ice cream in bed with that other woman.

Bile rose in her throat as she admitted she— Fleur/Clare—was the other woman.

As the minister began the call to worship, Clare mumbled something about the bathroom to her mother. She stumbled from the church, staggered over to the decorated Christmas tree, and vomited. When it was over, she decided not to run from the situation. She rejoined her mother and when the service finally ended, they made their way out to where Edmund greeted the congregation. When it was her turn to shake his hand, she looked straight into his eyes while her mother introduced her to the man she had been sleeping with for months.

If Edmund was nonplussed, he gave not a clue, just said, "How do you do, Clare? A Fleur by any other name would smell as sweet." The sound of his voice still made her tremble, made her crave ice cream.

He turned to the woman beside him. "Allow me to introduce my wife, Kirsty Campbell."

Kirsty was a Barbie-doll blonde with a nice round baby bump. "We go down to Richmond all the time, Clare. My folks live in Windsor Farms and Edward has all those committee meetings. You and I should get together sometime. Shockoe Bottom Starbucks?"

"That would be nice. I am sure we have a lot in common." Clare looked right at Edmund when she said it. "How about Cold Stone Creamery?"

She was relieved when she and her mother left. "Aren't they nice?" her mother asked.

"They are everything you said they'd be and more."

Clare spent most of the rest of her visit huddled under blankets in her old room, counting the stars on the ugly beige wallpaper.

Her mother plied her with her childhood favorite, fudge ripple, along with the juicy country gossip Clare usually loved, but nothing seemed to ameliorate the funk she'd fallen into.

"What's wrong with you?" her mother asked.

"Too much ice cream," Clare said as she finished the fudge ripple.

She wanted to call Edward/Edmund's wife to burst that happy girl's bubble, but decided against it. Kirsty was the one true innocent in this whole affair.

In her wildest moments, Clare fantasized about calling the Board of Deacons at New Prospect Baptist Church and blowing Edmund's cover but she didn't want to embarrass her mother.

She also fantasied about petitioning the Southern Baptist Convention to have Edmund barred from preaching. But there was a morals clause in her teaching contract, and she realized that could jeopardize her own job. Both she and Edmund had lied. But she wasn't harboring a husband and had never claimed to be a woman of God.

Back in Richmond, she picked up one of her journals and in a rush of adrenaline, wrote down the whole sordid affair, then tore it into a thousand pieces and locked them away in her jewelry box.

She did not call, text, or tweet Edmund after Christmas.

Then he called and said in his sexy voice, so southern Clare wondered how she'd ever been hoodwinked into thinking he was a Yankee.

"I have something special to give you," he said. "Something beautiful that you will love. I'm driving all the way to Richmond to bring it. Can you meet me? I know you hate me right now, but I can explain everything."

"There's nothing to explain. You are a preacher and a married man who's been cheating on his pregnant wife. End of story."

But in the end, she agreed to meet him, not at her house. No way was she going to allow him to wheedle his way into her bed again. He chose the time—midnight—and she the place, the ice cream aisle of Whole Foods. She wanted him to think about what he'd lost when he lost the delights of her bed, made sweeter by their shared fetish for ice cream. Their encounter would make a spectacle for the audience of Chubby Hubby, Willie Nelson Peach Cobbler, and Cherry Garcia, Clare's sweet men of ice cream, the only men she'd ever been able to count on.

What could he possibly say, she wondered as she drove through the quiet streets. That he was leaving the ministry and divorcing Kirsty so he could teach philosophy? That Kirsty was a young unmarried mother he'd rescued from unspeakable abuse? That Kirsty had an incurable illness?

Clare arrived first at Whole Foods. The parking lot was almost empty. When she went in, the store appeared deserted, not a cashier or shelf stocker in sight.

She established herself in front of the rows of ice cream and waited. As minutes went by, she rummaged through her large purse to pass the time. Trollop lip gloss, a bright red she had worn for Edmund. She'd throw that out first chance she got. The key to the jewelry box that held her ugly secret, she tucked into a zippered pocket. A piece of decaying wood from an abandoned church, a relic she carried to remind herself she still had a soul. And to her surprise, a knife. It was the stubby but deadly knife her father had used to geld steers and stick hogs. He had a name for it, Dynamite. She must have picked it up on the awful Christmas trip so she could feel a little bit of her father's protection. But her school forbade weapons of any kind. Carrying a knife, even a keepsake from her father, could get her fired. She resolved to find a safer place for Dynamite.

She glanced at her watch. Twelve-fifteen a.m.

Edmund was late. Had the bastard lured her here just to see if she would come—to make a fool of her again? She paced in front of the ice cream freezer and couldn't resist peering in to see if there were any new Ben and Jerry flavors. Maybe she should give Ben and Jerry another chance. She could almost taste Burnt Bourbon melting in her mouth.

It was twelve-twenty. She would give him till twelve-thirty. She heard footsteps echo in the empty store and turned. Bright lights illuminated him and she saw that he carried a panel of richly stained glass, as if he were an angel carrying a religious icon.

He smiled and opened his arms to her. "I come in peace, my darling. This is for you. I made it myself."

She found herself moving toward him as if the glass

were a magnet. "Beautiful," she said against her will. "Is it real or another mirage? Can I touch it?"

"I come to free you, not to fool you." Edmund held the stained glass over his head to catch the light. She took a step closer. Then she saw it. The panel was not what it appeared to be. Edmond had broken the glass at its edges, fashioning it into a sharp and deadly weapon. He grabbed her neck with his free hand. She looked up to see the jagged glass poised above her head, her carotid artery a vulnerable target for Edmund's murderous intent.

But he didn't know she'd taken a self-defense class when she first moved to the city. Instead of struggling, she slumped into him as hard as she could, spun out of his grasp, brought her knee up, and hit him hard in the groin.

Edmund dropped the glass which shattered on the floor. "Sweet Jesus," he moaned as he shielded his testicles from another frontal attack.

With that, she pulled Dynamite from her pocket and slid the sharp little knife into Edmund's soft belly and twisted and turned it.

"Thank you, Daddy," she whispered as she plunged her weapon again and again, finally sinking it into Edmund's most vulnerable part. She left it there, a ghastly erection. Edmund tried to run but collapsed in front of the ice cream freezer. He lay on his back in a pool of syrupy blood, shards of glass sticking to him like sugar sprinkles, Dynamite still rising up from his groin.

"Holy fucking Christ," he howled.

"Fine language for a man of God. Didn't your seminary cover the Third Commandment?" Clare hissed. She reached into the freezer, grabbed a pint of Chubby Hubby, and spooned its contents into Edmund's dying mouth with her fingers. Bubbles forming as he choked on the ice cream.

When it was over, she picked her way through blood and broken glass and made her way to the front door. She pulled her hood down over her face, slammed on sunglasses, and called out, "Clean up on aisle six."

In the parking lot, she almost collided with Edmund's pregnant wife. She felt a moment's panic, but Kirsty didn't recognize her under the hood and didn't notice the blood on her coat.

"Did you happen to see my husband in there? I sent him to get me some ice cream, but he's taking the longest time, so I came to find him. Can't wait another minute for my Phish Food Ben and Jerry's. You know how pregnant women are."

"Did not see a living soul." After all, Edward/Edmund was deceased. "But I too have always depended on the unbearable sweetness of ice cream." Clare spoke in a deep voice, hoping to fool Edward/Edmund's wife into thinking she was a drag queen out for a post-show pack of cigarettes. "Be careful, young lady. It's dangerous out here tonight."

She could see the headlines now. "Drag Queen Strikes

Down Holy Man in Ice Cream Aisle" and "Ice Cream Weapon in Random Act of Urban Violence."

Once home, in her rocker, with a tummy full of gelato and fudge, Clare thought of Kirsty and her unborn child. She winced thinking about having to listen to her mother going on and on about the murder of her minister. She shuddered to think of an innocent transgendered person accused of her crime in homophobic Richmond, and even more about Dynamite and all the DNA she left at the crime scene. Clare sincerely hoped they would not start collecting DNA samples from public school teachers.

Oh well, she thought, I will not think about any of that tonight. Maybe I'll think about it tomorrow after I make my snow cream. Snow cream full of raw eggs.

NAME THAT KILLER
J.D. Allen

The Client

Except for the fact his body had decomposed to mere bones, leaving an expressionless skull screaming silently over the pristine lake below, the photo of Henry Mitchell Neil was worthy of the cover of an outdoor magazine. He sat upright, resting easy on a rocky seat, cushioned by several years of ivy and moss. His hands were folded nicely in his lap. Wind, sun, and rain had faded and eroded his suit, but scraps of fine fabric told Jillie it was once an expensive suit.

"Mitchell's remains were found three weeks ago," the dead man's sister said.

Jillie looked up in surprise. The sister called him Mitchell, not Henry as the photo was labelled? Jillie wondered if his parents made that decision or if that was his own choice. Not being a Henry? Jillie got that.

The photo of his remains was laid out on Jillian Dolan's desk among several others. Another showed him straight-on, rather than in profile. A pair of close ups showed his clothing and the jaw bone that rested on crossed legs.

"Even though he's been there for five years, only a few of his finger bones were missing," his sister said.

Candice Neil-Upton sat opposite Jillie, prim in her pale blue button-down sweater and fake diamond necklace. Not one hair out of place, decent rings on her left finger. Maybe four total. Engagement, wedding and a couple of anniversary bands to boot. Long-term wife. She didn't seem too disturbed by the photos of her dead brother. Jillie tried not to judge.

"The police are going to close the case as a suicide," Candice continued. She tossed the next piece of evidence from her file onto Jillie's desk.

The dead man's sister had clearly rehearsed her pitch. Many clients did. As if to skew the sympathy in one way or another. Not that they needed to. Jillie got paid by the billable hour, whether she found what her client wanted or not. Having a strong opinion often hurt an investigation. Tainted one's thinking.

The "reveal" was the autopsy report. More pictures, sans the suit. Several shots of stuff—bones, a few bits of hair, the contents of Mitchell's pockets when he was found, including his wallet, his white-gold wedding ring, one quarter, two dimes, and two pennies. Forty-seven cents.

Who dies with only forty-seven cents while wearing a thousand-dollar suit, Jillie thought.

Lastly, a Casio solar-powered watch that was still keeping perfect time.

Keeping time for, she glanced at the estimated date of

death, five years. *Holy crap. I should get one of those watches.*

She couldn't help but picture the morbid situation as a great ad campaign for the brand. Dead guy on a hill, bulky black watch still strapped to his boney arm, and still ticking. Cue the voiceover: "You may die, but your Casio won't!"

She bit her lip so not to grin as while looking over the report. She made a humming sound and nodded her head to appear serious and cover any hint she found humor in Ms. Neil-Upton's loss.

"So it wasn't a robbery," Jillie said. "Anything at all missing? From the house? The car?"

"The police report said they never found his phone. Nothing was missing from his home." She sat straight, her hands folded over the now empty green folder in her lap. "It's in the police report I gave you."

Jillie nodded. She'd study that in detail over a glass of wine this evening. She glanced at the non-solar-powered athletic tracker strapped to her arm. It had buzzed at her three times today for sitting on her ass longer than it thought she should. The thing was in danger of not making two months, much less years in the woods like the Casio. Piece of crap. Her partner had given it to her for her fortieth birthday. Like Jillie wanted a reminder that her rear was spreading and she didn't move enough? Buzz. You fat slob. Buzz. Move a little would ya? Buzz. Buzz.

Happy Birthday.

"And his car." Candice's sharp tone brought Jillie's

attention back into the conversation. "They never found his car."

Right. Probably not robbery. She wrote that on the oversized blue Post-it pad she jotted thoughts on. So, she had a perfectly preserved skeleton on a cliff overlooking a lake. Five years missing. Insurance and property paid out to the wifey. Motive. Motive, and more motive.

"I have to ask this, so don't get upset."

If it was possible, Candice Neil-Upton sat even straighter. She nodded.

"Do you think he committed suicide?"

She didn't blink. "No. His finances weren't great, but that was the dot-com bust. Everyone was strained at the time. The market had crashed. And being a financial advisor..." Candice almost shrugged. "He was good at his job, Miss. Dolan. It meant something to him. His clients meant something. To give up, quit on them?"

Rhetorical question, answered with her incredulous tone. "He would have considered getting them through the crash and saving their money as important as saving their lives."

"And if there came a point where he realized he could not be the hero of their financial lives?"

She arched a pointy eyebrow. "He'd keep trying until he was."

The Scene

Jillie stumbled as she made her way over a pile of boulders. Okay, they were rocks, but they were big rocks. At least her stupid fit band would be happy with her step count for the first time since she'd donned it. Might even make the fucking goal today. It was an amazing fall morning, but hiking hadn't been on her to-do list in a few years. She was sweating more than she'd like to admit. If someone asked her, she would have classified the trek up to Henry's final resting place as an expert-level trail. Except, she'd left the marked path at least a mile back. The rest had been a trek through thick woods. She was about four miles from where she left her car at the trail head in the boat ramp parking lot.

Where the trail turned east, the map from the police report turned due west. The catalyst for finding the body in the first place had been a naughty puppy. The dog slipped his leash and took his owner on a wild goose chase that ended at one of the strangest crime scenes in years. Once found it would be treated that way until the ME confirmed it as a suicide.

She had to shimmy around a real boulder to find the right spot. No doubt about it when she did. Police tape still dangled from branches, as if they had to keep onlookers out way up here.

Who the fuck would climb up here to lookie-loo? she wondered. Cops and their procedures.

She retrieved the file from her pack. She'd brought all the data Candice gave her and some more she'd gathered from her source at the department.

She held up the photo of the remains to get the exact location. She placed herself in the spot. Legs crossed, hands in lap.

Wow.

The view was amazing. Not a bad place to spend eternity, in her opinion. The hidden cut-out in the rock overlook offered a great view of the lake from about eighty feet up. Even if anyone had smelled a dead body, Henry Mitchell Neil would have been obscured from the lake below by a stand of short scrub bushes along the base of the ridge. Anyone on a boat would only see rocks and leaves from lake level.

Except for the runaway puppy, they'd never have found him. Probably the best place to hide a body Jillie had ever seen. Strange place for a killer to know about. She scoured the area for an hour. The police missed no shell fragments or casings that she found. No indication of bullet damage to nearby trees or chips in the rocks. No knives, arrows, hammers, swords, or rope. No discarded pill bottles or needles to indicate the surmised overdose. And none of those things indicated in the evidence logs.

His bones were intact. No trauma indicated.

By all accounts he just came up here and died of amazing-view-overdose, or maybe a heart attack from the climb in dress shoes.

What the hell happened to Henry Mitchell Neil?

The Partner

Jillie liked full names. Thought a lot about them. She should. She had five of them. Jillian Adele Vance Agnew Dolan.

She studied the certificate on the wall behind a desk that was too clean for a finance guy—in Jillie's opinion. The desk should be covered with papers and forms that showed he was hard at work making money. The diploma proclaimed that Frazier McWilliam Xander had earned his degree in business management from University of Virginia. She inwardly smiled that his name was weirder than hers. Xs always won. Xander was defiantly German. She expected a portly man with an ill-fitting suit to enter the room. His hair combed neatly, his clothing loose enough to surround his belly, the extra fabric difficult to keep in check.

Her instinct was dead on. Frazier was a six-and-a-half footer with thinning red hair and freckles which were quickly turning to age spots. His coloring far more Irish than German.

He dropped backward into his overstuffed chair like a diver falling into the ocean. His feet even rose from the floor as the chair rocked back from the inertia.

"I understand you're here about Mitch." He didn't give her a chance to respond. "Not sure what I can add at this point." He dragged a finger under a bulbous nose.

You could add a hello and an introduction, she thought.

But she wasn't a client and would make him no money, and he clearly resented her being in his office taking up his time. Jillie was used that kind of treatment from men who thought themselves important.

Fine. "Did you and Henry Mitchell Neil keep key employee insurance on your partnership?" If he wanted to get to the point, she would oblige him.

He pushed himself away from his desk a couple inches, blinked a few times, as a scowl grew on his face. "I'm sure that has no bearing on the current situation."

"Then I'm not sure you understand why I'm here, Mr. Xander." She said it slowly. "The situation, as you called it, is a death. I have been hired to investigate it. Is there anything left of his property in the office?"

He shook his head. "No."

"How about a note? Was there anything in the last of your correspondence that might have indicated he was about to commit suicide?"

He shook his head but didn't answer within a beat so she added to the barrage. "And did you have the insurance or not?"

"We did not."

"Huh." Jillie re-crossed her legs as she pulled a note pad from her back pocket. "According to my notes, you made a claim of about two million dollars with Transport American Insurance once he was declared dead. Not that you notified the family of this claim."

He sighed and crossed his arms. "If you knew I had the policy, then why did you ask the question?"

Did she really have to answer that? "To see if you'd tell me the truth," she said. "To use it as an indication of how the rest of our conversation might go."

It was her turn to move on without warning. "So I ask again, do you have any of his personal property or old files of his in the office? Don't forget, I can tell now when you're lying."

He glared at her. She held the gaze, deciding that she wanted pizza for lunch. One of those new buffalo chicken ones the Hut had on the buffet. She glanced at her watch/fitness tracker. It was still an hour until they opened up the pizza trough.

Mr. Xander reddened at the neck and about the ears. After a huff, he hollered at the partially closed door. "Grace!"

For a finance guy, he was horrible at the game chicken. He flinched pretty fast. Maybe he didn't give a shit. He had his money and nothing to hide.

A tired-looking young woman with premature salt and pepper hair stuck her head in. "Yes, sir?"

"Is the box that belonged to Mitch still in the storage room?"

If it was, Jillie decided it most likely would not implicate Frazier McWilliam Xander in Mitchell's death, or he'd have played a better game.

Grace's mouth twisted to one side as she thought. "I think so."

He looked back to Jillie. "I doubt there's anything in there to help Candice. The cops looked at everything when he went missing. As his sister, she is, of course, welcome to it." He looked back to Grace. "Give it to Miss Dolan, and show her out."

He started typing on his keyboard on the otherwise empty desk. There weren't even finger prints. Too much shiny. She bet Gracie had to polish it every day before leaving the office.

"Thank you," Jillie chirped sweetly.

He didn't respond. She had been dismissed. Grace had already made her exit.

"Nice talking to you. Frazier," she added, just to be snarky, and followed Grace out.

The Wife

Jillie had read the interview with Leslie Lorraine Hart-Neil documented in the police report. What was with all the hyphenated names in this family?

She'd never been close enough to marriage to consider what she would do with her own name. Dropping Dolan and adding a new name seemed like an adventure to Jillie. Adding one more would push the it's-cool-to-have-something-different name thing into the realm of over-kill.

The officers who spoke to Leslie had noted she seemed cold. Quiet. Not as emotional as one should be if your spouse was missing. As if there was a template on that shit. They checked her background, her acquaint-tances, questioned her friends. Nothing indicated a lover, and they had looked. If no lover, then what motive would the woman have to kill her husband?

The insurance Leslie received when he was finally declared dead wasn't enough to give her an extravagant life. Five hundred grand. She had downsized, gone back to work herself, and managed to raise their daughter on her own, instead of remarrying.

Jillie had called ahead so there was no surprise when

Leslie Hart-Neil opened the door before Jillie reached the top step of the stoop.

"Candice wants to dig up old bones. She was always convinced that someone killed Mitch." Leslie held the door back to allow Jillie entrance. The place was neat, smelled like pink air freshener. Whatever sweet scent that shit was. Freesia, Rose? Jillie wondered. Leslie headed for the small kitchen.

"Even told people that I had murdered her brother. So now you're here. Coffee?" She held up a pot.

"Sure." It was the first word Jillie had managed.

Leslie poured. Jillie noticed a family portrait, at least ten years old, of Mitchell, their daughter Chris Lynn Neil—sharp, clean name; she liked it—and Leslie, all in matching white sweaters at the beach on a lovely day.

"If you're here to help her dig that up again, you can take a big sip of that Hawaiian blend, and be on your way." Leslie smiled as she said it, but there was a hint of attitude with it.

"She's convinced he didn't commit suicide."

"At the time, I didn't think it was possible either." Leslie's gaze darted to the portrait and back. "For Chris, if nothing else. Mitchell was a planner. He wanted everything perfect for that girl. We were on our way to saving for college, retiring early." She shook her head.

"But?"

She let out a little chuckle. "The bubble. The market crashed. He was under so much stress."

"Bad investments?"

She wrinkled her nose. "Not so much for us, personally. Our investments dropped, but not catastrophically. But some clients were very upset. He was constantly on the phone. I heard him give the same reassurance speech over and over. And he delivered it to me more than once. Hold tight. It will pass. But not everyone held tight."

"Meaning?"

"I remember a man who worked at one of the telecom companies. He'd try to play the odds. Bet on the falling prices or something. Short selling, maybe. Whatever it was, he lost everything. House, retirement, all of it."

"It's got to suck for a financial advisor to watch his client go through." Jill settled onto a barstool at the small island. It was cluttered with clean dishes and a stack of unopened bills.

"That one wasn't his client. He was Frazier's. The man jumped off an overpass onto I-40." Leslie hugged the coffee mug to her chest and shivered a bit. "But still, Mitchell felt the pressure. So when he disappeared, after a few months with no leads, not a word from him, I had to consider the fact that he'd given up." Her eyes went still and dark.

Jillie gave her a few heartbeats to feel that pain. "So you think he did?"

"Looks that way now, doesn't it? I mean up there by himself, no signs of struggle. All his belongings."

"The phone and car?"

"He left them in the parking lot. Someone noticed after a few days and took it." She tilted her head. "That's the only thing that makes sense, isn't it?"

"When you lay out the facts like that, yes."

Her brows rose. "But you believe differently?"

Jillie sighed. This one was boring. Cold cases usually were. All the heat of passion and anguish had been wrung out of the people involved. Leslie still wore her ring, still lived as a widow, but her pain had turned to a reality that was lived in, like an old, ripped sweater. You didn't particularly like it, but it was warm and always on the top of the pile.

"I believe my client is looking for an answer, I'm trying to find it," Jillie said.

"Good luck with that, Ms. Dolan." Leslie took a drink.

"Do you have any of Mitch's old records tucked around here?"

"I've moved twice since then. I kept things I thought were sentimental, but all the paperwork, it's gone."

"Makes sense."

"After so long, I didn't even need the old tax records." She set her cup down.

"So the marriage was okay? Happy family life? No affairs?" Jillie asked. The abruptness seemed to take Leslie off guard. She'd probably not heard such personal questions since the time of the disappearance.

She shrugged. "Like I said. He was stressed. I was young. We fought. But nothing bad enough to break us up. We loved each other, and we loved being a family." This time her gaze lingered on the portrait.

"Did you both have a will?"

Leslie rolled her eyes. "You did get that he was a financial planner, right? Of course we did." She took another sip. "I was beneficiary to our portfolio. Which was at an all-time low at the time. He had a modest life insurance policy because he thought the money for premiums would better invested elsewhere. And it probably would have been, but..."

"Crash."

"Exactly." She looked the picture again. Jillie was starting to feel the woman had not really moved on. Maybe she was still pining. Or struggling.

Jillie glanced at the stack of bills. Metro Bank on top.

"Chris and I got by with what we had. Mitchell had taught me enough to live modestly, and save as much as possible. We had wanted to pay for Chris to go to UNC. No loans. So I downsized. Saved. I think he'd be pretty happy with that."

Jillie would be. Her student loans were fifteen years old, and she had no hope of paying them off before *she* was a set of bones in the woods. "I bet he would."

There wasn't much here. Leslie hadn't gotten rich off her husband's death. She'd have been much higher on the horse if he'd lived and done a good job playing the market through the recovery. If she killed him, it was over passions long dead. And frankly, the woman seemed too soft to lure her husband into the woods, kill him, and leave him to rot. Something like that took some fire.

The Clue

Something didn't sit right. Jillie banged on the keys of

the old computer on her desk. Banged was accurate. No matter how much she tried to type more lightly it didn't happen. Two keyboards a year, maybe three, added to the cost of doing business. Pencil leads didn't stand a chance either. She broke them like mad taking notes. Heavy-handed, in more ways than one.

In its era, the dot-com bust made the news more often than a trashy celebrity with a drug problem. She needed to drill down locally, to see what was going on in the area. Context, and twenty-twenty hindsight, were her best tools for a cold case. And good old Google.

She poured a couple fingers worth of bourbon into a dirty coffee mug next to her computer. It was the cheap stuff and she didn't care. It went down a finger a swallow. She surfed through a bunch of articles about people killing themselves over the crash. The suicide Leslie had mentioned was there. Gregory Thomas Smith. Solid Midwestern, farm boy name. Seems Gregory had lost about three and half mill, wifey was leaving with the young'uns, and he had gotten the pink slip. Ouch. Jillie figured she might dive off a bridge over that. Being broke had its advantages.

She found four suicides in a two-week period in the papers. At the end of one of those articles, something caught her attention. Statistics about self-extinction for a few surrounding counties. They were mostly rural, but plenty of the big rollers of the tech industry lived out in fancy neighborhoods built close to the lake.

She spied a mention of a man missing from Pittsboro. The town just west of the lake. Different county. This man was the same age and general description as Henry Mitchell Neil. Jillie stared at the screen for a moment. The missing man's name was Mitchell Neilson. No middle mentioned. That bugged her.

She searched her records data base for Mitchell Neilson in Chatterson County. A couple came up. One had a DOB exactly two months off from Henry Mitchell Neil. She clicked through her database and tried to find a social security number or driver's license for Mr. Neilson. The DL search garnered her a picture.

"Well. I'll be dammed."

After a few more fingers of whiskey and time to ponder, she began to send emails.

The Sting

The blood pressure monitor on Jillie's fit band had finally dropped below the you-should-stop-now-before-you-die zone. She thought it fitting that she perched herself in the spot Henry Mitchell Neil/Mitchell Neilson had expired.

She sucked down a half bottle of water then immediately regretted it. Needing to piss when in the midst of a sting was not cool. And, of course, thinking about the possible need to pee made it happen. Shit. Shit.

She should go before the target arrived. She glanced up the hill above the crime scene. She hustled away from the rocky outcrop that had supported Mitchell's body for years. The trees grew thick and the undergrowth was thin from lack of sunlight. Mostly ferns. No goddamned fern was big enough for her to pee behind. She was not going to get caught with her pants down.

She walked farther into the woods, occasionally looking back to stay oriented, then found a pile of stacked trees that had all taken the fall at the same time, making a three-foot high timber wall between her and the site.

She was standing, trying to get her sweaty pants back up over her thighs, when she heard the sound of someone making their way up the trail. She shimmied and pulled, knowing her underwear would not end up in the proper location, but as long as her ass was covered, that was going to have to do.

She looked up to see a man. A hiker, boots, backpack, tan shorts, and a blue T-shirt. The backpack hanging loose on his back. She was still buttoning when he pulled out a gun.

The man turned, not surprised to see Jillie. "So. Are you looking for a weapon up here for real, or did you set a trap?" His gaze was dancing around, searching. Considering his options. "I considered both."

According to the marriage records Jillie had found, one of the other spouses was Stacy Neilson, forty-one, from Pittsboro. Married to Mitchell Neilson for seven years. A man? Stacy was a man. And that meant that Mitchell's big secret was worse than four wives. It was three wives and one hubby. Maybe more hubbies. What if they were all men?

"I thought anyone who might be worried they'd left evidence behind would come up and make sure." In the email sent at two a.m. she had implied she'd figured out where a weapon had been hidden.

"But he committed suicide, Ms. Dolan." The gun he pointed in her direction appeared to be a .380. "The autopsy says so."

"If you're aware of the autopsy results, you knew Mitchell was leading a double life." The implication was heavy. Because the autopsy records would only be released to Mitchell's wife. Or husband? "The Raleigh authorities only knew about his wife."

He nodded and grinned. There was more noise behind Jillie. She turned to see. It was Leslie. Also in well-worn hiking boots, but her clothing was much more North Face than his Old Navy. She had a knife.

"Ah." Jillie nodded. "You both knew. A conspiracy to commit murder."

"I found out." Leslie motioned Jillie back into the open. Leslie made her way to Mitchell's resting place. Looked over the edge. For an instant, she looked sad. But her eyes found Stacy and hardened. "I really thought this was the perfect spot."

Stacy shrugged. "Always knew discovery was a possibility."

"There is no evidence, is there?" Leslie asked.

"Only that the man had been living several lives," Jillie said, "and no matter how good an investor he was, no way he was keeping multiple partners happy when the markets crashed."

"I knew for a long time that Mitchell had others in his life. Stacy wasn't his only male friend. And so many women. Mitchell had a sick addiction to sex." Leslie touched Stacy's arm. "I reached out. Stacy had no clue. He thought he could build a life with Mitchell. I tried to break it to him gently."

"Wasn't that sweet of you?"

She shrugged. "We were just going to bust him. Make him give up the charade, and the others." Her voice still had that soothing motherly tone, as if she were talking about a misbehaving child. "Then Stacy pointed out that Mitchell's addiction was going to be the end of my family. My daughter's future."

"He used her. He used me," Stacy said, angrily. "He was a manipulating little—"

"You mean blackmail," Jillie said.

"Semantics. We convinced him to set up some accounts so we were both financially set to come out of the crash well-positioned."

Jillie eased closer to the rock formation to be better located. "So if you were milking that cow, why butcher it?"

Leslie Hart-Neil flinched. "He was going to..."

"Ah. Mitchell was smarter than you, huh? He got tired of the blackmail so you lured him up here and took him out. Which was it, the knife or the gun?"

"He committed suicide, once he knew we knew." But Stacy's nervous eyes and shaking hand gave his lie away.

"Sure he did. Way up here. All by himself. Dressed for a business meeting."

"We just wanted money. We didn't want him dead."

"And so you decided it was a good idea to open a joint account?" Jillie said.

They both took a step back.

"A joint account. To manage the investments, with a document he signed the day he disappeared?"

"You found that?" Stacy frowned. "Pretty resourceful for a cheap private investigator. Don't you need some kind of credentials to check on banking records?"

Cheap? Jillie prided herself on being one of the higher priced gumshoes around, with an immaculate reputation. "We've come a long way since Sam Spade. A statement sitting open on Leslie's counter made the search for accounts that much easier."

"That puts us in a far different situation here." Stacy puffed out his chest, stood taller. He was steeling himself.

Leslie was no longer the timid, mousy woman from the kitchen, woefully staring at the family photo. Her eyes were now tiger-like. Her knees slightly bent. She was as ready to pounce as Stacy. "I need to know if you told the police or Candice about us."

"Of course I did. I'm not stupid." But she had been drinking. She couldn't remember if she'd told Candice her plans or not. But Candice would be pleased to know she was right about her sister-in-law. And she'd get the money after all. Jillie wondered how the news her brother also had male lovers was going to go over.

Stacy raised the .380, pointed it directly at Jillie's heart.

Holy gunfight, Batman. She'd not come armed. The

plan had been to see who showed up and get the confession. She held her hands up and searched her mind for something she could say to put the man off the subject of that trigger long enough for the cavalry.

Bam! Bam! Two slugs walloped her chest. Jillie toppled back, crashing onto her tailbone. The back of her head bounced off the hard-packed surface. *Dang ferns.* Blackness shrouded her vision, and only little bursts of light broke through. The proverbial stars.

The bullets hurt worse than she'd expected, and a functioning breath took longer than she would have liked. She wondered what the heart monitor on the stupid sports tracker said at the moment? Zero? Two hundred ninety-eight?

Stacy and Leslie had shown up with a plan. But the one thing Jillie had on her side was that the two of them were amateurs.

They expected a fair fight.

Jillie was in a business where it never favored her to participate in a fair fight.

Two hidden cops rushed down from the brush farther up the hill. Guns raised and shouting. Jillie lay still and struggled to get her chest to raise and fall with any predictable pattern.

Detective Don Crutchfield bent over her.

"You okay, Dolan?" He pulled her into a sitting position. The vest she argued about wearing because it was tight and hot under her clothes had fucking saved her life.

She nodded through another set of labored breaths.

"Maybe you could have come out before he pulled the trigger?"

He snorted. The other officer was cuffing the pair. "Didn't think the man had it in him, really."

"They killed their husband. Why wouldn't they kill me?"

"You're not leaving them any money." He held out his hand. Jillie fished the wire and recorder out from under the bulletproof vest and gave it to him.

"You owe me a drink, Crutchfield."

OBSESSIONS
Bonnie Olsen

Back when I was hired, the boss—I'll call him DM—struck me as an unusually gloomy man. Fine with me, so long as gloomy didn't equal inertia. Research is funded by grants which are won on the basis of proposals, and those proposals are written by the boss—assuming he's not inert.

Our project was supported by a small grant, just enough to keep the lab going for a year while I dealt with a stream of incoming samples from clinics around the world: N'Djamena, Izmir, Tétouan, places I'd never heard of.

I was to streak each sample onto a special kind of agar that selects for the bacteria we study, grow it up, pick one isolated colony, grow *it* up, and freeze the results, then repeat the process again, and again, day after day. It's meticulous, repetitive labor—utterly unbearable for most people—but for me, my preferred element. I am a research technician, a very good one, in fact.

I may have had my doubts about DM, but the workplace itself was entirely to my liking: a small one-person lab—me—meaning I never had to deal with co-workers bent on expressing their oh-so distinctive personalities.

Better yet, this lab had an adjoining office—with door—for the boss. Once, I worked at a place where the boss's office was nothing but an alcove set off from the rest of the lab, and though I didn't have to endure co-workers, I did have to bear the boss's notions of conviviality. Two or three times a week, she'd call out through her non-door, did I want to go out to lunch, her treat? Would I like some Girl Scout cookies? Did I plan to attend so-and-so's birthday party down the hall? I left that lab mid-project—in fact, left the entire institution—and went to work at a lab with better architecture.

One day I was preparing samples for freeze-down, when somebody behind me said, "Hi."

I didn't reply. You don't, when microscopic droplets of saliva could contaminate your work. I am known for my impeccable sterile technique.

"Uh…*hi?*"

I closed my vial and plunged it into its dry ice-and-ethanol bath. The bath boiled up the way a cup of rum punch boils around a hot poker—but didn't boil over. I always get my proportions right. Satisfied, I turned.

The voice belonged to a scruffy fellow, longish greasy hair, ill-fitting boots, raggedy windbreaker: nothing I wanted anywhere near my lab bench. He affected an overly friendly grin. "DM in?"

A pointless question. DM was visiting his dentist, as the sign on his office door clearly stated. That was something I appreciated about DM, the way he posted a sign whenever he left, always specifying hour, date, and reason so I wouldn't have to deal with interruptions. I can't be gabbing with visitors when there's work be done.

"Um, can I wait?"

No point answering that. His grubby butt was already in my desk chair; his hands with grimy fingernails—I could spot them from across the room—already touching my desk, my pen, my notepad. I made a mental note to swab that desk and everything on or near it with seventy-percent ethanol as soon as possible.

But I had work to do.

Our long-term freezer is housed, unfortunately, in a facility shared by two other labs. Sure enough, Sheryl, a tech from down the hall, was there before me. An ambush? She closed the freezer door and leaned against it. "That wasn't Stan I saw down your way, was it?"

I was carrying a full complement of samples, dry ice, and ethanol; not my preferred condition, despite being properly gloved.

She said, "Scruffy guy? Kind of shabby? Bet he's waiting for DM—hope he is—that's *sure* to be exciting. Want to know why?"

She waited for me to ask why—which I didn't—and *I* waited for her to move her gossipy self away from the freezer door.

She said, "Well, the thing is, Stan used to work here. Had DM's tech job before you, and got *fired!* You should have *seen*—"

I reached around her, grabbed the freezer door's handle, and yanked.

She got the idea and I gained access. I have no time for gossip.

I could see why Sheryl was expecting excitement, though. I've often seen bosses fire somebody then pretend to be the friendliest people on earth. But I've never seen a fired worker return to visit his former boss. Unless it's for revenge.

When I got back to the lab, Stan the Fired Tech was asleep, head down, drool pooling on my desk.

But I had work to do. Colonies to pick, plates to streak; more colonies to pick, more plates to streak.

Suddenly cheers erupted behind me, and I almost dropped a whole stack of agar plates. It was Stan and DM falling into each other's arms like long lost bosom buddies. Difficult to fathom, but good to see DM so, well, *alive*. I almost smiled.

Nov. 13, 11:30 AM
LUNCH WITH STAN, BACK BY 1 PM

That's what the sign on DM's office door read, and I was glad. Stan's presence was a tonic for DM—and therefore a tonic for me. If that was Stan the Fired Technician's idea of revenge, it didn't seem to be working. In fact, I was expecting word of a grant proposal in the works any day.

JAN. 5, 11:30 AM
OUT WITH STAN

At first, the two of them just went out to lunch. Then they turned to playing some sort of car racing game on the computer in DM's office. It filled both office and lab with the roar of engines and masculine comradery.

I tried not to mind, because whenever Stan the Fired Technician stayed away for three or four days, DM would become gloomy again, and I'd have to worry about that grant proposal. But then Stan would show, DM would return to vibrancy, and I'd relax. Of course, I couldn't know exactly what DM did when he was alone in his office, but logically, grant writing would be on the agenda.

MARCH 10, 10:30 AM
OUT ALL DAY WITH S.

DM was more animated than ever, especially when he and Stan were talking G-force. G-force seemed to play a big part in whatever it was they were up to on those days they spent away from the lab.

Yet, though DM was animated, he didn't seem to be working on that grant proposal. In fact, he was hardly ever at his desk. I'd e-mail him my weekly report of samples received and processed, and all he'd write back would be, "Thanx."

But I'd catalogued well over a hundred samples thus far, surely enough for some kind of pilot study. I even included a line suggesting just that in my next weekly e-mailed progress report.

DM wrote back, "Thanx."

MAY 2, 10:00 AM
OUT ALL DAY WITH S.

Another in a growing string of *Out All Day* signs. At least the lab was quiet now, making this the best lab position I'd ever held. Unfortunately, it didn't look like I'd be holding this position long—not unless some other grant kicked in after our present one ended.

I never have trouble finding new positions because I am a good worker. But could the same could be said for DM? His professional reputation had to be suffering. A good technician would give her boss a nudge.

Instead of submitting my ordinary weekly report, I e-mailed him our entire catalogue of samples, their dates received, code numbers, countries of origin, locations in the freezer, and whatever unusual colony characteristics I'd noticed. At the very least, that last about unusual colonies should pique his interest.

DM's e-mailed response: "Thanx."

JUNE 18, 9:30 AM
ICBID CONFERENCE

ICBID stands for International Congress on Bacteriology and Infectious Diseases. This year's meeting was to be held at a certain conference center in Idaho. I've been there. It's a faux-rustic retreat that mixes luxury and informality to create a perfect environment for the exchange of ideas and promotion of collaboration. Better yet, it would be the perfect chance for DM to get his name added to some other researcher's proposal. I had my hopes.

The three-day conference ended but DM didn't come home. A full week passed after that, and still, I had no word from DM, not even an e-mailed "Thanx" for my regular progress report. At least, Stan the Fired Technician wasn't coming by to intrude upon my solitude.

Who did come by was the chair of our department. She hadn't heard from DM either, not a note, not a peep. Together, we rifled through his desk searching for clues about whatever travel plans he'd made, because he hadn't made them through regular channels; the chair already knew that.

We finally found a Post-it note reading "Sky Adventures" and a telephone number. I phoned, and together we listened on speaker as Miss Sky Adventures told us that yes, DM *had* reserved flight time on June 18, but not for any trip to Idaho. Sky Adventures is about parachute jumping.

Eventually, DM's body was found attached to a parachute snagged high in a tree. Stan the Fired

Technician has not been found, so they're calling him a missing person.

As for me, when I showed the department's chair my accurate, detailed, up-to-date catalogue of frozen-down samples, she agreed to write a glowing reference—another in my collection of glowing references. I am, as I said, a very good worker.

Sheryl waylaid me at the freezer again. "Wasn't that just horrible? Well, I knew some kind of revenge was in the works, didn't you? I mean, after what Stan was fired for and everything."

Another ambush. I had no time for this.

"But didn't you know? Stan the Man! Stan the *Dealer* Man, get it? Fired for selling laboratory ethanol to undergrads—and that was just the beginning. Reagent-grade caffeine, God knows what lab he was getting *that* from, but med students were wild for the stuff. Bar-bital—I think he was lifting that from some histology lab—you can get a real good night's sleep with barbital, but it's terribly addictive."

Yet again, she was blocking access to the freezer.

"See, with Stan," she said, "whatever addiction you've got, he's the man to feed it." She paused as if in thought, and when I made a move to go around her, added, "So doesn't that make you wonder what DM's addiction was?"

It didn't, but she went on anyway. "The way I figure

it, DM's addiction was to liveliness. You know, basic human interaction."

I pushed around her.

"Don't you want to know what *your* obsession is?"

I faked a sneeze and spilled freezing ethanol all down her leg. I had no time for this. *I* am not obsessed with anything. I'm just very, very good at my work.

SET THEM FREE, IF NEED BE
Courtney Carter

Obsession.

Rachael thought that was a perfect name for a perfume.

She reached for the egg-shaped bottle of amber liquid, popped off the top, and spritzed a generous amount onto her wrists, neck, and cleavage.

It wasn't her favorite scent. It was a little too spicy and a little too 1980s *Dallas* for her tastes, but she was seeing Mr. Klein tonight and that was the scent he liked the most. From something he'd said, she was certain his mother had worn it. Freud would have loved to sink his teeth into that one. Asking your date to wear the same perfume your mother preferred?

Oh, Mr. Klein, she thought.

She put the bottle back in its place among the dozen other perfumes lining her vanity, and smirked at her long-running personal joke. Imagine if she was seeing *the* Mr. Klein, rather than a regular client she secretly referred to by the designer's name. It was easier if she didn't think of them by their real names, their office-working, child-rearing, buying their wives presents identical to the ones they gave her so they wouldn't get confused-names. It allowed her to compartmentalize them and keep track without getting too attached. That's what they say, isn't it? You should never name a pet you aren't going to keep for very long. That way it's less of a struggle when you have to let it go.

Run! Be free, Fluffy! Or, whatever your real name is!

Rachael put the finishing touches to her ensemble: the diamond earrings Mr. Klein gave her for Valentine's Day that year—identical to, if also a slightly smaller carat size than the ones Mrs. Klein received—and a pair of low-heeled Jimmy Choos that matched her coral dress perfectly. Mr. Klein was stuck on the precipice of neither being a particularly tall nor a particularly short man, but she knew he liked it when she made an effort to keep her height under his.

The black Lincoln arrived precisely at eight p.m. to pick her up. She slid into the back seat, feeling the worn-in, buttery leather against the backs of her thighs. Rachael loved Town Cars, had never even considered navigating the city of Chicago any other way. Let the elite show-offs have their smooth Jaguars, their flashy BMW convertibles just made for being spotted in as they whizzed by. Give her a good old Lincoln any day, with a quiet chauffeur and plenty of Evian stocked in the back seat.

Rachael observed the entire world from the back of a Lincoln Town Car. She was a watcher by nature, a skill that often came in handy in her line of work.

When the car pulled up to the Peninsula Chicago Hotel, she waited for the driver to open her door, to help her avoid a small puddle as she stepped onto the curb. He was one of her regular drivers, Eddie.

"Have a good evening, Miss Barrow." Eddie tipped his cap and climbed back into the driver's seat.

She walked through the brightly lit lobby and into the hotel bar. Mr. Klein sat alone. He'd already loosened his yellow silk tie and unbuttoned the jacket of his navy Armani suit. Must have been a rough day. She pasted a sympathetic look on her face and tapped him on the elbow to get his attention.

"Hello there. Bad day, hon?"

Mr. Klein's face lit up. He stood to kiss her cheek, his nose sliding down to linger at her throat, breathing in a deep whiff of Obsession.

"You look lovely." He rumbled into her ear, then pulled out a bar stool for her and ordered her a drink.

The bartender brought a gin and tonic—heavy on the tonic, light on the gin—with an extra lime wedge in a little dish on the side. All the bartenders at the Peninsula knew to make her drinks on the weak side.

Rachael sipped her mostly-tonic and listened while Mr. Klein filled her in on the hardships of his day.

"First a junior partner at the firm spotted a hole in our biggest client's investment plan, then the damn house renovations got pushed back another three weeks, and don't get me started on Helen." He slugged back the last of his second martini. "She's been busting my balls since before the house work even started."

Rachael made the appropriate oohs and aahs of sympathy, even tittered at his rare display of crude language, but she never commented on his wife. The wives were off limits. In fact, she'd removed all synonyms of the word "wife" from her vocabulary.

Spouse. Significant Other. The Old Ball and Chain.

But she let Mr. Klein vent his frustration. It was part of the job, after all.

Eventually, he lost verbal steam and had enough Grey Goose in his system to turn them toward more pleasurable topics. His hand drifted to her thigh while they waited for the bar tab to be cashed out.

Rachael was rather fond of Mr. Klein. He'd been her client for three years now. His hair had thinned and he'd put on about fifteen pounds but he was a good client. He wasn't jealous or spiteful, if anything his only fault was that he just wasn't "good at monogamy."

His words, not hers.

They slipped out of the bar and stood close together in the otherwise empty elevator. They held hands down the hallway and before the door to their suite closed he reached for the zipper on her dress, and pulled her in close for another hint of perfume.

When Mrs. Klein showed up at her door three days later, Rachael was genuinely surprised. Few wives had bothered to track her down over the years, and this was the first one to show up at her apartment.

Mrs. Klein was blessed with a youthful appearance

for her age, whether by nature or cosmetic assistance, Rachael wasn't sure. She stood in the doorway, her tan slacks and mint green blouse pressed and neat, the straps of a five-thousand-dollar Hermes bag clutched in one hand.

"Are you Rachael Barrow?"

"Yes." Rachael straightened the red maxi dress she'd thrown on to answer the door.

Mrs. Klein's lips pursed together. "You're older than I thought you'd be."

"Oh?"

"And you're a brunette."

"That's right."

"That's not what I was expecting."

Rachael sighed. "Let me guess, you were hoping a twenty-one-year-old, blonde bimbo would answer the door?"

Mrs. Klein inhaled sharply, drawing her petite frame up, and said, "Do you know who I am?"

"Yes, I've seen your picture before."

"You've...you've seen..." Mrs. Klein's brief swell of fighting spirit died. Her shoulders slumped forward and Rachel wondered if the woman was about to cry.

"Why don't you come in?" Rachael opened the door wide, as if she welcomed her clients' wives into her home every day.

Tentatively, Mrs. Klein stepped into the apartment, eyes darting, possibly looking for something to make herself feel superior to her husband's mistress. Rachael's apartment was of modest size, but tastefully decorated.

SET THEM FREE, IF NEED BE

She steered the other woman to a seat in the living room and moved into the kitchen to make a pot of tea.

Soon they sat across from each other on matching couches with cups of tea steaming between them. Rachael waited for Mrs. Klein to speak.

When she did, she asked, "Are you in love with him?"

Rachael resisted the urge to laugh, only because she knew it would make things more awkward. "No, I'm not in love with your husband. He's a client."

"A client. I see." Mrs. Klein smoothed the fabric of her pants. "May I ask, how long he's been a client of yours?"

"Three years."

She made a tiny, high-pitched noise in the back of her throat. "And, how old are you?"

"I'm thirty-six."

"Thirty-six?" She gripped the edge of the couch. "*Thirty-six*? That's only five years younger than I am! That bastard doesn't even have the decency to sleep around with a girl in her twenties like a *normal* man going through a mid-life crisis!"

Rachael picked up her cup of tea, blew gently across the top, and took a long, satisfying sip.

"The way things stand, Mrs...." She stopped short of calling the woman "Mrs. Klein." "Ma'am. You have three options."

The other woman blinked watery eyes at her. "Three?"

"One, you can do nothing. Go on living your comfortable life and hope that your husband will stop seeing other women eventually. Although, we both know how likely that is. Men are creatures of habit, bordering on addicts." Mrs. Klein seemed like she needed a little more distance right now so Rachael stood and walked behind the couch. "Two, I can terminate my relationship with your husband, and you'll at least be rid of me. Of course, then we're back to the creature of habit theory, he might be faithful for a while but there's no guarantee. If he doesn't change you could always ask for a divorce, although I have a feeling that would hurt you more than help. I assumed you signed a prenuptial agreement?"

Mrs. Klein didn't reply, but the skin around her mouth tightened.

"Option number three," Rachael leaned both elbows on the back of the couch. "I can set him free."

"Set him free?" Mrs. Klein blindly picked up her own cup and put it back down without drinking. "How is that any different than breaking things off with him?"

Rachael studied the woman sitting across the room, studied her designer handbag and her clothes that no doubt came from a wardrobe that, if sold, could feed a small country for a year. What Rachael saw when she looked at this woman, what she saw in all of her clients' wives, was the person she could have potentially become. Rich, handsome men had promised her the moon if she'd only commit to them, but that commitment always seemed to be a tad unbalanced. At least in her experience.

Rachael enjoyed having a few of the finer things in

life, she just didn't see the point of giving up her freedom to get them.

"Have I mentioned that my mother was a pharmacist?"

"A what?" Mrs. Klein frowned.

"A pharmacist." Rachael smiled, returning to her seat across from Mrs. Klein. "Not a common practice for women in her day, but she was determined to finish school and build a reputable practice."

"What does that have to do with any of this?"

Rachael crossed her legs and settled back into the cushions. "Did I also mention that my father was another victim of habit? I do believe he tried to stay faithful to my mother, to our family, but he just wasn't good at monogamy."

Mrs. Klein shifted in her seat, smoothed the fabric of her trousers again. "What exactly are you trying to say, Miss Barrow?"

"When I was fourteen, they found my father dead in a room at the motel he used to meet one of his girlfriends. Heart attack. Of course, they questioned my mother because he was being unfaithful, but the autopsy didn't show anything out of the ordinary. He was an overweight man in his late forties who spent an inordinate amount of time trying to screw women half his age. His heart was bound to give out at some point."

Rachael waited.

Either Mrs. Klein understood the options Rachael gave her or she didn't. Either she'd make a choice or she wouldn't.

The Ansonia clock sitting on Rachael's mantel ticked the time away while she waited for Mrs. Klein to speak.

Mrs. Klein stood up, pushing her bag up onto one shoulder. Rachael followed her through the apartment to the front door.

"Thank you for the tea, Miss Barrow." Mrs. Klein spoke softly into the door. Her grip tightened on the doorknob as she drew in a sharp breath. She opened the door. "Set him free, then."

Rachael was at her vanity, carefully tracing the edges of her eyes with her new Chanel Noir Intense eyeliner. One of several gifts from her newest client, Mr. Chanel. A brand-new bottle of No. 5 now sat at the front of her perfume collection, the unopened box just waiting for their first official date.

With her makeup completed, Rachael reached for the half-empty bottle of Obsession and spritzed liberally until she was in a cloud of fragrance. She padded across the cool hardwood floor of her bedroom to the closet. Behind the built-in shelf holding her shoes, sitting flush with the back closet wall, was a slide-out panel. It held her birth certificate, Social Security card, a few photos of her mother, and a small lock box.

Rachael pulled out the box, dropping down on the floor of her closet, and flipped the rotating numbers until the combination lined up with a click. She lifted the lid and stared down at the five perfume bottles nestled inside.

Hermes.

Baccarat.

Bergdorf.

Gucci.

Dolce & Gabana.

All lovely fragrances, collected over the years. Some she'd liked more than others; none of them did she wear anymore.

She placed the Calvin Klein in its new home and locked the box.

"You look like you've had a good day, darling." Rachael pecked Mr. Klein on the cheek when he stood from the bar to greet her. The Peninsula bartender had her tonic with a splash of gin ready for her.

"It's been a fantastic day." Mr. Klein squeezed her waist. It appeared he'd already had more than one martini before her arrival. "No client emergencies at work and the house will be done next week. Hell, even Helen's mood has improved."

Rachael smiled. She sipped her drink and responded at all the right moments. It wasn't long before he paid the bar tab and they walked hand-in-hand through the lobby to the elevators.

Mr. Klein reached for her as soon as they entered their usual suite, but Rachael danced away. Crooking one finger, she guided him further into the room where her surprise waited. Champagne, chocolate-covered strawberries, even a small plate of petit fours in a kaleidoscope of flavors.

"How did I get so lucky?" Mr. Klein wrapped his arms around her from behind, nuzzled the hollow of her throat and breathed deeply.

Rachael lingered for a moment before walking to the table, hips swaying. She popped the cork on the champagne and poured them each a glass. Mr. Klein didn't like champagne, she knew, but he'd drink a toast to make her happy.

They toasted, they drank, Rachael feeding him a strawberry and a petit four, or two. When he offered her one, she declined until they'd "burned off a few calories."

Mr. Klein pulled her in close, ready for another breath of perfume and another night with her.

Rachael closed her eyes, thinking not of the man kissing her neck, but of the four or five drugs now making their way through his bloodstream, helped along by a rush of martinis and champagne.

One was known as the go-to for colds.

Another was a godsend when you had a headache.

There was even a handy herbal supplement known for easing anxiety.

But put them all together, well, that wasn't a very good idea.

The kicker? Each one was easily and legally obtained over the counter. Hell, the cold medicine was even buy one-get one free. It had taken some trial and error to find the right combinations. Poor Mr. Baccarat had taken forever to go.

Now, though, it worked out quite neatly. Rachael was never on the hotel's registration, her drinks were never charged to the hotel bar. She might be picked up on a security camera or two, but did the managers of this prestigious hotel really want anyone knowing they catered to people in Rachael's profession? Not likely.

Besides, no one would be all that surprised if dear Mr. Klein suddenly passed away from a strange combination of otherwise innocent drugs. After all, he was getting older, he probably just forgot he took one before taking the other, right? His wife could attest to his slipping memory, if she so chose.

Rachael wondered how long it would take for Mr. Klein to feel the effects. Maybe she had time to feed him another treat or two before taking the leftovers with her when she left.

Her thoughts were interrupted when he finally suc-ceeded in removing her dress. He moved like a man pos-sessed, so preoccupied with getting what he wanted that he didn't notice he was already started to fumble.

Rachael liked Mr. Klein. But if she learned anything from her mother it was that if you like something, you just might have to set it free for its own good.

And that was fine with Rachael.

Because now she was addicted to the thrill.

Just like he was addicted to her, and to the Obsession.

ALL CLEAR
Linda Johnson

My drive to work takes eleven minutes and forty-nine seconds, fourteen seconds longer than average. Three more cars making left turns onto Grant Street today. I pull into the parking lot and find my usual spot far from the other cars. I open my door and peer down, check for rats, spiders, snakes. One, two, three, four, five. All clear.

As I'm getting out of my car, Chris Turner pulls in next to me. Right next to me. Six empty slots on both sides of my car and he pulls in next to me. *Asshole.* I grit my teeth. My mind flashes red, my eyes bleed into my brain.

"Hey, buddy. How's it going, man?" Blond hair in a man bun, blue eyes, big grin showing off his dimples. I want to smash my fist into his perfect *GQ* face.

He yanks my lunchbox out of my hand and shakes it. "What's for lunch today?" He closes his eyes and puts his hand to his forehead like a fortune teller. "Let me guess: peanut butter and jelly sandwich, potato chips, apple." He opens his eyes. "Am I right?"

Of course, he's right. It's what I pack every day.

He hands my lunchbox back. Another big grin. "Just messin' with you, man. We're cool, right?" He drapes his arm around my shoulder and I break into a sweat. Breathe, breathe. One, two, three, four, five.

"What's Melody doing here so early?" I point to my dream girl, the girl he stole from me. She's smart, beautiful, funny, and a thousand times too good for him. I was going to ask her out, but he pounced first. When he turns to look, I duck out from under his arm.

"She's flexing today. Leaving early for a dentist appointment. I'll catch you later, buddy." He trots off. Gray mid-thigh shorts and a tight, black T-shirt flaunt his Ken-doll body, ready for his morning workout. When he's not coding, he lives at the company gym. Mornings, lunch break, after work. *Get a life, dickwad.*

I would never step into that germ-ridden petri dish of a gym: the sweat-soaked equipment, the chlorine-doused pool masking urine and saliva and God knows what other bodily fluids. I shudder. I don't need to exercise anyway. Stress-induced adrenaline jacks up my metabolism to supersonic levels.

I walk to my office building and, like a rat in a maze, make my way to my cubicle. Exactly ten-by-ten. When I moved in, I measured it. One side was off by three inches, so I insisted they adjust the partition. Gray fabric walls, bare and clean, not like Turner's cubicle next to mine. He's covered his whole office in posters of mountains he's hiked. I fantasize about him falling into a crevice and starving to death.

I power up my computer, pop open a Red Bull, and

take a swig. I open the file I'm coding, crack my knuckles and go to work. I'm the best programmer in the department. When I'm in the zone, the world disappears. Nothing can hurt me.

I don't hear Turner sneak up on me until he sits his ass on my desk. "Hey, buddy. How's it going? You working on the Baxter project?" He picks up my open Red Bull. *Don't do it, don't do it, don't do it.* One, two, three—he takes a gulp. *Fuck, fuck, fuck. What a prick.* He stands and peers at my monitor. He picks up my pen and points to the screen. "There's a better solution." He kneels in front of my desk, deletes sixteen lines of my code, replaces it with his, and hits the save button. He stands and slaps my shoulder. "Awesome, right, man?"

He's gone before I can respond, leaving behind my now-contaminated drink and pen, and his shitty code. I pull an antibacterial wipe from my drawer, rub down my keyboard and pen, and use it to pick up my can. I head to the men's room, pour the rest of my Red Bull down the drain, and toss the can into the recycling bin. I wash my hands and dry them on a paper towel.

Back in my cube, I use another wipe to clean my hands, then delete Turner's code. I stare at the monitor, willing myself to get back into the zone, but my brain is in deep-freeze. Those lines of code he deleted took me hours to write yesterday. They were perfect and now they're gone and I have to reconstruct them.

I try to work, but all I can think of is Turner. How he stole Melody from me, how he rewrites my code, how he laughs at me, how he embarrasses me in front of the other programmers. I want to wipe that fucker off the face of the earth. First it's just a flicker of thought, but then it takes hold. Why not? Why not rid myself and the world of this piece of shit?

The more I think of it, the more consumed I am. But how? No guns or knives—I hate blood. Other solutions: lure him to the rooftop and push him off, poison his coffee, tamper with his car brakes. Then it hits me—the most elegant solution: clean, bloodless, and painful.

My brain goes into the zone like I'm designing an algorithm, click, click, click, click, click. I have the who and the what, now the where: his office, the cafeteria, the bathroom, the gym? The gym, click.

I lean back in my chair and a sense of calm cradles my body. I will be free of my nemesis forever. I savor the moment, open a new Red Bull, take a swig, crack my knuckles, and go back to work. I reconstruct my code in a fraction of the time it took me to create it.

I watch for my opportunity. When I see Melody and Turner head to the cafeteria, I duck into her cubicle. I open her purse, grab her gym pass, and sneak out before anyone sees me.

On my drive home, I stop at a Home Depot. I hate to shop, to mingle with strangers, but I don't want to order what I need online. This way, there will be no record of my purchases and no wait for delivery.

Inside the store, my senses go haywire. Bright lights blind me, products in every size and color are stacked to the rafters, loud music pounds my ears. I close my eyes and take a deep breath. One, two, three, four, five. I can do this. I have to do this. I open my eyes and count one step at a time.

I find the Sani-wipes and scrub the shopping cart handle. I locate the aisles with the items on my list: a compact microwave with maximum voltage, a non-GFCI outlet, and several power cords. I keep my head down and make it to the check-out line.

"Hi, sir. Find everything you need?"

I glance up and register female, nose ring, chomping on gum. I nod and look down, breaking eye contact. Keep my eyes lowered until she calls out the total. I count out my cash. I want to count it again, but don't want to call attention to myself. I hand it over, take my change, and grab my shopping bags. I count the steps to the door. One, two, three, four, five, six, seven. Outside, I look around. All clear. I count the strides to my car, load up my packages, and drive off. Halfway home, my hands stop shaking.

The next morning, I launch myself from bed even before the extra early alarm goes off. I'm totally pumped. I have no second thoughts. My life will be so much better without Turner. Maybe I'll be normal again. I used to be, until Turner showed up and started needling me and needling me, like a tick sucking my life's blood. But now, all I have to do is get rid of him, and my life will be peaceful and calm and normal.

I drive to work and park in the adjacent office building's parking lot. I use Melody's pass to unlock the gym doors. I find the closest electrical outlet and swap it out for my non-GFCI outlet. I string the power cords together until there's enough play to reach the hot tub. The smell inside the pool equipment room makes me gag, but with the door cracked open, I have a perfect view of the pool and hot tub.

Turner shows up at five-thirteen, jumps into the pool, and swims laps for thirty-three minutes. Then he hops out and makes a beeline for the hot tub. I gaze around the pool area. All clear. I check my power cord connections to make sure they're tight. The microwave clock light is blinking so I know it's alive. I press the five-minute cook button so it's humming full-strength.

I push the door open and with no hesitation walk to the hot tub. Turner doesn't even notice me until I'm two strides away. "Hey, man. What're you doing at the gym? Going to try to put some meat on those bones?" He laughs. And then he registers the microwave, and his eyes widen. "What the hell?"

I hold it up over the hot tub like a trophy. Let him get a good look. "Adios, asshole!" I toss the microwave into the water. There's a splash, then an explosion, then a sizzle. Turner thrashes, then everything is still. His head dangles over the side of the hot tub, his mouth ajar. One, two, three, four, five. My mind is peaceful, calm, like a field of clover in the early dawn. I relish the moment, before I sprint into action.

I unplug the power cord and retrieve the microwave. I locate Turner's laptop in his locker, plug that into the power cords, and toss it into the hot tub.

The gym is still deserted when I leave at six-oh-seven. I race to my car, throw the microwave into the trunk, and drive to my usual parking space. I step out of my car feeling like a slave freed from his chains. The sun seems brighter than it's been for months. I turn my face up and soak in the rays, walk to my office building with a bounce in my step. Next to the sidewalk, flowers are blooming and I inhale their sweet scent. Butterflies flit from blossom to blossom, while birds chirp in the distance. Life is good.

I start my day: fingers fly over my keyboard, page after page of elegant code.

Melody rushes in and breaks my trance. "Did you hear about Chris?" she asks.

I turn my head, blink, and gaze at her beautiful face: heart-shaped, high cheekbones, bee-stung lips, cornflower-blue eyes wide with alarm.

"They found him in the hot tub, electrocuted."

I stand, ready to wrap my arms around her, tell her everything's all right. I'll wait a month or two for her to get over him, then I'll ask her out. We'll get married, have kids, everything will be perfect.

"They found a pulse, called nine-one-one. They think he's going to make it." She takes a step back. "I've got to get to the hospital." She turns and races from my cube, her footsteps echoing down the hall.

The pain in my head strikes me like a lightning bolt. I gasp and sink to my knees. One, four, two, five... all...all...all...I gaze down. Spiders crawl up my legs. I scrub them off, feel something move in my hair, fling a scorpion from my scalp. Something slithers out of my ear canal, a worm. I'm under attack. I run screaming full-speed toward a blinding light at the end of the hallway. The plate glass window shatters. Four stories down. One, two three, fo...

SOLITAIRE
Judith Stanton

My Solitaire app is my best friend, available any time of the night or day for a leisurely stroll through the suits, diamonds hearts clubs spades, or a sprint to finish the game.

No strolls or sprints with my husband, Walker Franklin Bailey, who expects me to have supper on the table every night at seven p.m., the moment he gets home from the upscale men's clothing store he inherited from his father, and from which he's outfitted every important local priest, politician, and professor, and oh, a couple of top-ranked football players here in Chapel Hill on their way to making millions in the NFL.

He handles all the bills, the stocks, mutual funds, and keeps us comfortable. I haven't earned a dime in years.

"Emmeline," he calls upstairs. "Honey. I'm home." A cliché if ever there was one. "What's for supper?"

Okay, I admit it. I was playing Solitaire and forgot to put his supper on the stove. What do I have for tonight anyway? Last I looked in the freezer, a chicken pot pie. Takes an hour, should have put it in at five-forty-five.

Didn't, because ten games in a row, not one posted a

single suit, let alone went to completion, which is some kind of record. I know, because I track my games in a palm-sized notebook I found abandoned at the thrift store, fifty cents. It has little lined pages, an elastic binding to keep it closed, a cover with a classic old-fashioned floral design I want to emulate in the new curtains I'm planning for my study.

Walker hates florals.

I turn back to my game. I love the slide of my mouse on my magenta wine-themed mousepad. I take another sip of cocktail hour Chardonnay. Solitaire is unpredictable but orderly and logical at the same time. Click on a card, click on another, and they fall into place.

"Honey? Dinner?" Walker calls up again.

"Pizza okay, darling?" I holler down.

My current game shows signs of completing after a boatload of no wins. When a game finishes, the screen lights up with fireworks and says, *You win.* I love that little pop of pleasure.

Walker stomps up our plantation-style curved oak stairs, his strides heavy as the defensive tackles he outfits for the big time. He watches Carolina football obsessively. When we were first married, I tried to learn the game, the rules, the plays, the names, so I could watch with him. Ha.

With a squeak, the door to my study opens. Feeling invaded, I minimize the screen.

"Honey," Walker says, "we had pizza last night."

Right. Frozen, meat supreme.

"Sorry."

Or not. I lost my love of cooking for him after learning of his third affair. Met the bitch. Fixed dinner for her and her husband, not knowing. My housewife gene dried up on the vine.

"Honey," he says again, sounding hungry. No doubt he thinks he busted his butt all day, always does, deserves his supper.

And no doubt I stayed home, and he doesn't give a flying fuck that Marisol cleaned the house this morning, that I checked up on her after every room, the floors, the stairs, polishing the sinks. After she left, I did the weekly grocery shop—all quick fix and frozen stuff.

"I can start salad in five," I say, faking cheerful. *Just let me finish my game.*

"Fine," he says. It's not fine with him.

A couple of minutes later, I follow him down the staircase, a palm sliding down the handrail, custom wrought-iron railings bowing out on either side. Mother's boy, his mom approved. He's shed the jacket of the Brioni suit he wears to impress his customers, ditched the Peter Millar tie, and opened the top button of his Peter Millar shirt. Sexy, not. And he already tuned into CNN, too keen an observer of economics and international politics to rely on the nightly network news rag.

I pick out the Majolica salad plates, Vietri Pesci to be precise, an anniversary present I requested from him back when I trusted him, long before I noticed his slow takeover of my life. *Let me do this for you, honey,* over and over, until, after a time, he was saying, *Can't you do anything for yourself?*

I tear off chunks of romaine from my grocery shop this afternoon, dress them with the bottled Caesar dressing, my version of cheating, add store-bought Caesar croutons, cheating again. Then in the one authentic thing I still do, I shave fresh Pecorino Romano cheese onto the plate, best quality I can put my hands on, like twenty-four bucks a pound.

"Honey," he says. "You should have used the Lenox."

Our wedding china, American. He doesn't believe it when I tell him the salad was invented by an Italian immigrant in a restaurant in Tijuana. His mother had her standards.

Still, he scarfs my salad which is fresh, crunchy and delicious but then turns on me, a purr that's like a snarl.

"No steak? You're pissing our life away at that damn computer."

Solitaire's my bliss, I protest inwardly.

He stands and grabs the collar of my yellow one hundred percent Irish linen camp shirt. He chose it for me, saying the haberdasher's wife must keep up appearances.

"I want my fucking steak."

Steaks, stakes. I look out the kitchen window to his garden. He stakes his tomatoes. He stakes peonies along his asphalt driveway. He stakes the places where he planted chrysanthemums until the loropetalum overgrew them and they died.

I look at the stake I hold in my hand, a high-profile

Wüsthof chef's knife. I could use it to slice the ribeye if I'd bought one. Or him.

"I'm going to put an end to this," he growls, and grabs a gleaming golf club iron from his leather Brooks Brothers' bag in the hall closet, "9" engraved on its sole. An anniversary present from me—his money, his order— and I shrink. He's only ever used his fists, and only when I pushed him too hard.

No illusions about diamonds, no more hearts.

He shoves me aside and storms up the stairs, his nine iron clanking behind him, scarring his expensive treads. I run after him. He breaches my sanctuary like he owns it, which he does. Then plants his legs in front of my laptop and lifts the club over his head, Paul Bunyan with his axe.

"No," I cry. "Please, God, no."

Walker drives his nine iron into its plastic casing, and I swear I hear a tinny silver moan. He slams it again, and I shudder at the sight of keys popping off my friend, its keyboard, its insides flayed open, motherboard shredded, red bits splattering around the room like blood, dark bits floating down like autumn leaves.

He stops, heaving—more, I think, from anger than exertion—and turns on me, hands on the shaft, knuckles white. "No. More. Solitaire."

I choke back sobs, outrage.

"Say, 'I understand,'" he goes on in the courteous, measured voice he cultivates to calm a nervous groom in for the fitting of his first tuxedo.

"I understand," I parrot.

I do not accept. Diamond hard, a gem of anger forms inside my heart.

He drops the club. "Clean up this mess. I'm going out to get a steak."

I pick up the nine iron and follow. He doesn't seem to notice I'm behind him or maybe he thinks I'm following him to fetch the whisk broom so I can execute his orders.

At the stairs, he spurns the handrail. He's golfing fit and proud of it.

From behind, I hook the club head around his ankle and pull. He cartwheels down the curving stairs, careens against the railings, bellowing.

I hear the crunch of bones splintering, hear him scream in pain.

He lands in a lump at the bottom.

I descend slowly, shaking, a hand on the rail every step of the way. Once down, I crouch within striking distance, sure he doesn't have a punch left in him.

"What are you waiting for, bitch?" he cries in a weak, hoarse whisper. "Call nine-one-one."

He looks pathetic, crumpled. Beneath his Peter Millar shirt, an arm is bent double at the elbow, and a broken bone pokes through his Brioni trousers. Blood drips from his nose and a corner of his mouth, trickles from one ear.

He's not moving, not writhing in pain as he should be.

"Honey," I say and lean against the wall. It's cool from the AC. "Call them yourself."

Judith Stanton

"Can't," he groans, then his eyes widen, horrified. His breathing is labored and his eyelids flutter shut. I take out my smart phone and call up my Solitaire app.

Diamonds, hearts and clubs dance before me on the screen.

Soon spades will dig his grave.

143

SILK STALKING
Antoinette Brown

I was awakened by the jangle of my phone.

"Martha? It's Roberta. Did I wake you?"

Of course you woke me. It's not even nine a.m. But that's not what I said. "I'm awake." I struggled to free myself from my blankets and sat up.

"You'll never guess what happened to the guest speaker after quilt guild last night."

"She caught her plane and went home to her posh lifestyle and mansion in Spokane or wherever she came from?" I guessed.

"No." Roberta paused for dramatic effect, as she always does. "She was hit over the head and left for dead in the parking lot outside the meeting room."

Now I was really awake. "How terrible. What about Joyce? Wasn't she taking the speaker to the airport?"

"Hit on the head, too."

I fumbled for my glasses. I swear I can hear better when I wear my glasses. "But they're alive, aren't they?"

"They're both at Chatham County Regional Hospital for observation. The police aren't allowing any visitors."

I sat up slowly. "Do the cops have a motive?"

"They were robbed." I could hear the outrage in Roberta's voice as it got louder and louder. "Someone stole the trunk full of fabric Alexi used to illustrate her technique!"

That was serious. "The fabric samples are pieces of art. Irreplaceable," I said and thought, and worth thousands of dollars. "Like the kimono that was lost in the mail last year. And the quilt stolen from the guild's show in April."

"Except nobody killed for those!"

"No one's dead yet," I corrected her.

"We have to spread the news among the whole quilting community, all over the world. We have to keep her art from being sold. Maybe even get the pieces back."

"Yeah, let's hope so." I needed a cup of coffee. I stood up. No use trying to get back to sleep, especially once my dogs heard that I was up. "Call me if you hear anything. I have to feed the dogs."

We crafters know that heirloom quilts and valuable fabric aren't stolen to be sold. They are stolen by other crafters who covet them. They won't be sold. They won't be displayed. They will spend decades in someone's collection. Someone's stash. Just like the trunk of silk stolen last night.

No one will see it again until I die and my kids give away my stash.

My name is Martha and I'm a hoarder. I am an addict. There, I've said it.

When do I suppose I first entered that state? When was it that "hoarder Martha" took the central role in my

personality? And why? What was the drug? Was it the
thrill of the hunt for the object of my desire or the pride
of ownership? I don't know, and it's too late to worry
about the details. I only know that that my closets are
stuffed with vintage clothing waiting to be deconstructed
and reused. My chests of drawers are packed with unfin-
ished projects. Quilt racks hold vintage and contempo-
rary quilts. Bins of fabric fill the bonus room. Hundreds
of quilting and sewing books fill the shelves in my office.
Sewing supplies are stacked on shelves that line my
bonus room. Baskets hold colored pencils, markers, and
dozens of seam rippers. I lose them all over the house
wherever I'm ripping apart vintage clothing and they get
buried so I have to buy new ones.

Every flat surface in my home is covered with fabric,
sewing supplies, half-finished quilts, deconstructed thrift
store clothing. The coffee table, the dining room table,
the stairs to the bonus room, the blanket chest. If it's
wide enough for a pair of scissors, it's covered.

But I do have a few saving graces. I can say that my
hoard is no larger than most. I'm able to fit it all into my
two-bedroom house. I never stored anything in my attic.
Some of my fellow hoarders have to rent storage units or
build sheds in their yards. And I only have two sewing
machines, one of which is still sitting in its box and has
never been used because I don't have a flat surface for it.

My son Dan fears I won't be able to pay my bills. He
worries I'll become dependent on him and his sister. He
doesn't understand that I'm really not that far gone.
Actually, I've never paid much for the stuff in my stash,

except the buttons. My buttons have made the transition from hoard to collection.

The fabric, ribbons, patterns, thread, and zippers I've bought mostly on sale or from thrift stores. Sometimes I accepted them from friends who were downsizing and needed to get rid of them. But I haven't accepted everything I've been offered, which I think speaks to my self-control. I only keep natural fabrics. Silks, cottons, linens.

My kids are embarrassed, naturally.

Dan called the Health Department. The Health Department sent out an inspector, but he didn't do anything because I'm not a public health risk. Despite Dan's concerns I'm not a filthy hoarder. No dirty dishes in the sink. No mold in the shower. Nothing in the attic that could start a fire. My son walks through the house when he comes over. He checks the fridge and the closets. I understand his anxiety. He can't bring his daughter or his dog over for me to babysit if the house is filthy. I think that keeping my house clean enough for my granddaughter also speaks to my self-control.

And until recently, I'd never committed a crime to add to my stash. I've shoplifted an expensive button from time to time, but who hasn't?

Fabric is hard to steal. It comes wrapped on large heavy bolts. Even remnants can be as large as baguettes. The only fabric I can steal comes in small cuts like fat quarters or charm packs of five-inch squares. I don't bother with them, but I have noticed that the clerks at my favorite store seem to watch me closely. I wonder if they can see the madness in my eyes. Perhaps they recognize it in themselves.

Of all fabrics, the one I most crave is silk. Silk comes from the cocoons of silkworm larvae. The cocoons are soaked in water to release fibers that are wound on spools. The fibers are woven into fabric on looms. Silk production is slow and labor intensive, which makes silk costlier than other fabric. It's also more beautiful than any other fabric and feels divine to the touch. Smooth and luxurious. Just last week a piece of eucalyptus and rose hand-dyed silk habotai sold for a hundred and nineteen dollars. It was barely two yards long and thirty-eight inches wide. I could never afford a piece like that.

I used to buy small pieces online, bits of vintage saris and fragments of ball gowns from the 1920s. Even they cost ten or twenty dollars apiece. From them, I created precious little leather wallet books. I page through the books at night, caressing the fabric. But that only made my greed grow. I wanted the good stuff and lots of it.

To satisfy my need, I devised an elaborate scheme to exchange cheap silk for better. A form of alchemy. I created a page on a popular social media site offering to exchange donated rectangles of silk to benefit a fictitious charity that was not explicitly identified. The goal was five hundred rectangles. I knew I could harvest that much silk from the clothing I purchased inexpensively from thrift shops, carefully deconstructed and now stored in large bins in my bonus room.

At first, only a few silk rectangles arrived in the mail. I dutifully sent scraps back in exchange. When I received a piece I didn't want, I substituted it for one of my discards and kept the process going. Eventually, after weathering ebbs and flows, I received a flood of silk: dupioni, raw silk, jacquards, and brocades.

I placed each treasured rectangle in an acid-free sleeve, along with any correspondence that was included, and put it in a notebook. I soon had five large notebooks of gorgeous silk fragments, all documented. I used up dozens of inexpensive vintage silk dresses and skirts and made room for more.

Finally the silk rectangles frittered out, and I needed a new source. Our local quilt guild invited a speaker from Washington State who dyed silk fabrics using a specialized technique. First the fabric was prepared to remove its finish and a resist applied to produce a design. Dye was mixed and added to a liquid solution. The fabric was immersed in the dye bath, drained and the color fixed by steaming. Then, the silk was rinsed in cold water and line-dried. She supplemented her presentation with samples of her dyed silk that we were free to examine. I fingered the silk and rubbed it on my face. It was soft and smooth and cool to the touch. The jewel tones were intense, vibrant, intoxicating. Emerald green, ruby red, magenta, and royal blue. I had to have them.

I tried to hide my excitement. "Are the samples for sale?" I asked the speaker.

"No, they're for demonstration only," she replied. "You can sign up for my class, and I'll teach you how to dye silk yourself."

Sure, I thought. Pay the class fee, fly to Washington,

pay an additional supply fee, and spend three days up to my elbows in chemicals. No way. I wanted them now.

What to do? I had to improvise. "How are you getting to the airport?" I asked innocently.

Joyce elbowed me aside. "I'm taking her to the airport." She helped the speaker pack her silk samples, yards and yards of them, into a dark navy blue travel case.

I thanked the speaker vociferously, said grand farewells to women I hardly knew, and made my way to the parking lot. I made a show of smiling and waving to cars in front of me. I took my time, spending nearly thirty minutes in the parking lot until only one other car remained. I drove out, circled around the building, and hid my Subaru behind the trash bins.

I took off one of my taupe support stockings and pulled it over my face. Not something I would want to do on a regular basis. If I had planned this in advance, I would have chosen a more loosely woven fabric for my mask, perhaps cotton gauze.

I opened the trunk of my car and dug out the tire iron stored under the spare tire. I put on a pair of forest green stretch gloves I stored in the car for cold nights. I'd seen enough cop shows to know that I didn't want to leave fingerprints.

I waited until I saw two women leave the building, struggling with the navy blue travel case carried between them and walking in the direction of the only other car in the dark parking lot. My heart pounded, and sweat poured down my face and back.

I approached them, waving with one hand and holding the tire iron behind my back with the other.

"Let me help you with that," I mumbled through my stocking. They looked in my direction. Before they could say anything, I rushed forward and hit the speaker on the top of her head with my weapon. She fell to the ground. Joyce screamed, backed away, and tripped. She struggled to get up but I yanked off her glasses and smashed them with my foot. Her screaming was getting on my nerves so I hit her on the head too.

I tucked the tire iron under my arm and tried to pick up the case. It was too heavy for me to lift, so I grabbed one handle and dragged it across the parking lot to my car. The sound of the metal edges of the case scraping on asphalt was deafening, but I would not let myself stop. I maneuvered it into my trunk, pulled off the stocking and gloves, and drove away. What possessed me to attack those two women? I have never hit anyone before in my life. What madness had come over me?

I had to get rid of the evidence. On the way home, I stopped at a thrift store parking lot where I emptied the case and ditched it. I drove home, pulled into my garage, and sobbed. Have I become incorrigible? After ten or fifteen minutes, I went inside and slept after ingesting twice my usual dose of sleeping pills.

Roberta called me the next morning. But of course, you know that. Later I unloaded my valuable cargo from the car and spread it over my living room floor. I handled each sample and admired its beauty. My little dogs came over to investigate, but I put them in their crates. No dog hair on this gorgeous hand-dyed silk.

It took eight trips up the stairs to move the fabric samples. I distributed them among my ten bins, all carefully organized by color. It felt good to have that part done, to have them where they should be.

In the end, I wish there had been an easier way. But silk, really fabric in general, is much too expensive to pay for all I need. And it's not like I killed anyone. Those women will be fine, and I bet that that speaker has a stash twice the size of mine. Three times!

I'll have to hunker down for a while until this blows over, but if I've learned anything from my experience it's that I must find more creative ways to add to my stash. Maybe organizing a silk-dying competition. Possibly hosting a workshop.

MURDER AT CARSON'S MILL
Don Marple

Snow fine as talcum powder poured over the hill and across the highway, swirled in eddies of wind and wrapped around me. I turned my back to the highway, buttoned my jacket, and watched the snow whiten the concrete walkway and the tops of the foundation stones in front of me, all that was left of my grandfather's general store.

I imagined the front of the store that I saw as a boy, two large plate glass windows on either side of an entry door. The window on the left had *O. C. Cunningham* painted in an arc across its length, and *General Merchandise* was painted across the window on the right.

Granddad, blue smoke rising from his pipe, would be standing in that door when my family drove in from Hartsburg, waiting for Martha and me to leap from the car and run to put our arms around him.

"Come on in, you two. Pearl's made some cookies and she won't let me have any till you're here." He'd put an arm around each of us and we'd race up the stairs to Grandma Pearl's warm kitchen for milk and cookies.

I heard the crunch of footsteps on gravel and turned.

A woman appeared, striding along the highway. She wore tight jeans tucked into leather boots and carried a canvas overnight bag over one shoulder. The hood of a black windbreaker covered her head and the bill of a cap stuck out from under it. She stopped and dropped her bag at the corner across from me, rubbed her bare hands together and looked up the road ahead of her.

I waved. "Hello!"

She looked up at me. "Is this Walker's Creek Road?"

"Yes, it is." I bounced down the steps from the walkway and started toward her.

She narrowed her eyes. "What's up there?"

"That's where the Cunningham general store used to be. The store and the mill on this side of the road burned down ten years ago, in 1968."

She looked me up and down. "How do you know?"

"It was my grandfather's store." I stuck out my hand. "I'm Ken Cunningham."

She shoved her hands into the pockets of her windbreaker. "Do you live here now?"

"I live in St. Louis, but this is a special place for me. My sister and I spent summers here when we were kids."

She wrinkled her nose. "There's nothing here now."

"Memories." I picked up a piece of gravel and juggled it. "I stopped at the Baptist church to visit the cemetery and came here to see where Granddad's store and farm used to be. I'm going to Hartsburg tonight for the twenty-fifth anniversary of my high school graduation." I lobbed the stone into Walker's Creek. "Most of my friends from the class of fifty-three will be there."

She picked up her bag and started up Walker's Creek Road. "I have to keep moving or I'll freeze."

"Are you going up the hill? So am I. Okay if I walk with you? I'm going up to see Granddad's house and barn on the other side of the hill—if they're still there."

"Come on, then." We walked up the hill together, leaning into the slope.

Walker's Creek made a black streak in the snow-covered grass to our right and below us. She pointed to the wooden stanchions that rose from the ground on either side of the creek. "What was down there?"

"The millrace for Boss Carson's flour mill. I used to walk through it and watch the pulleys and leather belts running. One summer when I came back I heard a diesel engine roaring. Boss got tired of waiting for the creek to rise."

She pulled in a breath, still studying me. "Do you have friends here?"

"Not anymore." I held out my hand, trying again. "I didn't get your name."

She stared at me for what seemed like a long time, then gave my hand a quick shake and release. "Mary Lockhart."

"Nice to meet you, Mary."

She stopped at the walkway to a house on the right side of the road. A mailbox on the post beside it said "Carson." The two-story white frame house was dark inside.

"Bye," she said. "Enjoy your reunion." She turned and went down the walkway to the porch, stepped across it and pushed the door open. She stood in the opening for a second, then disappeared into the darkness of the house.

It was getting dark fast. The reunion was on Saturday, four days from now, so I could spend the night here, see the farmhouse and barn tomorrow in the daylight and drive on to Hartsburg after that.

I walked back down the hill, got into my car and sat a while, staring at the snow dancing in the light of a pole lamp outside a gas station a hundred yards up the highway.

I started the car and turned onto the highway, heading away from Hartsburg, hoping that the motel I'd passed still had the red neon *Vacancy* sign lit.

It did.

I got up at eight the next morning, showered, dressed, walked across the road and into the sounds and smells of breakfast—bacon sizzling and coffee brewing—at Lizzie's Truck Stop. The restaurant was nearly filled with a group of men and women wearing blue and gold West Virginia T-shirts and a dozen bearded men in baseball caps with logos of trucking companies on them; they had to be the drivers of the semis in the parking lot.

Lizzie took me to a booth by the front window and brought me a mug of coffee. "Hi, darlin'. Cream?" I ordered scrambled eggs, toast and salt-cured ham.

Two deputies in gray uniforms with pistols and handcuffs on their black belts sat at the counter across from me, talking and shaking their heads as they ate their breakfasts. Customers and waitstaff came up to the deputies, spoke to them and walked away, their heads down. Others stood in clusters around the restaurant, speaking softly.

Lizzie slid my plate onto the table and refilled my mug. "Anything else, darlin'?"

"Everyone looks glum this morning. What's going on?"

"It's awful. Mary Lockhart was killed last night."

My breath left me. I sat back and stared at Lizzie, dumbfounded. "Mary Lockhart?"

"Up in Milton."

I couldn't believe what she was telling me. "Killed." I pulled in a lungful of air and let it out slowly.

"Who would do a thing like that? Such a sweet woman." She wiped her eyes.

I looked at my plate, my appetite gone. "Lizzie, I saw Mary Lockhart last evening."

She stared at me for a second, then backed across to the deputies and laid a hand on the shoulder of one of them. "Bud, this fella saw Mary last evening."

He came to my booth, Lizzie at his side. "Good morning, sir. I'm Deputy Sheriff Walter Graham. You saw Mary Lockhart yesterday evening?"

"Yes."

He took a black notebook from his jacket pocket. "Your name, sir?"

"Kenneth Cunningham. I saw Mary on Walker's Creek Road about six yesterday."

"Where on that road?"

"I noticed the name on the mailbox, Carson. I saw her go into the house."

He slapped his notebook shut. "Mr. Cunningham, you need to tell the sheriff what you saw. He's interviewing people at the high school. Finish your breakfast and I'll take you there."

I felt sick. "I can't eat anything. Let's go."

Deputy Graham and I walked into the Brane County High School ten minutes later. I expected to hear chatter, laughter, and clanging locker doors, but the students were standing around, talking quietly. They stopped talking and watched us walk by them.

A woman in a tan dress came out of a classroom. "Hello, Bud. If you're looking for Luther, he's in the office."

A few yards down the hall was a wooden door that had *Office* on its etched glass window. Graham opened the door slowly. Half a dozen adults were standing in a reception area. They greeted the deputy and stared at me.

A thin little man with round glasses and a monk's cap of gray hair opened the door to the principal's office, leaned in and said, "Luther, Bud's here with someone." He pushed the door open.

A stout man in a gray uniform came to the door. The silver badge on his jacket read "Sheriff." He studied me for a second, then shifted his gaze to Graham. "Yes?"

"Luther, this is Mr. Kenneth Cunningham. He saw Mary Lockhart yesterday evening."

The sheriff nodded to Graham, dismissing him. He looked at me. "How do you know Miss Lockhart?"

"I met her yesterday in Milton."

"What time?"

"About six."

I glanced around. People listening to us shook their heads and frowned—didn't they believe me? The sheriff backed against the open door and extended his arm. "In here please, Mr. Cunningham."

I walked into an office with a walnut desk and three leather chairs. Plaques and group pictures decorated the walls. The sheriff came in behind me, dropped a notebook on the desk and sank into the chair behind it. I sat across from him.

"Mr. Cunningham, I'm Luther Triplett, sheriff of Brane County. I need to talk to you about Miss Lockhart."

"What happened to her, Sheriff?"

"If you don't mind, I'd like to ask you a few questions. Then I'll tell you what I know." He put one hand on top of the other. "How did you meet Miss Lockhart?"

I told him where I lived, why I was visiting the town, how and where I'd met Mary, what we'd talked about, where we'd walked, and when I'd left her.

He leaned back. "What was your father's name?"

"John Lincoln Cunningham. Linc."

"One of O.C.'s boys." He squeezed his chin. "What was his sister's name?"

Was he trying to trick me? "He had two. Serena and Margaret Ann."

"Brothers?"

"Three. Burke, Mason and Will."

I must have passed the test. He flipped his notebook open and picked up a pencil. "You'd never seen Mary Lockhart before yesterday?"

"No, never."

"Was she carrying anything?"

"An overnight bag."

"Huh." He scratched his head with the pencil's eraser. "Was there a light on in the house when you got there?"

"No."

"You're sure of that?"

"Yeah. Not a light on anywhere."

"Did she turn on a light?"

"If she did, it was after I left."

He wrote something in his notebook. "Was the door to the house locked?"

"No—she went right in."

"Did she lock it behind her?"

"I don't know."

"Could you see her after she went inside?"

"No. It was dark in there."

"And you didn't go in with her."

Why'd he ask this? "I already told you I went back down the hill."

Triplett leaned forward on his elbows. "Mary Lockhart didn't show up at school this morning. The principal phoned the Carsons' house where Mary rents a room and got no answer. She knew the Carsons were away, and she was afraid Miss Lockhart might be sick or hurt, so she called and asked me to send a deputy by." He leaned back and frowned. "He found Miss Lockhart's body."

"How'd she die?"

"Don't know yet. I'm waiting to hear from the coroner." His blank expression told me he knew more than he was letting on.

"That's awful."

"She was a good woman and a good teacher. She hadn't been here long, but everyone loved her. I don't know why she'd be carrying an overnight bag. She was in school yesterday and was going to be here today." He tapped his lips with his fingers. "Describe her for me."

I closed my eyes. "I'd say she was five-six or seven."

"Un-huh." The sheriff stood up. "Excuse me." He went to the door and spoke to someone outside. He put his head back into the room and said, "Just a minute." When he came back to the desk, he carried a framed photograph of a round-faced, blue-eyed, smiling woman. "Is this the woman you saw?"

"No, it's not. Who is she?"

The sheriff squeezed his lips into a straight line. "Mary Lockhart."

Did I hear him right? "That's not who I saw."

"Mary was a chubby little woman. Maybe five-three, maybe a hundred fifty pounds. Cheerful. She had a high-pitched voice and laughed all the time."

"This is crazy. I've never seen that woman." I tilted my head. "Then who was the one I saw?"

"I'd like to know, too." He scratched his head again. "We'll get the coroner's report and one from the crime scene in a day or two, and I'm sure there'll be more questions for you. I'd like for you to stay around for a few days if you can. Otherwise, you might have to come back."

"I have to be in Hartsburg by Saturday for my high school reunion."

"You will be. The county will pay your motel bill while you're here and give you seven dollars a day for meals."

The motel room had been cleaned when I got back. The bed was made, fresh towels were on the racks in the bathroom, and the wastebaskets were empty. I was in the center of the room before I saw her standing in the far corner, barely visible in the shadow of the dark drapes—the woman I saw in Milton yesterday.

I backed away, toward the door. "You! What are you doing here? You're not Mary. Mary's dead!"

She held up her hands and looked at me with fear in her eyes. "I heard about it this morning, and I'm scared. It's going to look like I came to town and killed her, but I didn't. I never saw her."

"You knew Mary?"

"Yes, and I came to see her." She walked to the window and looked out. "She told me that the people she rents from were away, and I wanted to talk some things out with her. We had to do it without anyone knowing."

"Why?"

"If they found out, they would crucify her."

"Found out what?"

"She was so happy here. If they found out about us, it would be terrible."

"What would?"

"I loved Mary, and she used to love me." She looked toward me out of the corners of her eyes. "They fired her in Cincinnati."

"Good God." I squeezed my eyes shut, trying to hide my astonishment.

"After she got fired she just disappeared, and it's taken me a year to find her. I wanted to tell her I still love her and there are places we can go to live and make a life together."

"How'd she ever get a job here?"

"They were desperate for a Latin teacher and they jumped at her without checking anything. Not many people want to live in a hick town like this."

"Why'd she come here?"

Softly, eyes lowered. "To get away."

From you, I thought. "I see."

She gripped my arm and shook it. "You told me you hadn't seen anyone here and you were going on to Hartsburg last night. Why didn't you go to Hartsburg? You're the only one who saw me here."

"I stayed over last night to visit my grandfather's

farm. I heard about Mary Lockhart being killed when I was having breakfast at Lizzie's across the road this morning. I told a deputy that I'd walked up the hill with her last evening, and he took me to the sheriff. The sheriff showed me her picture." I shook my head. "Why'd you tell me that was your name?"

"I didn't want anyone here to see me, and I thought I'd made it when I got to Walker's Creek Road. I was rattled when I saw you. I didn't want to give you my name, and hers just popped out."

"What's your real name?"

She dropped into a chair beside the small table against the window. "Linda Decatur."

"How'd you get from Milton to this motel?"

"I stopped an old man in a pickup and asked him about a place to stay. He brought me here. He told me there's a bus to Charleston at three today."

I sat across from her. "You'll never get on that bus. The sheriff will be scouring the county for you. Someone will be watching every bus stop. You have to go to the sheriff and tell him what you did yesterday or you'll be in a ton of trouble. I can identify you as the woman who walked up the hill with me and went into that house."

"She wasn't there." She put a hand on mine. "You don't believe me."

"It doesn't matter. You have to tell the sheriff what you did yesterday."

"I can't do that—you don't understand!" Her eyes were pleading with me. "You've got a car. Drive me away from here."

"If you try to run away, you'll be telling him you're guilty." I held out my hand. "Come on, I'll take you to him."

Linda and I climbed the well-worn steps of the grey stone courthouse and went through its revolving door half an hour later. The sheriff was standing in the hall, talking to a deputy. He squinted at me. "Well hello, Mr. Cunningham. Who is this with you?"

"Sheriff, this is Linda Decatur. She's the woman I saw in Milton yesterday. She wants to tell you what she did while she was here."

He eyed Linda. "Is that what you want to do?"

"Yes, sir."

He opened his door and motioned for Linda to pass in front of him. "Come on in." He followed her into his office, leaving me outside.

I sat in a chair outside the office and flipped through back issues of *Field & Stream*, swallowing my impatience, until the sheriff opened his door. "Come in, Mr. Cunningham."

The sheriff sank into his chair, picked up a pencil and rolled it between his hands. "You did the right thing, getting Miss Decatur to tell me her whole story." He shifted his gaze to her. "Withholding information bearing on a serious crime can get you in a lot of trouble."

"I'm sorry, Sheriff," Linda said.

"Let me tell you where our investigation stands. Miss Lockhart's body was in the kitchen. She was killed by a blow to the head from a blunt instrument." He pursed his lips. "We think we know who did that."

He tapped the desk with the pencil. "The Carsons have a son, Harold. A bad boy. He got Ruthie Skidmore pregnant a year and a half ago. The judge gave Harold two choices: marry the girl or join the Army. Her parents wouldn't let her marry him—no one with any sense would—and they're raising the child. Harold enlisted, and six months later he deserted."

The sheriff leaned back and put his hands behind his head. "The Carsons have kept the light on in that front window ever since he went away, hoping he'd come home. So when both of you told me it wasn't on, I knew something was wrong. Someone came and turned that light off, and it wouldn't have been the Carsons or Mary."

He shifted his weight in the chair. "We have fingerprints from the kitchen and from a bottle of wine we found in the mud down by Walker's Creek. We've delivered them to the State Police in Charleston. They know it's a murder case, so they'll tell us whose they are right away. I don't expect them to be yours, but I need for both of you to stay around till I get the reports on them. Once we know none of the prints are yours, you'll be free to go."

"Both of us?" I asked.

"Right."

"But I didn't go in the house!" I said.

"I went in, but I left right away," Linda said. "I didn't see Mary, and I never went into the kitchen."

"So you say." He smiled but it didn't look like good humor to me. "You'll both be at the motel, right?"

I was having breakfast in Lizzie's on Thursday when the sheriff slid into the booth across from me. His tie hung loose and he needed a shave.

"Looks like you been rode hard and put away wet," I said. "What's wrong?"

"The bulb in that window lamp at Carson's had burned out."

"No!"

"And Harold Carson's been in the stockade at Fort Knox for a month."

"Oh, my God. Linda?"

"We got the report on the fingerprints this morning. Her name is Wanda Carruthers. From Cincinnati. Her prints were in the kitchen and on the wine bottle." He rubbed his red eyes. "She's in the Wood County jail. Two of my deputies are on the way to Parkersburg to get her."

"What happened?"

"She slipped across the road last night and crawled into the sleeper cab of a Pacific Intermountain driver she'd propositioned at Lizzie's." He covered his mouth and yawned. "She was still sleeping in the back when he got on his CB at three this morning and told a good buddy what a hot babe he had on board. A state trooper heard him and pulled the truck over this side of Parkersburg—he thought she might be the runaway they were looking for. The driver told the trooper where he'd picked her up and he called here to check her out."

"You're sure it's her?"

"The description fits, and her motel room is empty."

I lifted my mug. "Sheriff, do you know what was going on between Linda and Mary?"

He lowered his glasses on his nose and peered at me over them. "No. You?"

I shook my head slowly.

"Good," he said. "Let's keep it that way—just you and me."

THE WINDMILLS
Gina Lea

"Now don't you be spending all that money in one place." Mr. Sprout chuckled as he handed the slip of paper to Emmett.

Emmett clutched the check between his two gnarled hands, like it would slip away if he closed his eyes. His mouth remained fixed in a frown even in this triumphant moment. "So this is for them first few turbines standing out there on my land, eh?"

"Of course. Thirteen state-of-the-art Garnesa Wind Turbines that will be up and running shortly, producing twenty-six megawatts of energy. Enough to power over twenty-five thousand homes. May even turn tonight with all that wind we're expecting." Mr. Sprout pulled out his handkerchief from the pocket of his vest, wiped his brow and the top of his bald head. He took his suit jacket off and laid it on the chair next to him. "Mighty hot today. I take it you aren't using your air-conditioner yet."

Emmett, still grasping the check, looked up at the man across the table from him. "Couldn't afford to, but I reckon I can now. I was hoping this first payment would be in cash."

"Now, Emmett, you wouldn't want that much cash lying around." Mr. Sprout said. "Anybody could come in here and steal it. Best to put it into the bank. You do have a bank account don't you?"

"Hate banks," Emmett grumbled. "Sneaky sons of bitches find ways to take all your money and then tell you it's your fault you can't pay your bills."

"Well, my company won't pay you in cash. We prefer direct deposit. I'm making an exception to drive this check out to you." Mr. Sprout stood and walked over to the fireplace where a breeze was coming off the ceiling fan. He wiped his forehead again and leaned against the mantel, drawing back in disgust when his sleeve came away dusty.

"Hah!" Emmett put the check inside a lockbox sitting on the table. "I don't want no bank account so you'll have to keep delivering those checks." He watched Sprout try to brush away the dust and dirt from his shirt.

"Had to let the cleaning girl go. Maybe, hire her back now." Emmett glanced around the dingy, dirty living room. The dining room table groaned under the weight of bills and stacks of unopened mail. The kitchen counters overflowed with dirty dishes. Every corner of the floor had large dust balls stirring in the breezes from the fan.

"But, Emmett, how do you pay your bills?"

"Cash, good ol' American cash. Good enough for my father and his father before him!"

"But don't you still have to go to the bank to cash

checks?" Sprout wiped the back of his neck with his handkerchief.

"Yep, those thieves charge me every time but at least they don't get to keep my money. Now when did you say the next check will come? Need to get a haircut." He pulled his hand through his dingy gray hair that hung in greasy strands down over his frayed collar.

"Now you'll have plenty of money for haircuts and anything else you want." Mr. Sprout chuckled again, then stopped when he saw Emmett wasn't smiling. "This is just phase one. Phase two will add another fifty wind turbines producing another hundred and two megawatts of energy. That's enough to power another forty thousand homes. And the best news is, you can still farm the land between the turbines."

Emmett shook his head. "No more farming for me. This land 'bout killed me. Broke down my back and feet. Turned my hands into a mess of arthritis knots. This land has been in my family for three generations but it done turned sour on me. Can't grow tobacco anymore or even a decent garden. I'd sell it if I wasn't afraid my ancestors would haunt me." He walked over to the sideboard and pulled out a box. He opened it, removed a small square of paper and sprinkled tobacco across the middle, before rolling it up into a tight cigarette.

"What about your family?" Mr. Sprout asked, looking at the pictures on the mantel of a young boy, a girl and a woman.

"Both kids are grown and gone. Son's a teacher over in New Bern and daughter's married and living in

Georgia. My wife, Ronnie, left when times got hard. Divorced me for some fancy, slick businessman in the city. Course he still hasn't married her. Heard he's one of those newfangled taxi drivers now, hah!" He rubbed the side of his forehead where an old scar throbbed.

"Don't 'magine my kids'll ever come back home. Can't blame 'em. Hate farming myself. Have all my life. Blasted equipment's too expensive and 'bout killed me more than once. Near tore my head off when the housing on that cursed combine tried to crush me. Was trying to fix that ol' piece of rust so she'd run better, that's gratitude for ya." He rocked from one foot to another. The clock on the mantel struck three times.

"Hey, how 'bout you give me a ride into town, so I can argue with that fool bank about cashing this check?" He picked up the lockbox and glared at Sprout daring him to say no.

"Well, I suppose that will be all right this one time." Mr. Sprout picked up his jacket, anxious to get out of the hot farmhouse. "You should open a bank account, Emmett. It's not safe keeping that money here."

"Don't you worry 'bout that!" Emmett said darkly. "I know how to protect what's mine." He jerked his head to the rifle hanging over the fireplace. "Now let's hurry up before that worthless bank closes. Don't mind if I smoke, do ya?"

That evening, Emmett stepped onto the front porch, rubbing his belly full of steak and baked potato. He sat in his rocker, pulled his pouch out, and rolled his evening cigarette while he looked out over the farm.

The first gloom of night had painted shadows across his two barns, the deserted chicken coop, falling-down smoke-house, and moss-covered root cellar. The land was as neglected as the farmhouse and buildings around it. Abandoned crops lay wasting in the garden, picked clean by the blackbirds who mocked the disintegrating scarecrow. In the field, scrawny tobacco had turned brown and bent back to the earth as if it couldn't wait to return to the soil. Even the trees near the farmhouse were scraggly and bent, limbs long overdue for trimming, broken from past storms.

The crickets chirped from the bushes near the barn and the night became darker with clouds blocking the moon.

Emmett lit his cigarette and took a long draw. His mouth dropped open, causing the cigarette to fall, "Ouch, durnit." He snatched the cigarette off his lap. He turned toward the sight that startled him. Off in the distance the silent turbines had lit up and glowed bright as beacons against the black sky.

"Well I'll be danged. Didn't know they did that." He tried to laugh but snorted instead. "Well, guess you can light up the farm as much as you want as long as you keep making me piles of money."

He sat back and rocked, smoking his cigarette and thinking about the things he could buy now. Maybe one of those fancy new TVs. A new car. His old truck had gone kaput last month forcing him to beg rides into town. "Cain't spend too much though. Gotta save plenty. Taxes will eat a lot and that electric co-op would take more than their share. Better be careful." He felt his head droop and thought about going to bed, but the crickets were singing him off to sleep right where he was.

He caught himself before he fell out of his rocking chair. "What the heck?" He strained his neck forward and squinted trying to see out into the fields. The windmills were dark now. A deep rustling came from the turbines nearest the farmhouse, like something large moved in the dark. Whispers carried on the light breeze, across the fields and up onto the porch. Emmett was sure he heard voices mocking him.

He jumped up, opened the screen door, went through it so fast it slapped in protest. He came back with his rifle. "Whoever you are, come out right now or I'm gonna blast you to kingdom come!"

The night returned his threat with silence. Even the crickets fled. He glared at the fields but all was quiet with the sleek, silver turbines lit again and glowing. Emmett rubbed the back of his neck and lowered his rifle. "Must-a-been that shot of whiskey I had. I swear I heard something." He took two steps down and thought hard about prowling around the farm but decided his feet hurt too much to try.

"Guess it's time for bed." Emmett climbed back up onto the porch and into his house, locking both the screen door and the front door for good measure. He slammed the bolt across the top of the front door and circled around to every window to make sure they were secure. Finally satisfied, he went into the kitchen to fetch the cleanest glass he could find and slam back a long drink of water even though he wanted another shot of whiskey from the bottle he had opened that night.

Emmett glanced over to the worn-out dog bed in the corner of the living room. It sat cold and silent. "Maybe get a new dog," he said and went to bed.

That night Emmett tossed and turned. His dreams turned into nightmares. Something hid in the fields, rustling and creeping closer and closer. He tried to scream for help but no words came out. All he could do was open his mouth wider and wider as the swirling sounds grew louder and more menacing, devouring his fields, consuming his barns, the smokehouse and now whirling in the farmhouse. He'd be eaten too. They'd get his piles of money. He had to get out. Had to wake up. Get his rifle. Scream for help. It had to be those damn turbines. Had to.

He woke up late the next morning. His mood was as sour as the taste in his mouth. He dressed and went out to the kitchen, looked longingly at the whiskey bottle. "Later," he promised himself. "Tonight. But right now, I got more important things to attend to."

He trudged out the front door into the yard and strode over to the root cellar. He turned the key in the lock and flung it open with enough force to nearly smash the door apart. He stomped down the steps and over to the far corner where he'd hidden the lockbox. His hands trembled as he put the key in the lock and opened the box. There inside lay all the piles of hundreds the bank teller had grudgingly handed him.

Emmett sighed like a baby suckling on its bottle. He stroked the piles once, twice, before closing the box back up and turning the key. He hid it deep in the far recesses of the cellar before climbing back out into the sunshine.

"Just stupid fool dreams. That's all."

Three weeks later, Mr. Sprout pulled up as Emmett sat nursing his third cup of coffee on the porch that morning.

"Why, Emmett," Sprout said, "you look awful. Are you sick?"

Emmett rubbed his eyes, dragged his hand over his face, feeling the sharp stubble on his cheeks. He looked down at his rumpled dirty clothes then over to Mr. Sprout, dressed in his usual immaculate, three-piece suit, and wing-tip shoes.

"Some of us can't dress as fancy as others, Mr. Sprout. Not sick. Tired." He slugged back another shot of coffee laced with the whiskey he'd been adding the last few days. "Need to know something 'bout them durn turbine things, them windmills?"

"Certainly, Emmett. That's why I'm here, we are so pleased with the progress and want to get started on phase two as soon as possible."

"Now hold on a dang second. Don't know if I want to put any more of those blasted things on my property.

Somethin' funny's going on at night. I got to ask you something, Mr. Sprout," Emmett sat forward, staring at the fields and lowering his voice. "Can those things get up and walk?"

Mr. Sprout took a step back. "Walk? Really Emmett, are you pulling my leg? Of course they can't walk."

Emmett stood up and paced to the end of the porch. "Something's going on out there. Some sort-a rustling, stirring noises. Like those things are moving around. And voices. I tell you I hear voices. I never should have done this. I hate machines and they hate me, been trying to get me ever since they tried to cut my head off back in oh-nine. Blasted combine nearly got me that time and that cursed tractor sitting over there in the weeds 'bout turned over on me last year."

Mr. Sprout shook his head. "Now Emmett, I think you've been out here on this farm too long. That's just your imagination. Of course the turbines make noise. We told you that before you signed your contract. But move? Impossible." He stepped closer to the porch and calmed his voice. "I think you need to get into town more. Be with people. Why, I ran into your lovely ex-wife, Veronica, the other day. She's back in town and we had the nicest talk."

"Veronica? Hah! Is that what she's calling herself these days? What does she want?" Emmett continued staring out into the fields.

"She's worried about you out here all alone. She heard about your good fortune—"

"What'd you tell her?" Emmett demanded. "You tell her about my money?"

Mr. Sprout put his hands up in protest. "I didn't tell her any details. That is all confidential, but someone told her about the wind turbines and she wanted to know how it was going. How you are. She seemed genuinely concerned."

Emmett shook his head. "In a pig's eye. The only person Ronnie's ever been concerned about was Ronnie. Don't you tell her a thing about our arrangement, you hear me? She'll come sniffing around, trying to take my money."

"Of course, Emmett. Of course. You need to calm down. Now, we'd like to proceed with phase two. You good with letting us add more turbines next month? It'll mean a lot more money for you."

Emmett's eyes fogged over. He'd have to get a bigger lock box. "Sure. Sure. I signed didn't I?" Emmett rubbed his gnarled hands together before rubbing the scar on the side of his forehead. "Don't want to go back to farming. That's for sure."

"Splendid," Mr. Sprout turned to go. "Take care Emmett. Drink plenty of fluids."

Emmett nodded at Sprout who got into his car and pulled away. He pulled the flask out of his pocket and poured another shot into his coffee cup. "Well, now, if you say so."

* * *

That night the dreams were worse. Emmett tore himself out of sleep and listened to the rustling sounds outside. He shivered under his covers even though it was a warm night. He went to the kitchen to pour himself a drink. He pulled the curtains back and peeked outside, sure he saw shadows moving across the yard. "Leave me alone!" He ranted, banging on the wall next to the window. An eerie glow lit up the fields as the turbine lights came on.

He rubbed his head and rocked back and forth. "I should take my shotgun out there and blast those things. Out to get me, I tell you, Max."

He looked over to the empty dog bed. "Talking to a dog that's long gone. Run off." He massaged his scar. "No that's not right. Max wouldn't leave me. He loved me. Only thing that ever truly loved me. Dead. Right. That's right. Max died. Why can't I remember how?" He stopped and listened to the rustling outside. "Durn turbines gonna drive me crazy!"

He slugged back another shot then slunk into his bedroom and back under the covers. "Morning, got to make it to morning. They can't move in the daytime." He slipped back into his nightmares.

Emmett was locking up the root cellar when the big, worn-out Eldorado pulled up. A tall woman wearing a silvery dress stepped from the car and looked around before approaching Emmett.

"Good morning Emmett." She removed her sunglasses, closing them up with a snap. "Same old dusty farm I see." Each word filled with disdain.

"Ronnie." Emmett snorted. "What are you doing here?"

"Veronica. I go by Veronica now." She glanced over the fields at the tall, shiny turbines. "How are you Emmett? I'm worried about you. Living out here alone." She stepped closer to him and stroked his arm. "We may be divorced but I still care."

Emmett pulled his arm from her grasp. He spat on the ground then strode over to the porch and into the house.

Veronica followed him, picking her way up the creaky stairs and past the listing screen door. "Emmett, you know I still care about you. We were married thirty-six years, you can't brush that off with a little piece of paper."

"You had no problem brushing me off when you wanted to marry that slimy businessman of yours. What happened to him? Word is, he's a real loser now." Emmett took a slug from the coffee cup sitting on the kitchen table wiping his mouth with his sleeve.

Veronica stepped back for a moment, her mouth a thin straight line while her face turned red with effort. "His name is Ken. He wants to marry me, but now is not the time. He's not set yet."

"Not got enough money, more like it. You marry him, you can't keep raping me for alimony every month. You got that fancy degree I paid for. Git yourself a real job and stop stealing from me. It's not right, me having to pay for you and your loser boyfriend. That's right, I know I'm keeping him in that fancy liqueur he likes to drink while I sip on rotgut whiskey. Well, no more. I'm set now and you can't have any part of it, so git!"

Veronica shook her head. "I know you're getting lots of money from that big company. The one that put those windmills on our land. Everyone in town's talking about it. That nice Mr. Sprout confirmed you're loaded now." She preened at Sprout's name. "It's only fair I get half that money."

Emmett grabbed her arm and yanked her out onto the porch. "It's not 'our land!' It's mine. Been in my family for over a hundred years. You ain't getting one stinking dime of that money!"

Veronica struggled as Emmett pushed her toward the porch stairs. "You're wrong Emmett. I got a lawyer, and he says half that money should go to me. I have rights!"

Emmett grabbed her throat and began to squeeze. "That's my money." Veronica's face turned red. "My land. You hear me? Nobody's taking it away from me." He sobbed as he throttled her neck so hard, her hair whirled around her face. Veronica's eyes slowly closed as her choking noises became fainter.

Emmett heard a rustling noise and looked up. "Nobody. Not even you stinking windmills!" Emmett shouted at the fields, releasing Veronica who fell backwards down the stairs landing at the bottom with a hollow thud.

Emmett stared at the pile of clothes that held the body of his ex-wife. "Ronnie?" He squatted next to her and lifted her head. He felt something wet and saw blood.

* * *

A car door slamming woke Emmett from a fitful sleep on the couch. He grabbed his rifle and stumbled out onto the front porch. He looked around. Where had Ronnie's car gone? Had she really been here? Or was that one of his nightmares?

"Emmett?" Mr. Sprout waved and came toward him.

"Don't take another step!" Emmett held the rifle aimed straight at Sprout's head.

Sprout held his hands up. "What's going on Emmett? I'm just here to see if you set that bank account up."

"You sicced her on me, didn't you? You're in cahoots with her. First you talked me into putting those blasted windmills on my land. Paid me lots of money 'cause you know how desperate I am. Those things are alive. Creeping around at night trying to get me. Whispering in my head. Trying to find out where I hid the money. Now you go and send that greedy ex-wife of mine to steal it." Emmett aimed the rifle up in the air and fired. Sprout fled toward his car. "That's right, run, Mr. Fancy Pants. The next shot will be your head."

Emmett watched Sprout's car pull out in a cloud of dust. The sky was getting darker as a storm approached. He rubbed his ears and waved his rifle toward the turbines. "I hear you," he shouted. "Out there getting ready to walk. Roaring day and night. You can't have my money."

He ran toward the root cellar, fumbling with his keys, crying and moaning as he slipped the lock off the door.

Lightning lit up the yard as he stumbled down the steps. Emmett whimpered as the rustling noise grew louder and the shadows closed in around him.

He pulled the lockbox out of his hiding spot and dumped it on his lap. The whistling of the wind and crack of lightning grew louder as Emmett put his hands up to the sides of his head. "Get out. Get out of my head."

Sheriff Cody watched Doc Runyan close up the body bag. He looked around the desolate farm, watching his team comb the place for Emmett's missing ex-wife, Veronica, whose car was parked behind the farmhouse.

"I could be wrong," the doctor said, "but I think he died of a brain aneurism. My guess is, it was a ticking time bomb, ever since his head injury back in 2009. He flat out refused to let us do an MRI. I tried to tell him he needed to be checked, but you know Emmett. Just insisted I stitch him up and let him go home. Probably had no chance. Even if we found it in time, I doubt it was operable. Autopsy will confirm."

"Would that have caused him to jabber that crazy nonsense Mr. Sprout said he was talking? Something about those turbines getting up and walking. Trying to kill him. You think that was the aneurism talking? Would that cause him to kill his wife?"

"We'll never know. If I lived out here alone like he did, well, I might go a little crazy too." Doc turned to the sheriff. "I'll call you as soon as I've completed my findings."

"Sheriff." A young deputy followed by another officer came out of the barn and strode over to the two men. "We found Emmett's wife, Veronica. Dead in the barn. Looks like she was strangled but didn't die right away. Blood on her head. He might have struck her or she fell in the fight. Tried to drag herself out of the barn before collapsing. My guess is the blunt force trauma's what killed her. And it looks like something was in there with her. Something big made a hell of a mess. Never seen a barn so torn apart!"

"Guess, I'll need to take a look." Doc said, following the other officer.

"Sheriff, we found something else odd. When we were out searching the fields." The deputy scratched his head. "Looks like the ground around some of those big turbines has been messed with."

"What are you talking about?"

"Well it looks like someone tried to dig those turbines up. Grass is torn to pieces around a bunch of them and the base of those things are exposed."

"Makes no sense. Based on what that Sprout fellow told us, I'd a thought Emmett would have been too afraid of them to get that close."

The sheriff looked out over the fields where the turbines stood silent and tall in the gloom of sunset. "Doc must be right. Emmett had a ticking time bomb in his head, poor sucker. Scraped by on this farm all alone, getting poorer every year, losing his health, money and family. Finally has all the money he needs and his mind snaps." He turned to his deputy. He pointed to the turbines that lit up the sky with an eerie glow. "Look at them things. As big and powerful as they are, if they could pick up and walk, we wouldn't stand a chance. Wouldn't stand a chance at all."

THE CASE OF THE BATTERED BUNGALOW
Liz McGuffey

Good evening, folks and welcome to True Crime Stories. *I'm Dan Banter, your host for tonight's show. Our investigators will reveal to you the facts and the mystery that still surround this fascinating crime that we call "The Case of the Battered Bungalow."*

On May 25, 2015, Mr. Victor Zuckerman, a ninety-four-year-old Los Angeles native, rammed his 1976 Oldsmobile Ninety-Eight repeatedly into the house at 2309 Flagmoor Place in the Hollywood Hills, right here in Los Angeles. It seemed as if he had calculated the space between the middle stone pillars of the house to make sure his tank of a car could pass through. His aim was perfect. The front wall withstood the impact for the first few hits, but eventually it collapsed. Once the facade was breached, Mr. Zuckerman continued to attack the interior until the house was destroyed. A neighbor, drawn to the loud commotion, heard him scream, "Bleep you, Falstaff" with the final strike. Who is Zuckerman? And who is Falstaff? How are they related? When we return, we'll tell you more about this strange and tragic event in Hollywoodland.

Architect Vic Zuckerman first met talent agent Michael Falstaff in 1961 at the Intermission Café, a coffee shop convenient for a quick lunch or snack on the grounds of MGM Studios. Vic was sitting at a small café table with his back to the room staring at an unopened copy of the *Architectural Record* when Michael approached him, "I hear you're an architect."

"Yes. So?"

"I need an architect."

"I stay busy here at work and have no extra time for a project outside of work."

"You sure, friend?"

"Sure."

"Okay, buddy. See you around."

After that Vic and Michael spoke cordially when they ran into each other, but they were a contrast in appearance and personality. Vic kept to himself. He was a slight man, with piercing blue eyes and dull, wispy, dishwater-colored hair that seemed to gray daily. Unless he was doing close work, his pewter-rimmed eyeglasses were pushed up on his forehead. He wore battleship-gray gabardine pants and matching shirt with charcoal leather sneakers. He spent most of his days on the set and wore a suit and tie only for special meetings. He drove a tan Volkswagen Beetle. At forty, he was content living his life as background rather than foreground. He was so nondescript that his colleagues at work called him "Base Coat."

Vic's life outside of work centered on his daughter, Ronni, whom he had raised alone since her mother left them years earlier.

Michael, on the other hand, was a gregarious sort in his late twenties who sought conversation. An upstart in Hollywood with ambition to make it big, he was handsome but could stand to lose a pound or two. His signature uniform was loose-fitting flax-colored linen pants, a bold-colored silk shirt that was never intended to be tucked in, and Gucci loafers with ecru silk socks. His thick brown collar-length hair swept back in a gentle natural wave and his eyes were like faceted tourmaline stones appearing green, yellow, brown or a combination of all three depending on how light hit them. No one knew his natural skin color because he maintained an even tan year-round on his unblemished skin. His snow-white teeth were extraordinarily straight and seemed to gleam when he smiled.

If Vic's life was domestic and quiet, Michael's was the exact opposite. He was a freelance talent agent without an MGM entry pass, so he had to bribe the guard almost daily to get into the MGM lot. He knew every young woman who wanted to get into the movies. Known around town as an aggressive talent scout, this partier liked to drink and regularly frequented popular night spots late into the night. He drove a used but shiny 1955 Thunderbird convertible. Appearance was more important to him than substance. He thought he could hire Vic much cheaper than a private practice architect and once he had made up his mind, it was done deal.

About a year later Michael approached Vic again. "I'm renting a modernist house in Malibu now but I want to design and build a unique house in Hollywoodland. I want a home that combines bungalow and modernist styles, custom designed by an architect."

"Hmmpf," Vic replied.

"You're an architect. Want some extra work? Real work as an architect?"

"I don't think so, Michael. I have all I can handle here designing sets."

"I already own the lot in Hollywoodland. I have the idea for the house. I just need an architect to help me with the final details."

"I'm busy. Find someone else."

"Let's talk later, Vic."

Vic knew men like Michael, men whose salesmanship never faltered. Vic knew he'd be back. Men like him never gave up.

For some background here, viewers, the house that Mr. Zuckerman trashed was one of the last bungalows remaining in Hollywoodland. Most had been demolished and replaced by sleek modernist houses. The one at 2309 Flagmoor Place could more accurately be called a bunga-loid, retaining the exterior appearance of a classic bungalow, but with open interior spaces like a modernist design. The neighbors hated it, considered the folksy exterior hopelessly out of date, although it was so unique that L.A. Today ran an article about it.

The front porch ran the full width of the house, supported by stone pillars topped with square wooden columns tapering to the coffered ceiling. The front door, made of heavy wide-planked wood with a single pane of glass in the upper half, opened directly into a great room with the living area to the left and the dining space to the right. The galley kitchen, located behind the dining area, opened to a hallway leading to a half bath and a patio shielded from the sun by a pergola covered with wisteria vines. A spiral staircase on the back wall of the great room led to an open loft beside the enclosed master bath and the only bedroom in the house. The nine-hundred-square-foot house was a perfect size for a single occupant, and an anomaly in Hollywoodland. It was a quirky house, no doubt.

But why did Zuckerman trash the Flagmoor house? Did Falstaff have a history with this house? If he did, what was it? After a station break, we'll take you back to the origins of Vic Zuckerman's obsession with destroying Michael Falstaff. Please stay tuned.

Vic was attracted to Sybil the moment he saw her in 1942. In fact, one look was enough to cause his heart to race and his breathing to become labored. The asthma that had plagued him since his youth and the fact that he was a junior in UCLA's School of Applied Art kept him out of the war. He went to the office where she worked as an administrative assistant, their eyes met, and something inside of Vic sparked. The next day he returned on the false pretense of inquiring about registration for the next semester, and asked, "Would you like to see a movie sometime? *This Gun for Hire* with Veronica Lake and Alan Ladd is playing at the student union Friday night. I'm dying to see it. We could grab a hot dog and beer before the show starts. What do you say?"

"I don't even know your name."

"Vic. Vic Zuckerman. I met you yesterday. Remember?"

"Oh yes. You needed a transcript?"

"Right. What do you say to a date Friday?"

"I guess so," she said with a smile.

Their relationship blossomed in quick order and they were talking of marriage in just three months. At the end of the second semester, they tied the knot. They saved money by living in student housing but even on their tight budget they always allotted movie money, their favorite pastime living in the country's movie-making capital of Los Angeles. Vic saw every new Veronica Lake movie, in fact seeing each one several times. After a while, Sybil let it be known that she was tired of Lake's movies, but they were like an addiction to him.

Vic's infatuation with Lake drove a wedge in their marital bliss. Sybil told him she thought a baby would bridge the abyss that was growing between them.

Vic fell in love with his daughter when he first viewed

her through the window of the Beverly Hills Hospital nursery on Thursday, May 31, 1945. Vic insisted on naming her Veronica against Sybil's wishes. Against her greater protestations, he nicknamed her Ronni. She seemed to be perfect in every way and he doted on her from the beginning.

Every day after work, he barely greeted Sybil, but swooped Ronni in his arms and headed out the back door to play with her and their schnauzer, Jiggs. Or they were off to the park as Sybil called to them, "but dinner's ready now." His saddest days were when he had to work late, as he often did, and missed his time with Ronni.

Sybil sashayed around the house in her short shorts trying to get his attention, but he had lost all interest in her and in sex as he became obsessed with his daughter and with protecting her from any real or unimagined danger. Ronni was small, blonde, and beautiful just like her namesake. He wanted more than anything to spare her the downward spiral that Lake was following. Lake was a has-been before she was thirty.

One day in 1954 Vic came home to an empty house to find a tear-stained note written in Sybil's shaky hand-writing, "Ronni next door at the Andersons. I can't take it anymore." Vic and Ronni never saw her again.

* * *

As the sole supporter of a nine-year-old, he could ill-afford the long, unpredictable hours of a commissioned architect. He needed a regular schedule and when the position designing sets and overseeing construction at MGM opened up, he went for it. He earned less money but had a predictable paycheck every month. His training in architecture and more than ten years of experience in the field sealed his hiring by MGM. Designing building facades for MGM suited him perfectly.

As Ronni grew, he barraged her with constant questions, "Did you brush your teeth? Did you eat candy after school? Did you brush after that? Are the tires on your bike inflated? Did you talk with Aunt Audrey about that, you know, becoming a woman? What about pencils, notebook paper?"

"Dad, pleeeease. The only thing I need is a bike basket so that I can take Jiggs."

By the time she was sixteen, Vic struggled to meet Ronni's material and emotional needs. She was beginning to assert her independence, second-guessing the thoughtful advice he doled out. Her clothes budget quadrupled and she asked for—and expected—a car for her sixteenth birthday. Her grades dropped and she fell out of advanced placement classes. She lost all interest in college, looking for acting workshops instead.

* * *

"You're going to college, young lady," he told her every time the subject came up. "I always expected you to go to college so that you could get a good job. I want you to be able to take care of yourself. I won't be able to take care of you forever."

"You want me to be a nurse and clean bed pans? A teacher babysitting bratty kids?"

"I want you to find a career that will support you financially, but one you like."

"I just want to act. If I can make it big, I can take care of you."

Ronni found Vic poring over an old dog-eared edition of *Architectural Digest* and enjoying a quick coffee at the Intermission Café. When he saw her, he took his car keys out of his pocket and held them out for her to take.

"Thanks, Dad. See you at six," she said as she collided with a man entering the café. Their eyes met, they both apologized, and they glanced back at each other as they continued on their ways. Vic caught the moment between them and frowned.

Michael approached his table. "Do you know that pretty girl?"

"She's my daughter. She's sixteen, for God's sake. Don't even think about her."

"All right." Michael laughed at him. "Let's talk business. Do you see any ideas for my house in that old magazine? You must need some extra money with the added expense of a teenager. Come on, say you'll design my house."

"Why don't you hire a real architect?"

"You're a real architect, Vic. You can cut me a deal and I'll give you extra pocket change. What do you say?"

Vic was worried about paying for Ronni's college education. He suddenly realized that Michael's constant pestering him about designing a house could pay off. The fee would help defray the cost of Ronni's college education. So he agreed.

Vic felt utter disdain for Michael Falstaff, and at first only the thought of the extra money kept him working on the house plans, but gradually Michael's enthusiasm inspired him and he began to enjoy the process. They met often, changed and tweaked, tweaked and changed, until between them they had designed one damn quirky house. Michael signed the contract, Vic hired a con- tractor, and they broke ground in November 1962.

Michael's lot nestled into the side of a hill, offered no view of the surrounding hills or of the city. It was less than half a mile to a ridge with the city spread out below, but there were no sidewalks in the Hollywood Hills and the narrow, curvy roads didn't afford safe walking.

One Saturday near the end of construction, Vic convinced his busy daughter to drive out with him to see the new house. And he rued that day forever.

Ronni's baby fat had long since melted away and

playing on the tennis team had honed her body and given her a golden tan. Her muscles were defined and firm but not overly developed like a ballet dancer's. She looked great that day in hot pink shorts and an old white T-shirt that revealed her tight midriff. At eighteen, she was a stunner.

As they arrived, they saw Michael with his arm around the waist of a tall redhead, peering in one of the front windows. "Vic, I'm glad you're here. I hope you have a key. This is Eva from Kansas. She's…" His words trailed off as he saw Ronni climb out of the car. He pushed his sunglasses to his forehead and their eyes met. Vic knew at once this meant trouble.

Vic's life began to unravel after that day. Ronni insisted on going with him to the house every weekend on the chance that she could see Michael. But she now carefully selected her clothes and set her hair. At eighteen, she was of legal age and Vic could only appeal to her intellect.

Welcome back, viewers. Our investigation has revealed that Zuckerman's daughter, Ronni, was a model child who adored her father as much as he adored her. Mildred Anderson, who lived next door to Vic and Ronni when Sybil left, talked to us from her assisted-living facility. "Ronni was a dear. A beautiful, obedient child. She made straight As, never had to be coaxed to do homework, helped her dad around the house, took care of the dog. She babysat kids around the neighbor-hood. All around good kid."

But by her teen years, she changed. Her grades dropped, she had no interest in college, she cut tennis practice. This wannabe starlet in 1961, with long nat-urally blonde hair, looked eerily like her namesake, Veronica Lake. To Vic's dismay, she was interested only in acting workshops. By the time she was eighteen, she had fallen in love with a man, talent agent Michael Falstaff. It wasn't unusual to see this handsome couple, who loved to party, shouting and shoving each other after a drunken night on the town. Rumor had it that she was nice arm candy for Falstaff and more beneficial to him in that role than any part he could have ever found for her, given her extreme good looks and limited acting ability. And like Veronica Lake before her, Ronni Zuckerman's life would end early and in tragedy.

Vic Zuckerman never recovered from the loss of his daughter. And he never forgave Falstaff. But why did Zuckerman wait almost fifty years to seek his revenge? When we return, we'll explain.

Vic was powerless as he watched Michael seduce Ronni and escort her around town. The tabloids showed them at the Pink Pussy Cat, or Dino's, or Whisky á Go Go, or wherever the beautiful people of L.A. hung out. In the photographs, by the end of the night Michael still ap-peared unmussed and smiling whereas Ronni's clothes were disheveled, her hair unkempt, and her eyes glazed over in a drunken haze. Vic watched his daughter relive the life of her namesake, but with sensationalism instead of newsworthiness, with infamy instead of fame. His heart ached and ironically, he took to drink himself as he watched his daughter spiral down into alcoholism and promiscuity.

Five years later as he turned off the eleven o'clock news and savored a pleasant booze buzz, his phone rang. He picked up the receiver and before he could say anything, he heard, "Mr. Zuckerman? Are you Victor Zuckerman?"

"Yes, yes, I am. Who is this?"

"I'm Ann. I'm a nurse at Cedars-Sinai Hospital. We have your daughter here. She's been in a car accident."

"What? What happened? How is she?"

"We have her sedated, Mr. Zuckerman. The hospital is on Beverly Boulevard—"

"I'll be right there."

Vic found Michael in the ICU waiting area, sobbing, apologizing, pacing around, favoring his left ankle. It was the first time he had ever seen Michael other than perfectly ordered: His rumpled clothes were torn, grass-stained, and covered with dirt, his Gucci loafers scuffed, and his left eye was swollen shut.

"What have you done to my daughter?" Vic gave Michael a shove and realized how powerless he was against a younger, stronger man. If Michael fought back, Vic was in trouble, but Michael only turned away.

"Oh, God," Michael says holding his head in his hands. "I swerved to miss a cat or something in the road. I lost control. The car rolled down an embankment. My car is totaled. We were both thrown out. I couldn't revive Ronni, but she was still breathing."

Later Vic learned that Michael had landed on soft ground, shaken and bruised, but remarkably with no broken bones. Ronni was not as lucky. She landed at an odd angle on a boulder that severed her third thoracic vertebra and the underlying spinal cord, leaving her permanently paralyzed below the waist.

When Ronni could leave the hospital, Vic took her home and cared for her, just as he had when she was a child. He wheeled her to the same park where she used to play. He bought her a schnauzer puppy, but she named him Doom. She lived for just eight years, years spent in a haze of opiates, barbiturates, alcohol, and bitterness.

One day Vic came home to find her splayed out in her wheelchair with empty vials of morphine and Seconal beside an overturned vodka bottle. She had no pulse when he called 9-1-1.

Even after she died, his neurosis convinced him that he could still take care of her. He kept her bike in the closet and inflated the tires every month or so. His walls were adorned with framed photographs of Ronni at every age through her teens. He thought she was most beautiful in her senior prom evening gown. He kept no pictures of her after she started seeing Michael, but he did keep tabloid clippings of the two of them in a desk drawer. Every year on her birthday, he placed an urn of Asiatic lilies on her grave.

Vic lost his daughter twice, once to Michael Falstaff and finally to her physical passing. Vic never sought revenge but he also never experienced any solace from the resentment and hate he harbored for Michael Falstaff. When Michael died of cirrhosis at age fifty, Vic raised a glass in celebration and as he dusted the framed photographs of Ronnie, he called out to her, "Don't forget to feed Jiggs."

At ninety-four, Vic was frail and feared he wouldn't be able to take care of his daughter much longer. In the spring of 2015, he moved from his apartment at the retirement home to assisted-living. As he packed, he discovered a crumpled envelope among Ronni's things. In it he found photos he'd never seen before of Ronni and Michael together in the bungalow. They gave Vic a shock, a realization that his nightmare started when he agreed to build that bungalow and it would end with it.

On May 25, 2015, Vic got up at seven o'clock as usual, shaved his smooth, pallid face as usual, and sat down to enjoy his oatmeal and the *L. A. Times* as usual. After that, nothing was usual. He pulled the yellowed architectural drawings out of the back of the coat closet and with a ruler calculated the exact distance between the two middle stone pillars fronting the bungalow.

Then he precisely measured the width of his Oldsmobile. He fired up his Olds, stopped by the florist to pick up an urn of Asiatic lilies, and took them to Ronni's grave.

He then drove to 2309 Flagmoor Place and rammed the bungalow repeatedly until both of them succumbed.

Victor Zuckerman's life was ruled by his obsessions. The first one: Hollywood sensation Veronica Lake. He was so haunted by her beauty that he named his daughter after her and transferred his adoration to Ronni. When he wife left, he devoted his whole life to the girl's care. He became consumed with the design and construction of Michael Falstaff's bungalow, and blamed himself and the bungalow for bringing the two of them together. He mourned Ronni's journey down the same tragic path that led Ms. Lake to alcoholism and debauchery. Then that horrible car wreck left Ronnie crippled for life, both mentally and physically, and dead at age thirty.

But on Ronni's seventieth birthday, Zuckerman got his revenge. With the final lurch of the car, both Zuckerman and the bungalow collapsed leaving him buried in the rubble. As the first responders dug him out, they heard him murmuring, "Veronica, Veronica." The ambulance sped away with sirens blaring. At Cedars-Sinai he was pronounced dead.

Good night. Please stay tuned for our next True Crime Story.

GLITZ AND GLAM
Sharon Bader

A broken zipper can be fixed. I'm not sure why I'm so upset about a broken zipper. I will sit here on the tufted ottoman in the middle of your closet, eyes closed, while I count slowly to one hundred to calm myself.

You may be curious to know how my obsession with your clothes—such amazing couture—led to this moment. It's a short story that began several months ago, when you married Mr. Moneybags. You invited me, your destitute little sister, to move in with you until I found a job. The first thing I did was to sneak into your lingerie chest and borrow a pair of Victoria's Secret thongs. I loved the feel of silk and the look of sheer lace against my skin. I got bolder when you failed to notice the pair was missing. Scarves, purses, anything that languished in your closet became fair game. Those thigh-high boots you thought you'd left at your ex-fiancé's Mardi Gras party? I wore them with my newest mini-skirt, the one with the heart-shaped cutout over each bun.

Those small raids on your closet led to that confrontation last week when you discovered the beer stain on your leather pants. I had so admired the way they snugged that tight ass of yours, I just had to wear them. I'd have gotten them cleaned after you flew to New York the next day for an interview, but you decided to take them with you. I'd never heard such a soul-wrenching scream. You descended on me like a hawk on a rabbit, accusing me of theft and destruction of property. Such venom in your voice! What did you expect? That I would fall to my knees and surrender to your tongue-lashing with humility and sorrow? Cower behind your closet door?

I'm almost sorry about the black eye.

I do admit I was at fault for borrowing the pants in the first place, but the blame actually lies with the gal who sat next to me at the bar. I told her that I admired her silver and turquoise necklace but that it did not do justice to the citrus-plaid jumpsuit, lime-green boa and black knee-high boots that she sported like a lion tamer in drag. She shouldered me so hard that my mug wobbled as I brought it to my lips and beer splashed all over the front of my...um...your...leather pants.

You called me an ungrateful slut. Really, that was your best shot? Sure, you've shared clothes with me in the past. Worn or out-of-date handoffs. But since the leather pants episode I strut through your closet—a feast for the senses—only when I know you'll be out for an extended period of time. I've died several times now and gone to heaven in your closet. I love the glittery vision of your jewels and gems, secured with such care in the nine drawers of your jewelry armoire. I luxuriate in the smell of leather shoes and bags, the texture of cashmere sweaters, the prickle of wool in your coats and jackets.

Oh, about that fox-fur jacket, I wore it with the leather pants the night they got beer- stained. I was amped that evening because I felt like a model. A star in the limelight. Gorgeous in leather and fur. I nestled my cheek against the jacket collar so much my neck got stiff. The fur was softer than a lover's caress. But, someone lifted the jacket from the back of my barstool while I was dancing with this stud who also wore leather pants. Smooth leather massaging smooth leather as we slowly danced. Talk about luscious.

I hadn't noticed your name and number on the label inside the jacket. I'm glad I wasn't home when the manager at the Olive or Twist Pub called to say he had found it. It's a good thing he knows you so well at his establishment or you may not have gotten the call. Your revenge attack on my belongings, however upset you were, horrified me. You ripped up my ten-year collection of *Elle* and *Style* magazines and opened the window to November winds. Glossy paper shreds littered the floor of my room and danced on gusts of cool air blowing in the window. You sliced up my prized—my only—pair of Christian Louboutin boots. The attack was overkill. I was sure I could never forgive you.

And then tonight...painful, painful slander.

You said my blue spiky hair was outlandish and not stylish with any type of outfit, including band tees over ragged jeans. How would you know? That's not your world. Then you screamed at me, twisting the truth, telling me you're slender and sexy and I'm fat. I am not fat. Weight is just distributed differently on my body than on yours. You think you're sexy. Maybe to some you are, but I am sexy and smart. Intelligent. And, to educate your nonexistent artistic sensibilities, tats are an acceptable and expressive form of body art.

After listening to your idiotic sound and fury, I needed to reaffirm my SQ. That's Sexiness Quotient to you. While you dressed for your date this evening, I planned how I would later slip into the black beaded gown you bought two weeks ago: deep V-neck, cinched waist, beads and sparkle. I had to prove to myself that the fitted sheath would fit my curves. I longed to swish the diaphanous overskirt, weighted with beads and sequins, with every runway step I took. I wanted to wear a gown that made me feel slender, sexy and beautiful. I'd emulate Audrey Hepburn in *My Fair Lady*, wearing an exquisite beaded gown, a gown so classy it sang to me and my body hummed along in harmony.

After you left on your date with Dan in that strapless to-die-for Halston rose-pink dress—mmmmm, I may try that one next—I raced to your closet. It was easy to pick the lock.

The dress slipped down my up-stretched arms and past my shoulders like melting ice cream on a summer day, fell over my hips and puddled slightly on the floor. I reached for the small tassel on the zipper pull and started zipping, my left hand stabilizing the gown at the bottom of the zipper while the right tugged upward on the tassel. I held my breath as it closed over my lower back, my hips, my waist…my waist…deep breath…and finished at the neckline. I paused in front of the gilded full-length mirror that you had tucked into a corner of the closet. Definitely high SQ reflected back at me. I felt encased in beauty. Pride and satisfaction pulsed through me but I took shallow breaths until I felt secure within that snugness.

I searched the cubicles that house your shoes, eager to find the perfect pair. I needed stiletto heels to give me enough height to keep the gown from dragging on the floor. And then, perfection: open-toed suede with black beaded accents. I bent over to pull on the first pump and felt the zipper split open at my waist. A whisper of cooled air finger-walked across five inches of exposed skin.

I never expected you back so early.

Hearing that familiar hiss of your anger, I panicked. Your earlier words swirled through my head, overlaid with new invective, battering my ego and my confidence. I spun to face you, shoe in hand.

…ninety-eight, ninety-nine, one hundred. I am calmer now. I keep my eyes closed for a few moments longer and draw a deep breath, sweeping a lightness through body and soul, erasing guilt and fear. I stand and pirouette, laughing, into the semidarkness of your bedroom, arms outstretched, elated by the rustle of silk and the chatter of beads tapping against beads, the bloodstained stiletto pump still in my right hand.

My gaze shifts from the pump to the back corner of the room. Your body lies crosswise on the bed where it had fallen, one knee bent over the edge of the mattress, hands clenched in frozen fists over your flat, flawless abdomen. SQ approximately zero, sis. The stiletto heel that bored into your heart? Well, I'm not sure blood stains will come out of suede. Too bad.

I saunter back to the mirror.

A zipper can be fixed, you know.

THE TWO-FACED DOG
Ruth Moose

For months we slept with her ashes—Margaret Rose. I had no idea. Ugh. I shudder to remember. At first, I didn't know this, had no inkling in the world. Of course I had never checked every shelf in his bedroom closet. Had not peeked in his closet at all. He did his own laundry, sent his shirts out, suits to the cleaners. I admired his self-sufficiency, how he'd learned to do so much for himself since her death. Margaret Rose—the first wife. Blah. Ugh. So now I was living with her "remains" and that included her dog, a black lab named Chrissy. More blah, ugh. The devil incarnate in a sleek fur suit.

When I moved in with Martin, he'd had both of Margaret Rose's walk-in closets cleaned out; her clothes, her things. Every drawer, every rack, wall unit, shoe shelf, etc., clean as could be. I never knew if he did it himself or had the housecleaner haul everything away. Margaret Rose, the other woman, the other wife, her life, their life together. Gone, gotten rid of, except for two things. I'd have to live with the remains of Margaret Rose and worse than that, I'd have to live with the hound from hell, Chrissy. Her dog.

The day I hung up my meager wardrobe and began to settle in, that hound kept growling, snapping, snarling, nipping at my heels, did everything but clamp those sharp teeth into me. When Martin came home and I told him, he laughed, said I imagined things. That Chrissy had never growled in her life. And of course, to prove me a liar she came over, sat beside me, licked my hand, smiled her sweetest smile. She was so cool butter wouldn't melt in her mouth. Two-faced liar, I wanted say. Liar. Liar. Liar.

When Martin wasn't around, Chrissy spent a lot of the time in the master bedroom, in a pink wing chair by the bay window overlooking the water. She'd sit and stare out for hours. Of course, that must have been Margaret Rose's chair. I noticed Martin never sat in it. Nor in the chair in the dining room, the one Chrissy would lie under half a day, head on her out stretched paws, the picture of depression. If I tried to sit in either chair, Chrissy growled, bumped my legs almost hard enough to knock me over. I soon gave up, let her have both chairs. If Martin noticed any of this, and I don't think he did, he never commented. And I knew, if I had said anything, I would be accused of my silly "imagination" again.

Mutual friends introduced us, so before I met Martin I knew that Margaret Rose, his first wife had been dead a year. Cancer, of course, breast. Both. He'd had a rough four years caring for her but it made him the sweetest, tenderest, most considerate man I'd ever dated. We dated for three quick-paced months, then married, had a wild and crazy honeymoon in Costa Rica, and I moved into his house in the Hamptons.

I'd walk through the rooms and wrap my arms around myself. A dream. Was this really me? I felt like the luckiest girl in the world. Married to a real prince of a fellow in every way, successful and generous. I even had a home office that overlooked the gardens and the pool for my interior design business. It was all beyond belief.

Except for Chrissy who kept her distance, but watched my every move with those burning, black as hell, lying eyes.

The friends who introduced us said Martin was so full of grief they were really worried about him. He'd lost fifty pounds, wasn't sleeping, was letting his life slowly leak away. And tears. They had never known Martin to be a man of tears. True, he was the saddest man I'd ever seen. It was a couple of dates before I got a real smile out of him. And even then, little, half-smiles. Droopy eyes, distracted. But after a while his eyes lit up when he saw me, and he said I'd made him come alive again.

I tried to make up for all he'd lost in every way. And it was all ideal except for that damn dog. And now finding the ashes. My God, what does one do with one's predecessor's ashes? In the bedroom, no less. I knew I had to do something.

So I started small; first thing, got rid of that pink chair, which left Chrissy to pace and pace in the bedroom. Then I ordered all new furniture. Whew.

The day it was delivered, I met Martin at the door,

said "I've got something to show you." But Chrissy jumped in front of me, leaped, grabbed his coat and pulled him toward the bedroom, like the snotty little tattletale she was.

I followed, opened my arms wide. "Surprise," I said. "Out with the French Provincial, in with the Stickney. The whole room. It's collectable. You'll love it. Very male."

He didn't say a word, just turned around, grabbed Chrissy's leash and they went for a long, long walk.

But to me that damn dog's heart was black as her fur, her soul burnt in hell like the ashes in that urn on his closet shelf. Cursed day. The day I first saw the box, I thought oh, how lovely, how thoughtful. A gift. A surprise for me. We did have a six-month anniversary coming up. What a wonderful man!

I lifted the gold colored box down from the shelf. Tall and square, but not the right shape for lingerie, much too big for jewelry. And like Pandora, I knew I had to open it. Inside was a sparkling blue, green and gold cloisonné urn. Uh oh. I knew without lifting the lid it was Margaret Rose. My God, here she'd been in our bedroom all these months. Watching. I quick closed the box, shoved it back on that shelf and shut the closet door, then leaned hard against it, as if to bar her from our lives, our lovemaking. Of course, she didn't see anything. Margaret Rose was ashes, bits of bones. She was dead. Why was I so spooked? And what was I going to do about it? How does one bring up the subject of one's predecessor's ashes? Say, something like, oh by the way,

I found a box of ashes in your closet when I was cleaning today. (How often does one clean the top shelf of one's husband's closet anyway?) So what did I do? Nothing of course. I said nothing. But I burned inside.

Life continued on its every day path of me settling in and that damn dog reminding me every day, every step, I was an intruder, an outsider and totally unacceptable.

Next I tackled the dining room. Out with the cherry Queen Anne, in with the glass and brass mod look. Fresh, clean, clear. The table reflected the Wyeth original paintings I bought, small ones of course, but original. And the twenty-foot-long glass dining table showed off the hand-knotted silk Persian rug underneath.

Lovely, lovely. The colors made the room come alive. Made me come alive, not that Martin ever really noticed.

Chrissy took to staying in Martin's den more and more. I loved it. And all my changes in the house.

Martin never commented on any of it. Just got a blank look when he walked into a redone room. I learned not to expect anything positive or negative. He'd just leash up Chrissy and walk and walk.

Then I redid the living room: all leather, more glass and brass. His den I left alone. Somehow, I felt that was one place Margaret Rose never put her dainty little foot and it was the place Chrissy stayed most. A relief. His den, his dog now that the house didn't seem to belong to her anymore. Not that Chrissy was any nicer to me. He didn't seem to notice at all. I could have been a piece of furniture.

If I walked her, those few and far between times,

other dog walkers and their dogs knew her, petted and talked to her. Of course, she smiled! So sweet. And they'd say how devoted Chrissy had been to Margaret Rose. What a lovely sight they made, owner and prized pet. How elegant Margaret Rose always dressed and walked. Blah and ugh I muttered under my breath while nicely nodding.

Of course, Chrissy could do no wrong, bitch dog that she was. All smiles and wags, cute little licking tongue… those eyes…she even had the baby doll lashes and she was all Martin's. If she had been another woman acting like that toward him, I would have scratched out her eyes.

The minute Martin came in a room, she fawned at his feet, nuzzled his hand, rubbed against him around and around, wap-wapped her tail on my pricey silk Persian rug.

"My sweetheart," he said. "How's my darling girl. My precious."

I swear when my back was turned the two of them locked lips. Yuk. Doggie drool. Now you wonder why my kisses got fewer and fewer. Not even good night. Of course, she began to sleep with us. Three in the bed and always his arm around her, her head snuggled in his chest. She even watched him shave, something I used to do after a night of you-know-what. Not that we did that anymore, especially with you-know-whose ashes on the shelf.

All Martin's tenderness seemed to go to Chrissy. He took longer and longer walks with her; early in the mornings, late at night. I went on to bed and was asleep most times when he came in. The two of them together were like lovers, only aware of each other, no one else in the world.

To me he'd come in and say, "Dinner ready?" His voice a growl and he never even looked at me. Me, who had spent the day, all day, every day, just slicing and dicing, shredding and zesting...just me and *Mastering the Art of French Cooking.*

Yes, it was my hope to win him back. You know that old saying about the way to a man's heart being through his stomach. I had surmised from the lack of cookbooks, not a single solitary one to be found in the whole house, and certainly not in Margaret Rose's kitchen, that she had never so much as lifted a spatula. I bought the books and began. I made a new recipe a day, from vichyssoise to quenelles to coq au vin, to gratin Jurassien, to tarte a l'Ananas, to trois cremes aux beurre, I almost wore out the pages of Julia's tome. Plus, at farmer's markets I bought the freshest local vegetables, even massaged kale to make a salad with pomegranate vinaigrette. All those tiny seeds stained my hands like blood. My caramelized flan was a work of art. When I brought it to the table, lifted my butane torch to flambé it, I thought he'd be impressed but he only said, "Tea?" while my fabulous dessert went up in flames in front of him.

Tea? I wanted to scream. Tea? You want tea? For the moment, I wanted to flambé him!

Meanwhile Chrissy at his feet gave a single bark, got a hug and called, "Darling dog. Sweetheart. My precious."

Chrissy got whole sentences. I got monosyllables.

The worst part was when he wasn't here. Chrissy snarled at me, nipped at my legs when I walked past. Growled under her breath. Once she sunk some of those needle-sharp teeth into the calf of my leg so deep I had to have stitches.

"What did you do to her?" he asked when I called from the emergency room. "You must've done something."

He even accused me of being jealous. Of a dog? His work maybe, but a dog can be handled. Unless she's Chrissy. When I suggested we get rid of her, he hit the ceiling. Absolutely not. He wouldn't hear of finding her another home. Why should he? She was perfectly fine right here. This was where she belonged. Her home.

"You're perfect right here. Aren't you, sweetheart?" he'd say and she'd come to his side. Fawning and licking.

I walked her, fed her, avoided her. The enemy on my hearth. When she took to shitting on my silk, hand-knotted Persian rug, I knew this was the end.

So last night, the minute he opened the door, I met him before he could reach straight for Chrissy's leash.

"Wait," I said. I wore my heavy pot roast perfume and when he inhaled a deep whiff, he brightened up.

"I'm starved," he said and for the first time in a long time, he didn't immediately look around for Chrissy. "What's that wonderful smell?"

And it was a most delicious smell. It had distracted him as I'd hoped.

He sat down, carved the roast on a platter in front of

him, took a bite. "This is so lean." He smacked his lips on the juices, couldn't stop smacking.

"Must be grass fed. Where did you get it? Local farm? You've got to tell them how great this is. When can you go back?" He tucked in knife and fork though it was so tender he could have eaten it with a spoon.

I told him there was another roast just like this one in the freezer. He didn't have to worry. Plus, there were ribs I'd barbecue next week.

He ate the whole roast, then sopped the gravy with my homemade bread. Gravy I'd thickened with ashes sifted to delicate flakes and carefully seasoned with herbs to counter any bitterness. He almost licked his plate he enjoyed the meal so much.

When he stopped to notice I was eating only a salad, I said my system was a little off and the kitchen had gotten so hot while I was cooking, I'd lost my appetite.

He only nodded, paused a bit and went back to eating and mopping up the gravy.

When he couldn't eat another bite, he leaned back in his chair, put his hands on his stomach and for the first time looked around for Chrissy. "Chrissy, Chrissy," he called, went room to room, opened even the closet doors, checked the basement, calling, "My sweetheart, dearest dog, oh Chrissy my love. Come, come to your sweetheart."

In the kitchen, I rinsed my salad plate, put the roasting pan in to soak and thought, Oh my dear, you can call till the cows stomp and blow in the barn but that dog won't come. Still, she's closer than you think, my darling husband, oh so much closer. She's very near your heart.

A LOOK TO DIE FOR
Britni Patterson

I stared up at the giant banner, where my best friend's face was blown up and air-brushed into sixteen feet of dewy perfection.

Said friend was jiggling with glee next to me. "Can you believe it?"

I squinted at the picture. "Where's the mole on your cheek?"

Nari, my best friend since we were six, punched me in the arm. "It's a beauty mark, Rosa. And the whole point is flawless Korean skin, thanks to traditional Korean beauty products and our cultural secrets!"

I gave Nari the side-eye. She was three inches taller than me at five-foot-seven, and four sizes smaller thanks to a diet and exercise regimen that made me want to stop at Burger King. She also had perfect skin the color and smoothness of real ivory, dark brown eyes with impossibly long lashes, and hair so shiny I could almost see my reflection in it.

"Cultural secrets?" I said. "You mean like the need for SPF nine-thousand sunscreen so we don't make like vampires in the sun?"

Nari rolled her eyes at me. I had made an effort before coming to the International Cosmetics Expo hitting Raleigh this week. For her sake, I put on mascara and dug a lipstick out from under my vanity. I'd even made sure my jeans didn't have any holes in them. But next to me, Nari was a vision. She was dressed in a modernist take on a *hanbok*, with the traditional wrapped *jeogori* made of a deep blue silk that made her skin glow, but instead of the huge bell-shaped skirt of heavy embroidered silk, hundreds of long layers of habotai silk in shades of pinks and lavender floated around her. Fresh flowers were pinned here and there in her skirts, and in her hair, in an artless braid that took four hours to create. And, of course, a crystal tiara on top.

She said, rather acidly for a fairy princess, "You know my grandmother was *hanui*." A traditional name for a practitioner of *hanbang*, the Korean name for traditional medicine. Herbal remedies, cupping, acupuncture. Old ladies in bikinis scrubbing twenty pounds of skin off your back no matter how much you cry and bleed and promise to tip them more if they let you off the table. And of course, cosmetic aids.

"As was my great-grandmother, and my great-great grandmother. My family has been making beauty products for ten generations. Just because you consider BB cream too complicated a skincare step doesn't mean we're all unenlightened," Nari said, with a meaningful squint at me.

"I think I'm supposed to feel the burn, but I have no idea what you just said," I said to her, with a carefully blank expression as I sipped the complimentary ginseng and fungus tea I'd been offered by Nari's aunt, Ji-huen. ("It will clear your complexion," she said. Kindly.)

"Well, maybe you'll learn something today, Rosa. You're not getting any younger, you know."

"I'm a private investigator, Nari, I don't have time to stop and do essences and masks and all that crap every day. I'm only here because you said you wanted support. If this is some kind of weird make-over plan, I will spill my tea on your clothes."

She made a face. "It'd be good for you, but no. I...well, I'm worried about *imo* Ji."

"Why?" I asked. My tea tasted sweet, sour, and herbal all at the same time. I couldn't decide if I liked it or not, but I kept drinking it in hopes I'd find out.

"This is her big chance. K-beauty is so big right now, and our family has genuine traditional recipes, the real stuff. If she can get some investors, she'll be able to launch national, and I'll be the face of *Salanghada* Cosmetics all over the U.S.!"

Salanghada has no English equivalent, meaning the act of love, to love. The slogans were all over the banners. Natural love—Salanghada. Love yourself with Salanghada. Love is beauty. Beauty is Salanghada. And so on.

"What's to worry about? She's got genuine traditional recipes, freaky hipster tea, and your smiling face. She'll be fine."

"Not if that bitch Chang has anything to do with it," Nari muttered.

"Who?"

Nari jerked a thumb to another big booth across the room. Bright pink signs reading *Genuine K-beauty imported from Seoul* were plastered all over it.

"Dina Chang. She's importing all kinds of cheap shit and repackaging it, while imo Ji is making everything with real, local ingredients."

"You don't have to sell me," I said. "But what can Chang do to your aunt?"

"She's already reported her three times to the Better Business Bureau for selling K-beauty product that doesn't come from Korea, which, oh my God, really? We're Korean! And she tried bribing two of imo's chemists to get her formulas last month. Then she sent out some anonymous letters to the stores in Raleigh carrying her stuff saying that the seaweed masks were causing rashes."

"If you can prove it was her, surely that would be a good defamation suit."

"Yeah. It would be. If we could prove it," Nari said, meaningfully.

"Ah." I should have known.

"You don't have to go full detective or whatever it is you do, but could you keep an eye out? Today's the day where only vendors and investors are here. If Dina's gonna screw my aunt, it'll be today. Please, Rosa? I'll buy you lunch."

I definitely should have known. Nari was a master at getting me to do things I didn't want to do, from the time she made me pull her around the neighborhood in a wagon so she could practice being in a parade, to the time she talked me into being the ugly sister to her Cinderella for a talent show. Spending the entire day in a room full of people dedicated to spending thousands of dollars on self-centered perfectionism was pretty close to the absolute last thing I wanted to do. I had intended to come in, admire the ad poster, congratulate her, and sneak out.

"I already have lunch plans," I tried.

Nari's big eyes got bigger, as her lower lip quivered, "Please, Rosa? Please? I'm really worried. I know you hate this stuff. Dinner too?"

"What about Ji-huen? Is she going to want a detective in Walmart jeans hanging around her booth?" It was my last chance.

Nari made a face. "I mentioned it to her. She told me not to. She didn't want to impose. She felt it was rude."

"It is, Nari."

"Well, maybe a little, but you're my best friend. We're blood sisters. That makes imo Ji your aunt too!"

My conviction wobbled as imminent tears threatened to ruin Nari's eyeliner. She really was worried. I sighed. "I'll stick around for a bit, but if I don't see any reason to be worried, I'll split after lunch, okay? And you'll owe me dinner too."

"Okay! Thank you!" Nari bounced as her smile threatened to blind me with its whiteness.

A bell chimed three times, followed by a lovely voice saying, "Ladies and gentlemen, the doors will open in five minutes. Ladies and gentlemen, five minutes until the doors open."

"I've got to get to the booth!" Nari turned and fled, a faint trail of petals and the scent of gardenias in her wake.

Nari's aunt had gone all out. She had built a stage that stood three feet above the floor. It was set up like a deluxe spa, with a comfy-looking lounge chair, a heavy oak mixing table, and shelves holding various ingredients and medicinal plants. Potted hibiscuses surrounded the display, their tissue-paper petals matching the pinks and purples of Nari's skirt.

Nari climbed to a small crow's nest platform another eight feet above the stage. She could be seen from the entire room, glittering and impossibly beautiful, her filmy skirts wafting like ocean waves in the delicate tides of the air conditioning.

I found a good spot next to a security guard. I sat down in an empty folding chair he wasn't allowed to use, and he gave me an evil squint. I lifted the tea cup to him in a mock salute and settled down to watch. From there, I could see both Salanghada's and Dina Chang's booth.

The next hour was filled with more Armani and Gucci suits than I'd seen in one room before. People with personal assistants taking notes and carrying swag. A woman with an updated Jennifer Aniston hair-cut, carrying a black bag with "Vogue Editor" embossed in gold, talked constantly into her phone. I found myself staring at one woman, barely ninety pounds, as she stomped through the room in four-inch heels. The left half of her head was completely shaved, but five-foot long platinum dreads grew from the right side and skimmed the floor in her wake.

The Salanghada and Dina's K-beauty booth were mobbed. Nari was right. Korean beauty was super-hot. Suddenly, she appeared next to me.

"My feet are killing me. Can I sit down?" She'd been standing, smiling and waving for an hour. I stood up and let her have the chair.

"Have you seen anything?" she asked.

"Nope. Dina left her booth once, making the speediest bathroom break ever about ten minutes ago."

"Nerves. Good," Nari said with a savagery that startled the guard next to us.

"So, what, it's ten hours of schmoozing?" I asked.

"No. The first hour is for getting acquainted, handing out schedules and freebies. Product demos start now and go on throughout the day. Imo Ji is going to be mixing up all her stuff right there on stage, to demonstrate how authentic and pure everything is."

"Huh. What's she demoing today?"

"First one she's doing is the ultra-hydration crème with sea-weed mask."

"Is that the one with the snail goo in it?"

She nodded. "She's going to pick a random audience member so it won't look rigged."

"That'll be fun."

Nari stood up. "I've got five more minutes to hit the bathroom and get some water, then I'm back up there."

"Aren't you going to eat something?" I asked. I knew she hadn't eaten breakfast while being turned into a fairy princess.

She stared at me in horror. "And risk belching or farting or having to take a dump? Are you crazy?"

Reason number six hundred and seventy-three why I never envied my friend's model lifestyle. Even if my job required the occasional thirty-six hours in a car, I didn't have to worry about taco farts ruining my career.

Beautiful people swarmed. Conversations mingled; avid, interested, dismissive, gossipy. I didn't bother keeping track. Nari waved to me once she was back on the crow's nest.

Ji-huen was perfectly turned out in a long white wrap-dress over a floor-length black skirt, which gave the stylish impression of a lab coat. Nari's cousins, Hwuen and Sumi, had joined the display and they wore outfits identical to their mother's. Hwuen held up a giant ginseng root, with the earth still clinging to it, while Sumi carefully positioned the chair in the center of the stage.

The sound of a gong startled me. Everyone in the hall stared up at Nari who was holding a gong the size of a turkey platter. As the ringing faded away, she said into a microphone, "Live demonstration of Salanghada, five minutes!"

The crowds shifted toward the Salanghada booth. Dina Chang, her face determined, elbowed her way to the front. Her bright pink suit, the same color as her banners, made her easy to find. I stood up and started moving closer so I could see her more clearly.

Aunt Ji was setting the ingredients she intended to use out on the heavy table. A couple of small bottles, some seaweed soaking in a bowl, a thick white paste, small vials, and a mortar and pestle.

Aunt Ji turned and smiled at the crowd as soon as she had everything arranged.

"Salanghada is pleased to present the authentic recipes used by my family for over ten generations to maintain the beautiful dewy skin demanded for the flowers of the court! All ingredients are genuine, organic, and carefully prepared in the traditional Korean methods refined by my family over two centuries! I would now like to demonstrate the amazing hydration provided by our Moonlit Mask with sea-weed wrap! Any volunteers?"

A number of people held up their hands, but a large lady climbed up onto the stage like she heard a starter pistol and beamed triumphantly. She wasn't as expensively dressed as most of the people in the room, wearing a too-tight pantsuit, and there was nothing particularly outlandish about her hair or accessories. I figured she was a writer or blogger.

"Thank you, madam! What is your name?"

"My name is...is...Louise!" The hesitations were odd, but I chalked it down to the nervousness of being on stage.

"Louise! A lovely name. Come, sit in this chair, while my assistants, Sumi and Hwuen, apply our Refreshing Ginger and Hibiscus toner with traditional bamboo brushes!"

Louise glanced nervously at the table full of things, before sitting down heavily in the chair. Sumi carefully put a linen towel down around Louise's neck, and Hwuen flicked the toner on her face with the brushes, splashing it onto Louise's skin lavishly. A lady in front of me murmured, "Those brushes would be a big seller. Very natural. And that application! It'll inhale product."

Ji-huen smiled widely at the audience. "You see, in Korea, we do not rub toner into our skin, damaging it by forcing dissolved dirt and oil and harsh astringent back into the pores! No, we splash it, using it as a gentle rinse, to awaken our skin to receive the moisture and rejuvenating vitamins of the Moonlight mask."

Ji-huen began spooning things into a beautiful blue glass bowl. Two large scoops of the white gunk. A small plop of some clear jelly she described as "snail extract." Louise looked over to where Dina Chang was standing and then popped up from her chair, barreling toward the table.

Aunt Ji turned in surprise, "Miss Louise? Please sit down."

Louise said, "I just want to see what you're putting in there." She leaned forward, and bumped the table hard with her hip, as the cousins tried to escort her back to the chair. Little bottles and bits went flying off the table and into the crowd in front of the stage. People ducked back, as Hwuen and Sumi dove after everything.

"Find the tea tree oil," Ji-huen called, loud enough to be heard above the uproar.

I watched Louise. Her face was triumphant for a

moment, and then it showed dismay.

"I'm sorry, I'm sorry," she said and moved quickly back to her chair to sit down, her hands pressed tightly in her lap.

Ji-huen counted the bottles her daughters retrieved, then she said something sharp in Korean. Hwuen and Sumi looked alarmed and started searching again on the floor.

"Looking for this?" The voice came from Dina Chang, holding up a small bottle, just out of Ji-huen's reach.

Ji-huen gave her a tight smile. "Yes, thank you." She went to the edge of the stage and bent over to snatch the bottle. She carried it back to the table and dropped a healthy dose into her bowl. She straightened her white wrap and turned back to the audience with a reassuring smile.

"As I was saying. The air whipped into the mask allows it to moisturize without clogging, and the tea tree oil I have just added combines with the other materials to pull out the oil and impurities, which then allows for more moisture to be absorbed by the skin." She set the bowl down, and picked up another bottle. "Our reju- venating Essence of Peony and Starfish both perfumes and revitalizes." She sprinkled a couple of drops into the bowl and whipped it again with a bamboo whisk, the muscles in her arm pumping violently. Sumi placed another linen towel around Louise's neck, rather firmly, I thought.

"Hwuen, get the seaweed, please," Ji-huen said, as she

smeared the mixture onto Louise's face with a bamboo spatula.

Hwuen immediately covered the mixture with strips of seaweed handed to her by Sumi.

"We usually leave the mask for twenty minutes, but–"

Louise started wiggling and making noises underneath the mask.

"It seems like twenty seconds is too much!" Dina Chang called out, to a few appreciative titters from the crowd behind her. The laughter made Dina's smile wider, and she leaned forward, resting her elbows on the stage with the avid glee of a shark watching a sinking ship. Ji-huen's smile became fixed, and she glared at Dina Chang.

"The tea tree oil can provide a pleasant tingling, an assurance that your skin is being exfoliated and awakened—" Ji-huen said, a bit louder.

And then Louise screamed, or tried to. It was muffled into a horrible choking sound, as she started clawing the mask off her face.

"What did you do to her?" Dina Chang screeched at the top of her lungs.

Louise was flinging seaweed and creamy goop all over the place, her incoherent cries hoarse and desperate. Hwuen and Sumi stood there in shock. Ji-huen grabbed the seaweed water bowl, and flung the contents at Louise's face.

"Sumi! Towel!" Ji-huen snapped. Sumi jumped, and grabbed the stack of meticulously folded linen towels, and brought them to her mother, who began mopping the mask off.

"Stop! Don't scratch. I told you before, don't scratch," Ji-huen said, before standing back.

Louise's face was revealed, unrecognizable with swelling so violent that her eyes couldn't be seen and her lips were grossly oversized, their original shape distorted into pillows. Her skin was mottled with red hives and pale, shiny swelling, and her screams had faded into painful, terrified whimpering. She held up her hands, grasping for help. Her fingers were rapidly ballooning, red patches where she'd touched the mask. She wasn't screaming anymore, because she was gasping for air.

"Does anyone have an EpiPen?" Ji-huen screamed. "She is having an allergic reaction."

I was already dialing 9-1-1, even as purses rustled as people dug for their EpiPens.

Ji-huen held Louise and continued to mop the mask off her face. "Just lie still, lie still, Miss Louise. You'll be fine! Don't panic. Hwuen, call nine-one-one!"

"I already did!" I yelled, even as someone passed an EpiPen to Hwuen. She carried it to her mother and the crowd winced in sympathy as Ji-huen jabbed it hard into Louise's meaty thigh.

Louise's wheezing drowned out the murmurs of discomfort and the clicking of cell phone cameras, as the crowd stood there, uncomfortably shifting, not wanting to watch, but not wanting to leave. This sort of ugly disfiguration had no place in this world of pore-less perfection.

"I am so tweeting this," I heard from someone behind me.

Paramedics showed up a few agonizingly slow minutes later, pushing a stretcher, with six security guards clearing a pathway. They put Louise on the stretcher and wheeled her through the crowd.

Her face was clear of the mask, but the damage was undeniable. The crowd murmured angrily. Dina said, far more loudly than necessary, to the woman next to her, "That's the trouble with some of these homemade organizations. No quality control. No consistency. That's how lawsuits happen."

Some of the more expensive suits assumed disinterested expressions and melted away at the magic "L" word.

Ji-huen looked at the bowl, and sniffed it. Then she scowled, and stood up to get the tea tree oil bottle. She opened it, sniffed it, and turned on Dina like an avenging Fury. "What did you put in this bottle?"

Nari gasped from her platform perch, and waved at me frantically, mouthing, "Told you so."

Dina's eyes went wide and her mouth opened and then shut, before she said. "What are you talking about?" Her expression sharpened as she realized everyone was now staring at her.

"This isn't the tea tree oil I pressed myself. The color is wrong, there is no odor! You switched the bottles to ruin my demo!"

Dina glared at Ji-huen. "That's cute. You're just trying to cover your own mistake. We all saw what you did to that woman's face with your unscientific hoodoo!"

"How dare you slur our traditional medicine as unscientific?" Ji-huen towered like a goddess of righteous anger on the stage. "My products are made in carefully controlled small batches, while yours are made in giant vats by unskilled people paid with pennies. My ingredients, home grown in my garden, organic, free of pesticides or other chemicals. But you, you hired this woman to come and knock over my products so you could sabotage my demonstration. Everyone saw you touch that bottle. You must have switched them." She pointed an accusing finger at Dina Chang, who tried to take a step back, bumping against the crowd behind her.

Hwuen and Sumi stepped forward and flanked their mother, arms crossed over their chests as they glared down at Dina.

Dina Chang turned with a confident smile toward the crowd, starting to say, "Can you be...believe this," but the words and smile both faltered as she realized there were no friendly faces looking back. Her face turned back to stare up at Ji-huen, shock and realization warring in her expression.

"That—that's slander," Dina Chang managed to say, "You can't say that. You have no proof! How dare you." She pushed her way through the crowd and fled back to her booth.

Ji-huen took a deep breath, and smiled. "Ladies and gentlemen, we will be redoing this demonstration with the correct ingredients in one hour. Thank you all for your interest in Salanghada!" She, Hwuen, and Sumi began cleaning up the stage.

Nari came floating over to me. "Rosa! Rosa, did you see it?"

I looked at her. Her face was so open, so hopeful. "Yeah, Nari. But we should talk about it later—"

Nari grabbed me by the hand, and was dragging me toward her aunt with surprising strength for a fifty-kilo vegan.

"Imo Ji, Rosa saw what happened!"

The expression that Ji-huen turned on both of us, surprise and fear in her eyes, made us both stop.

She looked from one of us to the other, and managed a wobbly smile. "What did Miss Park see, Nari?"

Nari looked at me. "I don't...she didn't say yet." Her expression grew uncertain as she looked at my face.

"I saw a great performance," I said. "I hope you paid that woman well."

Ji-huen's chin lifted. "I don't know what you're talking about. Paid who? Nari?"

"Louise," I said.

"What? What are you talking about?" said Nari, "Rosa, you mean Dina paid Louise, right?"

"No." My eyes never left Ji-huen. "I mean your aunt set the whole thing up, to smear Dina. Now if Dina tries to claim that Salanghada has quality control issues, or brings this incident up, she'll ruin herself. Her word's been ruined."

Nari stared. "How? You can't know that, Rosa. Imo would never do such a thing." She turned to her aunt, reaching a hand toward her, but the words died on her lips at the defiant and embarrassed look on Ji-huen's face.

"Dina was causing many problems, Nari." Ji-huen whispered, glancing nervously around. "This way, no one got hurt but Louise, and she'll be better very soon. No one will listen to Dina, and after everyone sees our demonstrations go perfectly this afternoon, we will get the big contracts!"

Nari's hands dropped to her sides, and she said, confused, "I don't understand. I thought Dina..."

I said gently, "There's no way that Dina could have made a duplicate bottle in time that would fool someone who used these bottles every day. She also didn't put anything in it. I was watching her, and she used the same hand to pick up the bottle and hand it back to your aunt. She looked at the label, but otherwise she did nothing to it. Whatever made Louise react was already in that bottle. Add that to the fact that your aunt told her not to scratch, saying, 'I told you.' They had supposedly just met. When did she tell her not to scratch?"

"Maybe Dina switched it before the show!"

"When? Are you trying to tell me that none of the four of you would have seen her approaching the booth during set up? And the convention security cameras could disprove that in a minute."

Nari turned to her aunt. Her lips trembled. "But imo, that poor woman."

Ji-huen stared at the melting face of her campaign,

and whispered desperately, "Nari, I paid Louise, all right? But please, calm down. It was just, just a play."

"Except for the fact that you've discredited an innocent woman," I said. "And you risked Louise's life."

"I am *hanui*! I would never risk her life. It is just an irritant. And that woman is not innocent," Ji-huen hissed. "She's been trying to destroy my business for months with her lies. I had to protect our livelihood, our traditions, our family."

"Yeah, that makes it okay for you to destroy hers," I said. "Nari, I'm going to go. We'll do lunch another time."

Nari nodded, still looking stricken. "Oh. Okay, Rosa. Thanks for staying. I-I'm so sorry!" She turned and ran for the bathroom, silk skirts trailing like the tail of a comet.

Hwuen scowled at me. "You couldn't just keep your mouth shut? You don't understand the business of beauty culture."

Ji-huen said, "What are you going to do?"

I looked at all three of them, the fear, and the resentment in their faces. "I'm going home."

Relief warred with suspicion. Sumi said, "That's it?"

"Confucius says if one's actions are motivated by profit, one will have many enemies. You all deliberately injured someone, caused her pain in a way that would make your ancestors sick, using the traditional recipes that are the treasure of your family in order to strike at an enemy in a cowardly way. I hope the woman you injured is a reliable, honorable sort, because she can now blackmail you into eternity."

Ji-huen paled, her lips thinning.

I nodded. "Normally, I consider blackmailers the scum of the earth, but in this case, I think Louise is owed a little justice for injury. Better hope you don't make it big, because nothing makes leeches fat like another's good fortune." I started to turn away, and then I stopped and looked back.

"Oh. And if something unfortunate happens to Louise or whatever her name really is, better believe I'll find out, and I'll make a point of letting the officials know the truth of this incident."

"You are a horrible person" said Aunt Ji, her eyes stricken and her lips trembling. "I would, I would never…"

I turned back toward the door and kept walking. At the door, the gate guard looked at my special wrist band. "Leaving already? You know this is a one-time-only band, right?"

"Realized I didn't need any help looking in the mirror," I said.

He squinted back at the room as he cut my bracelet off. "Bet a lot of them in there would kill to say that."

"I wouldn't take that bet."

"Me neither. Have a nice day."

DEAD MAN'S HAND
Karen McCullough

Caroline's hand shook as she stuck the key in the door of her home. She hadn't been inside since that hideous night a week ago, when she'd found her husband's body on the floor of his office. The police had kept her out while they investigated his death.

Emptiness echoed through the place as she walked in, the silence louder than her footsteps on the hardwood floor of the hall.

She stopped for a moment in the kitchen. She'd have to clean out the refrigerator, replace all the staples, sort through the accumulated mail, do laundry. The white board over the desk caught her eye. It bore a note from George reminding her to pick up his gray suit from the dry cleaner. He must've written that between the time she'd left to go shopping and his death a few hours later. A tidal wave of grief washed over her, blotting out everything else. What was the point of doing anything with George gone? She dropped into a chair and cried, letting the tears flow in a way she hadn't been able to while staying with her sister-in-law.

When the spasm wore out, she blew her nose, and sat

up straight. Before anything else, she needed to face the hardest test, to go back into George's office.

She steeled herself and opened the door. The strange aroma that she'd smelled in her dreams since that night lingered—gunpowder, blood, excrement—and there was something new, a chemical tang. Nausea surged through her. She covered her mouth and made herself survey the dark stains on floor and wall.

When she'd had all she could take, she backed out quickly. Everything else could wait until the cleaners who specialized in crime scenes had done their job.

She retreated to the living room and sank into the couch. George had handled all the financial things, not just because he didn't want to talk about the cost of his gambling, but because he was also a control freak and it made him nervous to leave it to anyone else. Before his death, she'd lived with the stress of his gambling addiction. When he locked himself in the office for hours, when he refused to discuss their finances, she'd tried to convince herself it was all right. He gave her a generous allowance and the credit cards were never refused; no bill collectors ever called. Now, not only did she have to grieve for the man she still loved, she had to come to grips with how he died.

Her phone buzzed in her pocket. The caller ID said it was Jeff Campbell, her lawyer.

"Caroline?" Jeff said. "I hear the police are closing the case. Calling it suicide."

"They are. I still don't believe it."

"Even without a suicide note it sounds like the

coroner was convinced he shot himself."

"I know. But I'm not. We need to talk."

"Of course. This afternoon?"

She agreed to be there at two. As she hung up, the doorbell rang to announce the arrival of the cleaning crew.

While they worked, she retreated to a corner of the dining room and booted up George's computer. The police had found nothing incriminating on it, but they didn't know all the things she did.

There were several emails to and from his nephew on the day of George's death. The last one made her gasp and read it through twice.

Dave—

This can't go on. It's starting to drain my resources and you and I both know it's not healthy. One way or another, it's got to stop. I can't support this anymore. Let me know when you can come by to talk about it.

George

George had always treated Dave as the son he never had. Dave's mother, Margaret, was divorced and George was the only father figure Dave had. George enjoyed the role. He'd even loaned Dave the money to start his own engineering business. George told Caroline that Dave was repaying the loan on a regular basis and he was proud of him.

So, what did this mean? *What couldn't go on?*

She read through the other emails to and from Dave,

but they were all mundane business issues, setting up times to meet for lunch or a baseball game, questions about relatives, or discussions of sporting events and the fantasy football league they were involved in. Not even a hint of what had to stop.

The cleaning service continued its work. Their equipment was loud. The workers wore overalls and masks. She wondered when she could call her life her own again, then dug deeper into George's computer files. She hoped that somewhere in the laptop, she'd find the key to understanding his death.

Jeff Campbell was the family lawyer and a long-time friend of George's. When she was shown into his office, he stood and came to hug her. "How are you, Caroline? I'm so sorry about George. What a shock."

"Yes, it was. Is. I'm not sure how to go on. But I have to. George would expect it." And, she thought, I'll have to be strong if I want to figure out who killed him.

Jeff took her arm and escorted her to the client chair at the desk. Then he took his seat opposite her. "You already know how George's will was set up. Fifty thousand to his nephew, plus forgiveness of the rest of the loan. The balance of payments from their parents' trust go to Margaret for her lifetime, then the principal passes to her son. The rest of his estate goes to you. Most of his accounts and investments are already held jointly with you, so they pass to you automatically. One of his partners in the accounting firm has already approached me about buying out his share of the business."

"Can you manage that for me? I trust you'll get a fair price."

"I can. And there are papers to sign, of course." They spent the next thirty minutes dealing with the details of the estate. Once that was done, he said, "This wasn't the only thing you wanted to talk about."

"No. I still don't believe George killed himself."

"I get that. But there's not much you can do about it."

"But protect myself," Caroline said.

Jeff's eyebrows rose. "You think you're in danger, too?"

"I think it's entirely possible I'll find out *why* George was killed and that may well lead me to who did it. The police said there was no evidence of forced entry. The implications are pretty obvious. Plus, I found this in George's email." She handed the printout of George's message to Dave to Jeff. "So, I plan to change the locks, have a security system installed, and learn to use George's gun. I also want to leave a couple of things with you." She pulled out a sealed letter and handed it to him. "I put a copy of the email in here and some other things, too. This is to be opened only if something happens to me that isn't clearly natural causes. I have another copy that I'm giving to the police detective as well."

"You really think Dave could be involved?"

"I don't like to think so, but it's hard to see what else this message could mean.

His expression suggested he took her fears seriously as he pulled out a file folder, slipped the letter in, and then put it in his bottom desk drawer. "I very much hope you're wrong about this."

"I do, too. And it's still possible it was an accident, though I find that hard to believe. But I can't afford to take the chance."

Jeff nodded.

"One more thing. I need to know about George's gambling debts. Am I obligated to pay them?"

"It depends on who he owes and what kind of agreements he signed. Certainly the lines of credit from the casinos have to be paid. Have you any idea how much it is?"

"No. It will take some work to find out."

"Why don't you let me do that for you? If you want to just box up all his papers and bring them to me, I'll be glad to sort it out for you. In fact, since he was a friend, I can just come by and pick up everything. We might be able to pay the debts out of what you get for the sale of his share of the company."

Caroline hesitated. "Let me sleep on that."

"In the meantime, if anyone presses you about anything, refer them to me."

"Will do."

He stood when she did. "Take care," he said. His tone made the words more than just a social nicety.

Caroline's head buzzed and warning bells rang loudly in her brain. She just wasn't sure what they tried to tell her. The minute she got home, she called around until she found someone willing to come out that evening to change the locks. The security company promised to be there the next day.

Her first dinner alone in her house wasn't as traumatic as she feared since she'd often been on her own when George went on the gambling jaunts he called business trips. But he almost always phoned in the evening to talk. Never again. She let herself have another good cry, but refused to indulge the depression it brought.

The locksmith arrived as she finished her meal, and she did feel more secure, though lonely, once he'd handed her the new keys and left.

She knew she wouldn't sleep, so decided to face the office now and go through George's desk and files. The room smelled of carpet cleaner but she thought she could still detect a hint of the coppery scent of blood.

The desk's center drawer was full of paper clips, pens, pencils, a checkbook, and a few envelopes containing current bills. She glanced through them, noting totals and that none of the bills showed back charges or past-due notices. A second drawer held boxes of writing paper, a stack of legal pads, and a few smaller notepads. The third housed his collection of pipes, along with cleaning equipment and a humidor for the tobacco. The aroma brought back memories of their nights together. She shoved it closed.

The final two drawers held stacks of old computer printouts, newspapers, and printed booklets, relating to football, baseball, and basketball games going back several years. Most showed betting odds on various teams and events.

Caroline sighed and crossed to the filing cabinets. The top drawer held folders of paid bills, one each for the electricity, water, phone, cable, car payments, mortgage, and credit cards. None gave any indication of financial problems. Even the credit card balances were paid in full each month.

The buzz of the phone pulled her out of musing on the implications of all those neatly paid bills.

"How are you doing?" her sister-in-law Margaret asked. "This is your first night alone in the house without George. I'm sure it's lonely. I'll be glad to come over if you need company. Or help you start packing up his things."

She's trying to be helpful, Caroline reminded herself, though Margaret's idea of help usually meant taking charge of any situation and issuing orders. "I'm all right," she said. "I'm meeting with the funeral director tomorrow at ten to go over the details. You want to meet me there? We could do lunch afterward."

"Yes, I'll be there," Margaret said. "Do you need help with George's things? I know that must be difficult for you. Dave and I would be glad to come over on Saturday."

"I'll let you know." She took a moment to wonder if she was getting paranoid. Why did all the offers of help make her suspicious rather than grateful?

She ended the call, went back to the file cabinet, and paged through the rest of the bills, finding nothing of particular interest. The next drawer held sales receipts, warranties, and instruction books for everything they'd ever bought, including things they no longer owned. It was so like George to save it all and keep it neatly arranged, she thought, as she flipped through information for two vacuum cleaners that had passed on to small appliance heaven years ago.

Tears threatened again. She'd sometimes wondered if the gambling was a reaction to his compulsive need for order and control in every other aspect of his life. An outlet perhaps. But whatever anyone else thought, the gambling hadn't been bad enough to damage their lives. He wouldn't do that to her.

She paid closer attention to the financial records in the drawer below. Folders organized by company and year contained monthly reports from their various investment accounts. Several times over the past year, George had taken money from one or the other account, but in no case had his withdrawals represent a huge percent of the balance. Unless he'd drained all of the accounts since the most recent reports, she would certainly not be penniless.

At the back, she found the reports for the trust his parents had left him and his sister. Jeff had been the lawyer who administered it for him and Margaret. She saw the records of the orderly monthly payments to both beneficiaries.

She'd seen the reports on several occasions, though she never paid close attention.

They were arranged with the most recent closest to

the front. She planned just to glance over it, but one number on the top sheet made her stop and study the whole thing more closely. In fact, she read all the text as well as the numbers and graphs, but still didn't understand why there should be an unexplained withdrawal of almost one hundred thousand dollars taken from the principal. If that was a trustee's fee, it seemed excessive on a three-million-dollar trust. Had there been some kind of change in the fee structure?

She went through the rest of the reports page by page. Each month showed some dividends reinvested as well as the regular distributions, but in May, fifty thousand had been deposited without explanation. In March, another hundred thousand had been taken out, listed only as "miscellaneous fees." In January, a trustee's fee of fifteen thousand was noted.

Caroline flipped the page to the previous year. In November, forty thousand was deposited with no explanation other than "reimbursement." In August, another one hundred thousand had been removed as "miscellaneous fees." In May, fifty thousand was deposited and in March, one hundred thousand removed. In January, another fifteen thousand trustee's fee was noted. Reports from two prior years showed the same pattern, with the regular trustee's fee in January and other irregular deposits and withdrawals. Always the withdrawals were greater than the deposits.

That didn't make any sense. Unless someone was taking out loans against the principal of the trust. Who would be doing it though?

She booted up the computer again. George kept his checking account log in a program that tracked all his financial records. Scrolling through the transactions showed nothing to account for the large withdrawals from the trust fund. He had a couple of larger deposits, but she thought the end-of-year ones were bonus distributions from the accounting firm where he was a partner, and the others were likely the occasional gambling win. None of the deposits matched the dates or amounts of the withdrawals from the trust to say that he'd received those funds.

It was possible the money had gone directly to some other account, but she couldn't find it. George had said he ran everything through his checking account to track it. So, where had those funds gone? There weren't many possibilities. Margaret or Dave? Either might explain his email to Dave. Margaret had expensive tastes but she also had a decent-paying job and a substantial settlement from the divorce.

Caroline retreated to the couch to consider how she might figure it out. When she realized she was falling asleep instead of thinking, she gave up and went to bed.

First thing in the morning she called Detective Martinez and explained to him what she'd found and what she made of it. She had all her arguments mustered and ready, but he surprised her by not immediately rejecting the idea.

"You think you've found a motive for murder?" he asked.

"I'm pretty sure of it."

"The coroner's just as sure it was suicide."

"Did you see the note on the whiteboard in the kitchen?"

A moment's pause followed. "Something about picking up a suit at the dry cleaner," the detective answered.

"Right. And he wrote that sometime after I left to go shopping and before I got home and found him dead. Does that sound like a man who planned to commit suicide? George wasn't impulsive. If he'd decided to kill himself, he would've made preparations. He'd have left me a long list of instructions on what to do with his things, not a reminder about picking up his dry cleaning. That's the way George was."

Martinez paused again. "You have a point. But it's not enough to weigh against the coroner's ruling."

"I know. But I think I know how to get around it."

When she told him what she wanted to do, his response was loud and uncompromising. "No way. Don't you dare." Anger and concern made the words ring loudly through the phone line. "It's way too damn dangerous."

"I have to."

"I don't want to have to investigate another murder."

"I don't want you to, either, but I'm not safe now."

That quieted the detective for a moment. "I can't believe I'm saying this, but there are a couple of ways to ensure it. Revise that letter you left with the attorney and make sure everyone knows I have a copy. Or just hand over the documents."

"No. I'm not stupid, and that means I'm not safe.

Can't be safe because I'll always have access to the information no matter what I hand over. But in any case, I want justice for George more than I want safety. I'll take the risk."

"I can't let you take it."

"You can't stop me. I'm going to do it. But I'd much rather have your help."

The silence stretched out for so long she feared he'd hung up, then he said, "I'm going to regret this one way or another. We do this my way. You will do exactly as I tell you. We have to do this right to be sure it's airtight."

She agreed and told him she'd be there after she met with the funeral director and had lunch with Margaret.

The meeting went about as expected. Caroline had made several decisions about the casket and funeral beforehand. Margaret weighed in with her opinions and Caroline let her have her way on some of the less important things.

Afterward they went to an Italian restaurant for lunch.

"Have you thought about what you're going to do with the house?" Margaret asked over plates of linguini.

"No. Not yet. I need to decide what I want to do next before I can worry about that."

"What about George's things? Do you want Dave to come help you go through them?"

Warning bells rang in her brain again. Was there more to Margaret's pushing on George's things than simple concern? A less simple need to protect herself or her son?

"Not ready to even think about that yet. I'll let you know after the funeral." Caroline found it hard to keep her mind on the conversation and was relieved when they finished eating and she could honestly say she had another appointment and had to get going.

It took the detective and his people several hours to set everything up. By the time she made the phone call that would set the plan in motion, it was almost five. Her hands shook and it took all her will power to make her voice steady and casual as she asked for help with George's papers and said she'd be at home that evening.

Then she had to wait.

"Try to do your normal things," Martinez advised. "Cook dinner. Watch TV. Read. Whatever you'd normally do this time of day."

"I don't dare. What if I forget to concentrate on what I need to say when the time comes?"

"You won't. When the doorbell rings you'll snap into catch-a-killer mode."

"I hope you're right."

Caroline cooked dinner and watched television, but her mind could only be coaxed into paying half-attention to those activities. Time crawled.

When the doorbell sounded a little after eight that evening, she did jolt into full alert mode, mentally rehearsing what she needed to say. She checked behind her, saw all looked normal, drew a deep breath, and went to the door.

She struggled for a calm, normal smile as she let him in.

"Jeff. Thank you for coming." She kept her head down and sniffed, hoping to hide her nerves under the real grief. "I appreciate the help. I just don't think I can handle the paperwork."

She followed him into George's office. "Can I get you some boxes or bags for this?"

"That would be good." He answered absently as he approached the desk.

By the time she returned with a couple of boxes, he was going through the bottom drawer. "Anything in there you need?" she asked.

"Just what's in the top drawer." He shut the bottom drawer and went over to the file cabinets. He ignored the folders of paid bills in the top drawer and the instructions and warranties in the second. When he got to the third, he pulled out the folders of trust account reports and dumped them into the boxes without looking too closely. As he tore through the bottom drawer, though, his expression changed to concern and puzzlement.

Caroline picked up the set of folders she'd tucked away on a corner of a bookshelf and put them on the desk. "Are these what you're looking for?" she asked.

He straightened up and turned, approached the desk, and his eyes widened at the label. He stared at her. "You've looked through them?"

"You're a gambler, too, aren't you? All those business trips you and George took together. You encouraged his gambling along with your own. But you couldn't afford it as easily as he could."

"Wrong." He frowned and eyes flashed with anger. "He drew me into the gaming world, even though he knew I couldn't afford it." He paused and sighed. "If you'd just let me handle all of George's finances, you would never have known about this." He took a step toward her, pulling a gun from under his jacket.

Nausea roiled her stomach but she had to keep going. "George was worried that you couldn't repay the debt to the trust and that you wanted more. Did he tell you he was going to put a stop to your borrowing against the trust fund?"

"He threatened to. After he'd dragged me into his sordid mess in the first place."

"You'd be disbarred. Maybe go to jail."

"It was supposed to be an unfortunate accident. But suicide was even better. And now you're going to have to end it all, too," Jeff said. "You couldn't handle the grief. Too bad. Please don't try to struggle. I promise it will be quick."

She didn't dare look up. Breath clotted in her throat but she managed to choke out, "You found his gun again?"

"I took it out of the drawer in his desk while you got the boxes. You're going to use it." He stepped toward her keeping the gun aimed at her head.

"What was George doing when you pulled it out of his desk?"

"He went to the bathroom. I waited until he sat back

down and moved right up beside him."

"How did you know he had a gun?"

"I've seen it a couple of times when I met with him here. I'm sorry, Caroline. I hate to do this—"

"We definitely do not hate to do *this*," Detective Martinez said as he grabbed Jeff's gun arm, forcing it upward so that the bullet he fired hit the ceiling. A second police officer yanked the gun away, while a third got an arm around Jeff's neck and dragged him backward, to the floor, facedown.

Caroline bit her lip as she stared at Jeff. "Didn't it occur to you to wonder why I put it back in the same exact place after the police took it? You didn't check to make sure it was loaded, though, did you? It isn't."

Jeff glared at her but didn't say anything.

"Are you all right?" Martinez asked her while the others cuffed Jeff and led him away.

"Shaken and stirred, but okay. Better now that I'll have justice for George." She looked around. "I suppose your crime scene unit will have to make a mess in here again?"

"Not as much this time," he said. "You won't have to move out."

"That's all right, then." She shook her head. "But I'll have to get someone to repair the ceiling. Doesn't matter. So worth it."

INTERVENTION
Caroline Taylor

Dearest Younger Sister,

I know you didn't mean to do it. I'm just trying to understand. Wallace is quite upset, as I'm sure you can imagine. Nobody wants a criminal in the family. He claims he can barely hold his head up around town. Like some nineteenth-century paterfamilias, he has forbidden me to contact you. Thus, the Charlotte postmark.

I've been told I may not visit you unless you okay it. Will you?

We haven't been close, I know. But I truly want to understand what happened. The trial was a joke, in my opinion. Your legal representation was ineffective. Even Wallace agrees with me on that point.

Speaking of whom, please reply to the post office box number on the return address. In case they didn't give you the envelope, it's P.O. Box 390, Charlotte, NC 28201.

I look forward to seeing you. It has been too long.

—Your always older sister, Lucy

* * *

Lucinda—

After all this time? You must be joking. Go crawl back under your rock and don't bother me again.

—Martha

Dear Marty,

To borrow your own words, "after all this time," you still hate me? Surely you have more important things to concern you than whatever grudge you're clinging to. I know I haven't been the best sister, and I apologize if that has hurt your feelings. I have always felt I needed to look after you, especially when it comes to things Mom and Dad aren't aware of. I can't help wanting to do whatever I can to clear your name and get you out of there.

It can't be pleasant for you. In fact, I imagine it's quite horrible. I don't want you to suffer. So *please* let me visit. I really need to understand what happened and why.

The official version—that you deliberately dropped your hair dryer in the bathtub—just doesn't fly with me. You might have some serious problems, but you're no killer. Was it an accident? If so, why didn't the jury believe you?

You can still reach me at the Charlotte post office box.

—Your loving sister, Lucy

* * *

Dear Martha,

It has been three months and no word from you. I called the correctional facility and discovered that you still haven't put my name on your approved visitors' list.

I might have been a bit too frank when I told you I didn't think Tony was the right man for you. But don't imagine that Wallace was influencing me. He wasn't. Although he, too, thought Tony was not, as he put it, "our kind of people." If Tony had family here or at least somewhere else in the South, we would have been able to ease our qualms a bit. The wise-guy accent alone was off-putting, and the way he acted around you was disgusting—like you were nothing but bimbo arm candy. You might have been blinded by love, but the rest of us—including Mom and Dad, by the way—thought he came straight out of central casting for *The Godfather.* What else were we to think about an Italian from New Jersey?

That's why I'm on your side, Marty. I think it's more than plausible that Tony was the kind of male chauvinist pig who always has to be in charge. Given your personal issues, it's easy to imagine that you maybe weren't paying enough attention to him. His poor, fragile ego couldn't take it, and so he played tough guy with you. Made your life miserable. Was that what happened?

Please, Marty, let me come and visit. Mom and Dad want to know how you are doing. They're too far away and too old to travel all the way to New Jersey. They're wondering if you're being offered treatment. We all hope so.

Please.
—Lucinda

Lucinda—
Treatment! Fuck you. All of you. You think I'm some kind of addict? Get real. And, while you're at it, go to hell.
DO NOT PASS GO.
DO NOT write to me!

Dear Martha,
I'm only trying to understand, sis. If you didn't kill him, why are you locked up? Was there somebody else? A jealous girlfriend, maybe?
—L

Bitch. Tony might have had his faults, but he was not cheating on me. Now, do me a favor and GET LOST.

Dear Martha,
Dad is begging me to visit you. Mom cries all the time. Her hair has turned totally white from all the stress. Dad could have a coronary any day, he worries so much. They think you've been railroaded, that Tony was indeed mobbed up, and his pals bribed some jurors to vote for conviction. Dad says that happens all the time in

New Jersey. Or maybe the Mob bribed your lawyer to mount that shitty defense.

I would much rather talk this over with you face to face, but if you won't let me visit, I will continue to write. I truly believe that if you're innocent, you should be doing everything possible to clear your name.

Please let me help.

—Lucinda

Bossy Older Sister,

What part of FUCK OFF don't you understand?

Dearest Younger Sister,

I have hired an investigator to look at the trial record and see if there were any irregularities or anything else that might help you. Wallace doesn't know this and would not approve. I haven't told Mom or Dad either. I don't want to get their hopes up.

—Your loving older sister, Lucinda

L—

You might think you have my best interests at heart, but you seem to have forgotten what a lousy character witness you were! Dragging up all that old stuff from the past. Just because you were too goody-good to shoplift something you really, really had to have didn't mean you had to rat me out. And so what if I didn't ever return stuff to the library? Does that make me a murderer? Thanks to you, the jury certainly thought so.

Leave me alone.

—M

Martha—

I didn't have a choice! I was under oath, sworn to tell the truth. How was I to know the prosecutor would drag up all that old business? If I had lied—and believe me, I was tempted—I'd be in prison, too! Imagine what that would do to Mom and Dad.

If you blame me for your predicament, Marty, at least let me help you.

—Lucy

You can't.

—M

Marty—

Don't be so defeatist, sis. We can fix this, but we need to meet. I could bring Cameron with me. He's the investigator I hired. He'd like to hear your version of events. Then maybe he can take this thing further than that fool you had for a lawyer.

Wallace is going to California for a Mercedes dealers' convention in a couple of weeks. The timing would be perfect for me to visit you, and Wallace would never find out.

Please say you'll see me. Cameron, too. In case you need it for the prison officials, his full name is Cameron Bondurant (yes, those Bondurants), and he's a licensed private investigator with a law degree to boot. Anytime the week of March 13 will work.

See you soon?

—Your hopeful sister, Lucy

Dear Meddler,

Save your money. Not to mention your marriage.

Did it never occur to you that maybe I deserve being here? You see, I'm really not sure if I dropped the hair dryer on purpose or not. I was clearly not in my right mind. In fact, I was going ape shit. Tony accused me of neglecting him. He decided he was going to "cure me or die trying." (His words.) I told him there was nothing to cure. I even got down on my hands and knees and begged him to understand where I'm coming from. But he was absolutely heartless.

He locked my Kindle in the gun safe. It had Sarah Paretsky's latest on it! He took my phone away, wouldn't let me order anything from Amazon. He wouldn't even go in to work just so he could keep an eye on me twenty-four/seven. That's how he managed to keep me away from Farley's Bookshop while they were having a three-for-one sale of Janet Evanovich, Sue Grafton, and Patricia Cornwell. I've never had to go three whole days without anything to read. You've always had this crazy idea that I'm suffering from some kind of addiction. Not true. In fact, you and Mom and Dad will never understand one simple thing about me: BOOKS ARE MY LIFE.

Luckily, they seem to get it here at Edna Mahan Correctional. I even have a job in the library.

HER FINAL TRICK
Robin Whitten

"You might as well keep going." She didn't stop walking. She tried to put more distance between herself and the man who drove too close to her, the man who wouldn't stop talking.

"I really want to help you." His voice rippled through the heavy air.

"There is nothing you can do to help me. Please just go on." When she first heard the car, her mouth watered, her skin tingled. She'd hoped he was a John, a little money for a fix. Then she saw his car.

He crept along the dirt road in his Dodge Charger as she mostly staggered, sometimes tripped, her pace quickening over the railroad tracks that ran next to the road. She couldn't get away.

"Look, you're about to get drenched." His arm shot out of the window.

She stepped back, ready to run until she realized he only meant to point to the sky ahead. Dark clouds, black against the green of the pines, threatened on the horizon. "Can't you see where you're heading? What's about to happen?"

She stared at the ground, at the nothing. "It's already happened."

"What?"

She turned toward him, frustrated that he was still there. She knew she was filthy. Her hands, caked with many days of dirt, pressed against her dress, its hem flapping loosely in the cooling air. She had seen her reflection in the broken glass at the train station. Her hair, the color of dust, hung in greasy strands around her swollen face. A bruise, yellow and green, perfectly round, surrounded her left eye. She felt its familiarity, accepted its price.

The car drifted ahead of her a few feet and stopped. The passenger's side door swung open. "Come on, get in the car." She didn't detect any threat in his voice. "I'll take you wherever you want to go."

She tried to laugh but it came out a wheeze. "Officer, if it's all the same to you, I don't have any place to go." She wanted him to leave, drive away, so she could find a John. Only ten dollars and she could be high. No one would even think of approaching her with him around. Besides, he made her nervous.

She searched the sky, hoping for an answer, a rainbow maybe, but saw only dark billowing clouds. She looked to her left, toward the dense woods. Would the trees on the edge of the road provide any shelter? Maybe she wouldn't need the trees if someone picked her up, someone with a car, someone who had a trailer. Then she could sleep, one night, sleep.

"What's your name?" His voice, soft, not accusing.

The way he spoke startled her. His figure, a blue sculpture stood half in, half out of his car.

"Amy," she said. Lightening coursed through the darkness. It's jagged edges razor like in the cool air. It was getting closer,

"Let me take you to the shelter." He stepped away from the car.

Amy's eyes traveled the length of the railroad tracks, up and back. She should run, now, but her legs wouldn't move. Traitors, she thought. They never did what she asked of them, just like the people she let in, those few who saw the all of her. Like the men who held her close and said they loved her before they hit her. Traitors.

The officer placed a hand lightly on Amy's elbow and led her to his car. With the promise of warmth came uncertainty. She'd have a rough night at the shelter. She'd have to come down, become sober, without help. She'd done it before, sometime in the past. The memory of it was vague.

Amy pulled her arm away. "I can walk on my own. Officer Perry, right?" The letters on his name tag blurred.

He shrugged and followed her to his car. He bent close to her, close enough to smell her sweat soaked skin, and opened the back door. She knew she smelled bad, but he didn't flinch.

"Can't I sit in the front with you?" She leaned toward him, hoping he might glance at her full breasts and pink nipples, hard and visible through the thin material of her dress. Maybe he'd take her home, to his home. Maybe he could love her, hold her without the promise of pain. Maybe he'd be her last trick.

"No, Amy. It's against the rules." His breath, minty, clean, brushed across her cheek. His hand touched the top of her head, lightly guiding her into the back seat.

She shivered, surprised at how the warmth of the car crawled over her skin. She focused outside of her window. Was it cold out? What month were they in, October? When had Karin died? Karin, her best friend, pals since childhood. The last few days, her last fix, had helped her forget. Now, though, now she remembered.

Karin's face swollen, pasty, her lips purple. Amy had waved a hand over her open eyes hoping she might blink or turn her head. *Blood ran in ragged lines from her nose.* Amy always made fun of that nose, with its large nostrils, *better to inhale more juice*, pushed flat from being hit so many times. Karin's nasal voice. Amy closed her eyes. She'd never hear her voice again.

Officer Perry shut his door and turned on the ignition. The engine purred as the car bumped over the railroad tracks, pulling Amy out of her thoughts. She inhaled deeply, hoping she could keep it together. She really needed a fix. Her teeth chattered, her heart sent ripples through her chest. She poked his shoulder through the metal grate.

"Listen, you can drop me off anywhere around here. That corner over there." Amy pointed to an intersection, already occupied by three women dressed in short shorts and tank tops. Their hair piled on their heads like rats' nests, red lips pasted on their faces. Is that what she looked like? What if her mother saw her? She leaned back on the seat and closed her eyes. Her mother dead now two years. Everyone who meant anything was dead.

"Where do you live, Amy?" His voice, deep and soothing, sounded as though he cared about her. She knew better. They all acted the same, until they wanted something.

"Nowhere now. Nowhere." Everyone she loved gone.

"So how did you get so far from town?" Amy searched Officer Perry's dark blue eyes in the rearview mirror.

Please don't laugh at me, she thought. And don't feel sorry for me. Treat me like a normal person. She might have said this. She might have, as she had so many times in the past. But Amy wasn't normal. She couldn't be normal, not like other people. Not like her mother. Her mother, who forgave her when she left with him, her first lover, her first mistake. Her mother, who always took her in, held her when she cried.

Amy studied the houses, one by one, as they drove slowly down the main street of town. All of them had a porch, a front door, closed and locked, keeping in secrets, their own stories. Amy knew them, the men who lived in them. She'd been inside many of their houses, searching through their things, trying on their clothes, eating their food. Yes, she knew them. They were no better than she, with their lies.

Her eyes drifted to Officer Perry's neck. His hair was trim, no ragged edges. A spot behind his right ear caught her eye. The skin puckered, slightly pink, around a deep indentation. A small chunk of his ear was missing, leaving a slight divot in the cartilage. *A scream, a man holding his head, blood dripping.* The hair rose on her arms, her empty stomach turned. Her heart skipped a beat. Something about that scar stirred a memory, a thing. Amy stared at it. Her vision blurred. Her eyes felt tired, so tired.

"There aren't any lights on in the shelter yet." His calm manner brought her back.

Amy glanced out of her window at the large brick building that seemed wedged in by other buildings, pushing it back into a slight cul de sac, alone and hidden. It looked deserted, like every other building in this part of town. Deserted and unwanted like most of the people who ended up there. Like her.

He examined his watch. "Do you want to get something to eat?" He peered at her through his rearview mirror. "I can kick off for a half hour or so."

"I don't have any money." She slid low in her seat. What did he want from her?

"Well, then I guess I'll have to buy. That okay with you?" His voice smiled, his reflected eyes seemed concerned.

"You could just give me some money." She stared at him, hoping she looked sincere. "For food, I mean." She only needed a few dollars and she could feel normal again.

"I'd rather eat with you," the officer said. He studied the road.

It seemed as though they drove another half hour

before stopping at a small bar pushed all the way to the end of a dirt road. Five or six cars rested in the parking lot, all in a row, equidistant apart. A flashing sign over the front door read *Open*. He walked around to her door and gestured for her to get out.

"Do I look too bad for a regular restaurant?" She tried to pull her hair back into a pony tail but had nothing to hold it with.

Officer Perry raised a hand, as if to touch her, then let it drop to his side. "You look fine." He studied the bar for a moment. "I just thought you'd feel more comfortable here." She turned away, telling herself she didn't care. His touch would end the same as all the rest.

They sat in a booth in the back of the darkened bar, tucked behind the juke box. After they ordered, he placed his hands on the table. Her eyes rested on a green gem that filled the face of the class ring on his right hand. *The ring on the hand holding the bloody ear.* Was it the same? She jerked back into her seat, pushing away from the table.

He studied her for a moment and smiled. "Sobering up a bit?"

She clasped her hands together, her fingers turning white. Her body began to shake, then her chair. She thought her seat might break apart, so she grabbed its sides.

The waitress came back with a beer for her and coffee for him. She studied Amy, then the officer, and shook her head. Amy pretended not to notice as she raised the glass to her swollen lips and took a sip. Her hands shook, her teeth chattered. Please God, she thought, make it stop.

The man with the hole in his head, the ring on his finger, lay on his face. He groaned as the blood dripped through his fingers, over the ring with the green stone. The blood creating a ragged line that flowed into a small puddle on the ground under him. Amy closed her eyes. Maybe she was hallucinating. She did that often since Karin's death.

"I must confess, Amy, I've been looking for you for a long time." Officer Perry wrapped his long fingers around the coffee cup.

Amy tried to position herself for flight. She scooted her chair so that it sat at an angle from the table, facing the front door. She wasn't certain if she could run, but wanted to be ready. She sipped on her beer, her anxiety increasing with each swallow.

"You are definitely hard to find. Where have you been hiding?"

Someone else's hand, also covered in blood, held a handkerchief over the hole and pressed hard. Amy covered her face with one hand, held the bottle with the other and shook her head. *The man with the gun lying on the ground nearby, still alive, groaning.*

"What do you want?" she asked. She knew what was coming. He bought her dinner, now she had to pay. With blood probably, her body would be too easy.

"What do you mean?"

She could barely see him through her fingers. "I guess we can get a room if you want."

274

He removed her hand from her face, slowly, his touch almost a caress. Amy pulled away, then turned to study his face. His eyes registered confusion.

Officer Perry shook his head. "No, Amy. Listen." He raised an eyebrow at the waitress as she set their food down.

The angle of his head brought back another memory. *His face turned to look at her, blood on his cheek, dried and dark. "Call for help."*

"Amy," he said. "Don't you remember?"

A sharp slap. A heavy blow to the back of her head pushed Amy away from him and across the room. She scrambled for her phone, tried calling 9-1-1, then harsh, blunt pain to her nose and upper lip. She tasted blood. Her eyes closed and she felt more pain, on her breasts, to her back.

She looked back at the officer, the memory frightened her. "You're the guy with the bullet wound to the head," she said, her voice sounded flat, off key, even to her.

"Yea." He smiled, a dimple filling one cheek. "You saved my life."

Amy felt sick. The beer churned, threatening to come up. With life came responsibility. "I didn't."

"The doctor at the hospital said that if you hadn't put that pressure on the wound to my head, I might have died."

A ripple traveled through her, like the rush after her first hit. Relief. She let out a long, ragged breath. "I thought I hurt you."

"No." He touched her dirty hand, making her feel

even worse about her appearance. "The guy who shot me almost killed you as well. He beat you so badly that you had to be hospitalized. Don't you remember?"

"I remember waking up in the hospital." Amy smiled, finally relaxed, the urge for a fix fading. "That was three years ago, wasn't it? Why haven't I seen you on the streets before now?"

"Two major surgeries," said the officer, pointing to his head, "and a lot of rehab."

"I never knew what happened to him."

"You mean the guy who shot me?"

She nodded.

"He was killed trying to escape." His voice trailed off.

Her appetite returned. She picked up her hamburger and took a big bite. "I thought you were going to arrest me." Ketchup ran down her chin, creating a line of red along her dress, spreading, seeping along the white fibers. She swiped at it with her napkin.

"Listen," he said, his eyes were steady on her face, his smile gone. "I want to help you get cleaned up, help you get a job or go to school, whatever you want."

She stood, too quickly. Her chair toppled, creating a loud bang. Other customers turned to look. She felt heat rise on her face. "I need to wash my hands. I'll be right back." She walked quickly, tremulously, to the bathroom. How many times had she heard those words, believed them, believed in them?

Some time passed before Officer Perry stood and threw a few dollars on the table. The food, barely touched, sat in the same place the waitress had set it earlier. He made his way to the restroom and knocked on the one that read *Dames*.

"Amy, is everything all right in there?" He waited a few beats before he opened the door. A small window above the last stall sat open, letting the night spill through.

ABOUT THE CONTRIBUTORS

J.D. ALLEN was a Killer Nashville Claymore Award-nominee and a Mystery Writers of America Freddie Award-winner. She attended Ohio State University and earned a degree in forensic anthropology with a creative writing minor. She has a short story in the Anthony Award-winning anthology, *Murder Under the Oaks*. In 2018, her Sin City Investigations series launches from Midnight Ink. She is a member of the Bouchercon National Board, MWA, PI Writers of America, and her local Sisters in Crime chapter.

SHARON BADER hails from a small town in upstate New York, but lived most of her life in California before settling in North Carolina. She has always loved reading mystery and adventure stories. With a Bachelor's degree in Education and a Masters in Geological Oceanography, she taught for many years until she succumbed to the lure of technology and began to program lessons for computer-based training. She is an emerging writer with a strong interest in producing fiction, including mysteries, linked short stories and poetry.

ANTOINETTE BROWN is a mystery writer and reader. She lives in Apex, NC with her two small dogs. Her first published short story appeared in *Carolina Crimes: 19 Tales of Lust, Love and Longing* in 2014.

Hailing from a small town in North Carolina, **COURTNEY CARTER** has had a passion for reading and writing from a young age. She has served as both the membership committee representative for Triangle Sisters in Crime and as the chapter secretary. "Set Them Free, If Need Be" is her first publication credit, and she is thrilled to be involved with the latest edition of Carolina Crimes.

JAMIE CATCHER writes from her home in South Carolina where she lives with her family and a big, fluffball collie. She has a degree in English literature and can be found behind a book most of the time. She has written short stories for *Bella Magazine* and the Sisters in Crime anthology, *Carolina Crimes: 19 Tales of Lust, Love, and Longing*, published by Wildside Press. She has a love for all things British, and yes—shoes.

TONI GOODYEAR is a former journalist, winner of the North Carolina Press Association Award. Other past careers include ghostbusting (yes, really). Her short stories have appeared in the Anthony Award-winning anthology, *Murder Under the Oaks*; *The Killer Wore Cranberry: Room for Thirds*; *Kings River Life* magazine; *Carolina Crimes: 19 Tales of Lust, Love, and Longing*; and *Fish or Cut Bait: A Guppy Anthology*. A member of Sisters in Crime, she holds a Ph.D. in Psychology from the University of North Carolina at Chapel Hill.

LINDA JOHNSON is originally from Chicago where her first career was in advertising. When the cold and gray of Chicago got to be too much, she and her husband packed up their dogs and horse and relocated to warm and sunny North Carolina. After working for several years as the owner and manager of a hunter/jumper equestrian facility, she decided to trade riding for writing. Linda writes suspense novels and short stories and particularly enjoys creating smart, psychopathic villains. She is a member of Sisters in Crime and the North Carolina Writers Network, and has published two novels and several short stories. Online at LindaJohnson.us.

Obsessed with books, dogs, and creepy old houses, **SU KOPIL** writes short fiction about peculiar people. Her stories have appeared in magazines and anthologies including:

Woman's World; Murder Most Conventional; Flash and Bang; Destination Mystery; and *Fish or Cut Bait: A Guppy Anthology.* She is the owner and founder of EarthlyCharms dot com, a graphic design company that has been working with authors since 2000. sukopil.com or @INKspillers

BONNIE KORTA is a native Virginian and graduate of the College of William and Mary with a degree in English and American literature. She is retired from a career as a licensed clinical social worker. She studied creative writing at George Mason University, Radford University, and the Hindman Settlement School. Her writing has received awards from the North Carolina Poetry Society, the Poetry Council of North Carolina, *Poetry in Plain Sight*, and *Carolina Woman* magazine. She has been published in a variety of journals and on-line sources. She lives and writes in Pittsboro, North Carolina, and is currently working on three mystery novels, one set in the English Department at UNC; another the fictionalized treatment of the oldest unsolved mystery in Chapel Hill, the murder of Miss Rachel Cook, whose store became the location of the restaurant, Crook's Corner; and the third featuring Eudora Welty as a fictional character.

GINA LEA grew up sharing time between Southwest Ohio and the Deep South. She began writing and illustrating stories as a child, hoping to create the next great comic strip. Having fallen in love with the Carolinas at a young age, she found it a natural setting for her books. Gina draws on her experiences living in a small town and working in the coffee industry for inspiration for her stories. Kirkus Reviews called her first novel *Defining Destiny*, "An ideal and frothy beach book." Gina's next novel is her first traditional mystery set in the fictional town of Destiny Bay. She lives in North Carolina with her best critics, her husband and Zuzu the Wonder Dog.

KAREN MCCULLOUGH'S wide-ranging imagination makes her incapable of sticking to one genre for her story-telling. As a result, she's the author of more than a dozen published novels and novellas, which span the mystery, fantasy, paranormal, and romantic suspense genres. Awards she's won include an Eppie Award for fantasy and a Vixen award. She has also been a finalist in the Prism, Dream Realm, Rising Star, Lories, and Scarlet Letter Awards, and a semi-finalist in the science fiction Writers of the Future contest. Her short fiction has appeared in several anthologies and numerous small press publications in the fantasy, science fiction, and romance genres. Her most recent novel is *Wired for Murder*, the second in her Market Center Mysteries series. A former computer programmer who made a career change into publishing, Karen has been an editor, managing editor, and senior web editor for an international trade publishing company. She lives in Greensboro, North Carolina, and now runs a web design company that specializes in creating web sites for authors and other small businesses to support her writing habit. Karen is a member of Mystery Writers of America, Sisters in Crime, Romance Writers of America, and the Writers' Group of the Triad. A former president of the Southeast Chapter of Mystery Writers of America, she has served on the boards of MWA National and the Writers' Group of the Triad.

LIZ MCGUFFEY lives in Durham. She's a retired pharmacist who spends her time writing, traveling, and playing bridge. She's written and published scientific articles but now she's trying to figure out how to write creative fiction and non-fiction. In July of this year her essay, "Rediscovering Mary Hancock, Warrior for Whimsy," was published in the *North Carolina Literary Review*. She lives with her husband, Mike, and their dog, Rosie.

DON MARPLE has been writing fiction—short stories and one novel—since 2009. One of his stories, "Mara's Baby," won honorable mention in the 2103 Doris Betts fiction contest. The judging editor told Don it would make the basis for a good novel. He has written that novel and is seeking a publisher.

RUTH MOOSE'S first novel, *Doing it at the Dixie Dew* won the Malice Domestic St. Martin's Press Award. Its sequel, *Wedding Bell Blues*, was published by St. Martin's Press in 2016. She has published in *Ellery Queen's Mystery Magazine* and several Malice Domestic anthologies.

BONNIE OLSEN is a former research technician (surprise!) and—now that she's retired from that—a new writer. She spends her days chugging away on a multi-volume historical fiction series that's still in progress. This is her first attempt at writing a short.

BRITNI PATTERSON is the author of the Justice & Mercy mysteries set in San Antonio, Texas, in the Hill Country near where she was born and raised, and the Rosa Parks short stories set in Raleigh, North Carolina, one of which was a finalist for the 2015 Derringer Best Short Story. She enjoys writing traditional mysteries that invite the reader to try and figure it out, with capable, clever, and flawed protagonists. She also occasionally writes for Cracked.com, studies medieval book arts, watches *Ru Paul's Drag Race* religiously, and is a bullet journal addict. Find her on Facebook, Twitter, or at britnipatterson.com, because she loves hearing from readers.

JENNIFER RILEY moved to North Carolina thirty years ago, delighted to discover writer courses and critique groups. After earning a master's degree in English, she branched into computer software technical documentation. A technical report she assisted with earned her a trip to Rome, Italy. After her software technical writing, she entered a clinical trials two-year degree program. While sitting in anatomy, physiology, and biochemistry courses, she learned various methods for murder. Her core competency is the analysis and explication of literature. Creative writing has intrigued Jennifer for the past two decades.

SARAH R. SHABER is an award-winning mystery author from North Carolina. Her World War II historical mystery series begins with *Louise's War*. It features young widow Louise Pearlie, a government girl who works for the Office of Strategic Services, the United States' first spy agency. Shaber is also the author of the Professor Simon Shaw mysteries, *Blood Test*, and editor of *Tar Heel Dead*. Her first book, *Simon Said*, won the St. Martin's Press/Malice Domestic Award for best first traditional mystery. She was the Bouchercon15 (World Mystery Conference, 2015) Local Guest of Honor.

Novelist, poet, and scholar **JUDITH STANTON'S** *Deer Diaries*, her first collection of poetry, was published in 2016. A romantic herself, Stanton published four historical romance novels, *Wild Indigo* and *His Stolen Bride* with HarperCollins, and *The Mad Marquis* and *The Kissing Gate* with Leisure Books and Montlake Press. Recently, she published her first equestrian suspense, *A Stallion to Die For*, with her own Cat Crossing Press. As a scholar, she edited *The Letters of Charlotte Smith (1749-1806)*. This definitive edition of 400 letters helped restore Smith's reputation as the first Romantic poet and has garnered Stanton a nomination as a Distinguished Alumna at the University of North Carolina at Chapel Hill.

A lifelong book addict, **CAROLINE TAYLOR** has published several short stories in online and print magazines and anthologies. She is the author of two mysteries and one nonfiction book. Find her online at carolinestories.com.

ROBIN WHITTEN is a physician's assistant in family practice. Writing is her gift and her passion, one she has developed and explored throughout her life. She continues her search for the one story, the one word on the tip of her tongue, that she can put down on paper and share with the world. She has published in the *Red Clay Review*; the *Bethlehem Magazine*; the *Main Street Rag,* and has published a novella called *Epona.*

OTHER TITLES FROM DOWN AND OUT BOOKS

See www.DownAndOutBooks.com for complete list

By J.L. Abramo
Chasing Charlie Chan
Circling the Runway
Brooklyn Justice
Coney Island Avenue

By Trey R. Barker
Exit Blood
Death is Not Forever
No Harder Prison

By Eric Beetner (editor)
Unloaded

By Eric Beetner
and Frank Zafiro
The Backlist
The Shortlist

By G.J. Brown
Falling

By Angel Luis Colón
No Happy Endings
Meat City on Fire (*)

By Shawn Corridan
and Gary Waid
Gitmo

By Frank De Blase
Pine Box for a Pin-Up
Busted Valentines
A Cougar's Kiss

By Les Edgerton
The Genuine, Imitation,
Plastic Kidnapping
Lagniappe
Just Like That (*)

By Danny Gardner
A Negro and an Ofay

By Jack Getze
Big Mojo
Big Shoes
Colonel Maggie & the Black Kachina

By Richard Godwin
Wrong Crowd
Buffalo and Sour Mash
Crystal on Electric Acetate

By Jeffery Hess
Beachhead
Cold War Canoe Club

By Matt Hilton
No Going Back
Rules of Honor
The Lawless Kind
The Devil's Anvil
No Safe Place

By Lawrence Kelter
and Frank Zafiro
The Last Collar

By Lawrence Kelter
Back to Brooklyn

(*)—Coming Soon

10-20-17

CPSIA information can be obtained
at www.ICGtesting.com
Printed in the USA
LVOW07s2032210817
545810LV00005B/921/P

9 781943 402953